Walter Reid was educated at Oxford and Edinburgh universities. He is married with two children. His time is divided between the west of Scotland, where he raises sheep and cows, and the south of France, where he grows olives. He has written seven books on aspects of British twentieth-century history. He is a fellow of the Royal Historical Society.

To Janet, with thanks for her enthusiastic participation in the research.

For Heather,

Walter Reid

THE QUICKENING OF ALEC ROSS

a very dear friend,
from Walter
with love.

AUSTIN MACAULEY PUBLISHERS™

LONDON • CAMBRIDGE • NEW YORK • SHARJAH

Austin Macauley is committed to publishing works of quality and integrity. In this spirit, we are proud to offer this book to our readers; however, the story, the experiences, and the words are the author's alone.

A CIP catalogue record for this title is available from the British Library.

ISBN 9781528991896 (Paperback)
ISBN 9781528991902 (ePub e-book)

www.austinmacauley.com

First Published (2020)
Austin Macauley Publishers Ltd
25 Canada Square
Canary Wharf
London
E14 5LQ

20200917

Table of Contents

French Catalonia in the Second World War

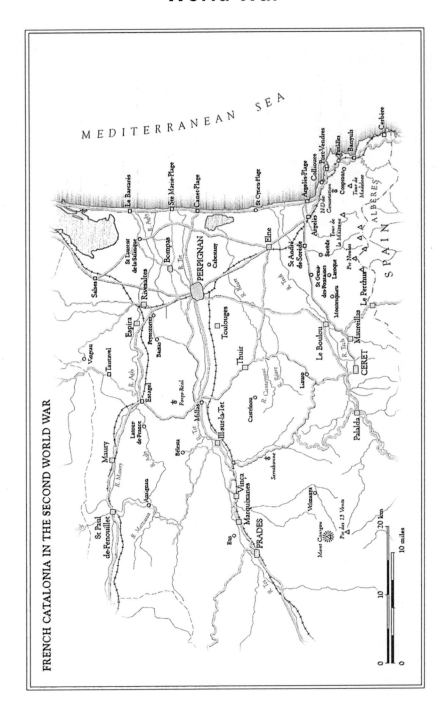

FRENCH CATALONIA IN THE SECOND WORLD WAR

Part One:
Perpignan, French Catalonia, 1940

Chapter 1

After a long day's spying, Alec Ross was walking back to Perpignan. It was a warm, spring evening. Behind him lay the Mediterranean. Ahead of him lay the summit of le Canigou, the sacred mountain of the Catalans on both sides of the border, French and Spanish. It was twenty miles away, but clear in the crisp air, the snow on its upper slopes amber in the rays of the setting sun.

The cloudless skies had kept the temperature high while the sun was up; now they allowed it to fall sharply. The early evening air was cool. Narrow wraiths of wood-smoke rose from fires lit to cook evening meals. In the stillness of the air, the grey smoke lay in horizontal bands not much above roof height. As Ross made his way towards the centre of the town, he could smell it, sharp and welcome, cutting through the coolness of the air. He was tired and hungry. His pace quickened.

The single cotton-cloud that often floated above the summit of le Canigou was absent today. Over Alec Ross too, spy and gentleman-artist, the man who had killed a wife and abandoned a lover, there floated no cloud of self-doubt or introspection.

Had he been asked, he would have been unable to say what, if anything, he was thinking about. He was self-absorbed, but not absorbed in thought. Serious mental activity had been dulled by the rhythm of his march, his speed disguised by the length of his pace. He wore an old khaki shirt, brown corduroy trousers and desert boots. At his side, a canvas case swung against his hip.

The approach to Perpignan was dominated by its one remaining city gate, le Castillet. He entered the town through this bastion of the old city, a looming tower of stone and the red brick decoration the local people called *cayroux*. Most of its narrow windows were barred. As in mediaeval times so today, it was used in part as a prison. On its inner side lay the Place Arago. Ross's goal was the Café Gambetta at the far side of the Place. As he walked across the place, le Castillet now behind him, he hardly noticed another of the daubs that had started to appear on the walls: *"Nourriture pour les français—merde pour les juifs"*—"Food for the French—Shit for the Jews".

At the Castillet's foot was a group of refugees from Franco's Spain. They had come across the border after the outbreak of the Civil War. Their numbers had increased since the fall of Barcelona. But now there was only a trickle. They had never been welcome. The Catalans of the north had neither enough food nor prosperity to see their fellow republicans of the south as other than a threat. The pitiful mass which made up *La Retirada* had at first been held up at the border by French border guards. Defeated soldiers, mothers with babies in their arms, and the old and sick had stood in the cold for days on end, facing the bayonets of their northern cousins.

They had come for refuge to France, the birthplace of liberty, the source of the Rights of Man. A hundred thousand men, women and children crossed the Albères, the foothills of the Pyrenees, in the first wave, and within two weeks of the fall of Barcelona a further half a million refugees arrived. They did not know what awaited them.

Eventually, they had been allowed to squat in and around Perpignan. Some were confined behind barbed wire on the beaches, where they had been inspected by Marshal Pétain, the hero of Verdun in an earlier war, still awaiting his destiny in the current one. Others remained at liberty. The system didn't acknowledge their existence and wasn't particularly concerned to bother itself with them. These tolerated *sans-papiers* were the people who congregated daily around the station, in the open space of les Platanes, and especially at le Castillet.

Ross had become used to seeing them and their plight, their begging, their hunger. But over the last few days, he had noticed a difference. A few weeks earlier, France herself had fallen to Fascism, and the aged Marshal Pétain had found his destiny, ruling France as the puppet of the Nazis. Now there was no longer even the hope that France could protect the refugees from the forces of oppression. Pétain's France might prove worse even than the rule of Franco from which they had fled. The dispirited huddle was no longer animated by gossip and camaraderie. It stood listless and silent.

Ross had seen too that the Spaniards were no longer the only people who congregated in the Place. At first, the refugees were unwelcomed but largely ignored; however, since the fall of France and of democracy, the slimier elements of society were emerging into the light, like slugs from under stones. Round the three sides of the square that faced the ancient Castillet, swinging sticks and batons, were supporters of the Marshal: unprepossessing bunches of thugs, some of them formally uniformed, others wearing scraps of any official-looking clothing they could find. There were weathered veterans of the earlier war and of lawless skirmishes, but others little more than children, amongst them boys as young as ten. If the older thugs, who called themselves the *Milice,* were a version of Hitler's Brownshirts, the youths, the *Jeune Milice*, were Hitler Youth on the cheap.

The thugs studied the refugees. They themselves were observed unnoticed by a man who loitered in an angle of the Castillet tower. He wore a blue serge suit, shiny and threadbare. He had sharp features, a whiskery moustache. He was bare-headed, his black oiled hair growing from a widow's peak.

There was a strange silence. The refugees hardly spoke, and the strong men and spotty boys of collaborationist Vichy only muttered amongst themselves in low voices. They stared down the broken Spaniards. The sense of menace in the square was inescapable.

Because of that—perhaps only because of that—Ross noticed something that might have escaped his attention a couple of weeks earlier. Three or four hobbledehoys wearing the homemade uniform of the *Jeune Milice* were jeering at a young woman. As Ross passed, they pushed her. She fell heavily on to the cobbles. He could see a youth preparing a kick for her ribs. She did not ask Ross's help, but her eyes met his.

Ross had no sense of sympathy. His reaction was not so much concern for the girl as a feeling that it wasn't acceptable that ill-assorted youths with no legal status should control events. He was himself the creature of an ordered society. Disorder offended him. He could not do nothing. But he didn't do very much. He didn't hit anyone. He didn't threaten anyone. All he did was to snap at the boys in a tone of contempt, telling them to get home to their parents.

When he thought about it, very much later, Ross wondered why his uncharacteristic intervention had been so effective. Was there some authority in a forty-five-year-old man with a military background? He had spoken French, though he could equally well have used Catalan, but did they detect a hint of a foreign accent? Or were they a little ashamed of what they were doing, glad to have an excuse to stop? They hadn't looked it, and they didn't just slink off. They paused in their assault, surprised to have their authority challenged. They looked for guidance at the older men who stood nearby. Ross didn't break his gaze on the louts, so he didn't see what instructions they received, if any; however, after a moment or two, the boys silently walked away. They did so slowly, their eyes fixed on Ross, trying to save their dignity by letting him know that he hadn't heard the last of them. If they had been older and better-built, the threat might have been more effective.

What Ross did next was a little thing, but no less out of character. He offered his hand to the girl to help her to her feet. He wasn't aware of any electric charge passing between them. He nodded to her and continued on his way. She didn't smile or speak, but when he reached the Café Gambetta, he saw that she'd followed him.

***

Georges Cadot was already at their usual table. Ross greeted him and sat down. The girl was still behind him. He noticed that she checked her pace when she saw Cadot in the uniform of *brigadier* of gendarmes. But she continued into the café and sat on her own at the next table.

Cadot was amused. His large, square countryman's face was as animated as Ross had ever seen it—or at least his eyes were: his mouth was as inexpressive as ever beneath the heavy moustache, his expansive cheeks unperturbed.

'Well, my friend, what is this? Our bloodless Englishman has some blood after all?'

'Georges, Georges, you *know* I am not an Englishman.'

'I know that we've naturalised you, but Englishmen are born with umbrellas within them to stiffen their backbones, and there is no operation known to medical science which can remove the umbrellas. You will always be an Englishman at heart—but until today, I would have said you had no heart. What then has happened? The Alec who has so few human needs has found himself a little friend after all?'

Ross told Cadot about the encounter. The gendarme affected not to believe him: 'I am glad to think that you have a more human appendage than an umbrella. For my part, Alec, I should much prefer your little Spanish partridge to my weekly *rendez-vous* with the widow Lagrande whose moustache I cannot help but note becomes increasingly luxuriant. But you saw your partridge first and you must have her as long as you pay the price.'

'I shall not have her, and there is no price to pay.'

'You have learned little in your long life, Alec. There is always a price to pay.'

***

Cadot was well through his meal when Ross and the girl had entered the café. Ross ordered his usual *boules picoulat*. The dish still tasted meaty enough, but its composition was not what it had been before the war.

He turned to Cadot: 'I read in *L'Intransigéant* that the Maréchal, with his respect for the peasant life, applauds the fine French cow and the brave French horse, but I think there is more of the latter than the former in the *boules* today.'

Cadot agreed silently, and added, 'But you must not overlook the heroic contribution of the gallant French sawdust.'

Ross glanced at the girl. She was not looking at him. Her eyes were fixed in the middle distance, her hands clasped together. He told the waiter to give her what he was eating. She looked at him, acknowledging his response to the request she hadn't made. She didn't smile or speak, but she met his eyes. It was Ross who had to speak.

'Why were they doing that to you?'

She looked at him in surprise. 'Because they said I was Jewish,' she said.

'And are you?'

'Yes, I am a Sephardic Jew.'

'How did they know?' asked Ross.

She looked at him steadily, but said nothing.

He looked at Cadot. 'How?'

Cadot said simply, 'They know,' and turned to the girl, sharing a truth from which the Englishman was excluded.

'Anyway,' said Ross, 'why would it matter—I know the *Milice* hate the communists, but I never thought they cared about Jews. That's a German obsession.'

'I'm afraid, my dear, innocent Alec,' said Cadot, 'you will find that many here share that obsession. Ask your little friend. The Maréchal has many supporters who hate the Jews far more than the little German does. I read last week of the new laws that are coming. We shall soon be interning the French Jews as well as the Spanish communists. So make hay with your little friend while the sun shines. And now I must leave you. As you know, it's Wednesday and Wednesday is for the widow Lagrande, much as I should prefer to stay here and play draughts with you and gaze on your companion.'

He sat for a moment more, and when he rose, he added, 'But before I go, my dear, Alec, I must counsel caution. What you did in the Place today was no doubt admirable, though it is not something I should have expected from you. But be careful. These men are dangerous and now they are the men of power. I shall always do what I can for you, but I am no longer what I was.'

'You are a *brigadier de gendarmerie*, Georges.'

'I am a gendarme. That may have meant something in the past. The priest, the schoolmaster, the gendarme—they counted for something. But it's different now. For a start, I am sure you will have learned at school that the French Gendarmerie was divided into two bodies, a civilian one and a military one. Not any longer. Now the administration for its own reasons has created fifteen separate bodies. We spend most of our time squabbling and fighting between ourselves while the Germans run things and the criminals operate freely. You have seen for yourself these little bastards in their *Jeune Milice* and if they are not enough, we have now got a *Garde Française* and a *Jeune Front*.'

'But you represent authority, surely?'

'Authority? There has never been authority in France, not even under Napoleon. Before the last war, French Catalonia, *Catalogne du Nord*, was hardly part of France. My Catalan father didn't know he was French till 1914 when he was told to fight for France. He couldn't speak French. He didn't understand what his officers were telling him. He lost his leg and his two brothers for a France that never did anything for him. What do you imagine he felt about French authority? And now the venerable Maréchal, whose image surrounds us, tells us to dance to the tunes of the Germans, while the lanky General from the safety of London bids us fight them. Vichy tells me to do one thing. The rich and silent who keep the Maréchal in power tell me something quite different and very unpleasant, and soon our new friends in the Gestapo will be here to tell me something different still. I say to you, Alec, these boys in the Place wearing scraps of the abandoned uniform of a village postman will soon have as much authority as I have ever had.'

These were the most strongly felt sentiments Ross had ever heard Cadot express. The gendarme looked slightly embarrassed by the strength of his views. He left, bowing to the girl. She had finished her *boules* and had used all her bread to mop up the gravy. Ross had eaten only half of his.

He offered the plate to the girl, who took it without embarrassment. She ate it unselfconsciously. Ross, finishing his wine, studied her. She must have known his eyes were on her, but she was unperturbed. She was in her early twenties, very thin, her fine fair hair cut very short. Boyish but attractive with wide eyes and an open countenance. She was wearing a black jersey and black trousers, and was carrying a bag like a military small pack. Ross paid his bill and looked out the door. The girl followed him and as they left the café, put her hand in his.

'Inez,' she said.

It was now dark and quite cold. The wood smoke was still heavy on the air. The refugees had left the Place. At the foot of the red brick Castillet stood the same short man, rat-faced, his hair oiled and swept back from its widow's peak.

As they turned out of the Place, Ross saw another scrawl, *Merde aux Juifs.* Beneath this was a rough drawing of a caricatured Jew hanging from a gibbet, his mouth stuffed with ordure. Inez saw it too. She passed it without evident reaction. But Ross felt a moment of nausea.

Chapter 2

As they walked towards Ross's lodgings, his reaction to the girl's presence was confused. He had never walked hand-in-hand with a woman before, either at his suggestion or at that of the woman. The gesture might be innocent and bereft of sexual significance, or it might not. In either case, it was an intrusion and assumed a compliance on his part that should not have been taken for granted.

But he had no decision to make. For all her fragility, Inez displayed a self-assurance for which his limited acquaintance with women had not prepared him. It was she and not Ross who was in control.

And so they continued in silence for the short walk to Ross's apartment on the Rue des Cordonniers. The flat was entered by its own front door at street level. A narrow stair led to the first floor, where a single room provided the living and working area. An open staircase led to the floor above, the small bedroom and a bathroom.

Still on the street, they disengaged hands. The girl looked at Ross with a smile that hinted at amusement. Ross opened the door and stood aside. Inez entered first, as of right, and as Ross followed her up the stairs, watching her buttocks and thighs moving against her trousers, he felt the mucus thicken at the back of his throat.

She stopped in the living room and took stock. Then she moved around, frankly inspecting the room, unembarrassed by the knowledge that Ross was observing her. After some minutes, she continued upstairs to the next floor and the bedroom. Ross stayed in the living room. He considered what would happen next. Sex—either as a payment to him or for payment by him—seemed likeliest, but given her self-possession and quiet authority, it was far from impossible that he would be expected to control his appetites and sleep on the couch. Physically, the other option had its attractions, but an attraction that was qualified for Ross by the abandonment of self-control, a sacrifice to be resisted.

As always, it was preferable not to take the initiative, not to venture the human contact; better to respond to events rather than to shape them. He sat for some time, looking round the room.

He was a man who thought very little about others, and not at all about what others thought of him, but he found himself wondering what his apartment told Inez about him and the life he led. The room was frugal, tidy to a Spartan degree, almost ascetic. Its occupier was a man formed by institutions, who had not sought to soften or humanise his surroundings. There were a few books, far from new, an unexciting mix that might have come from a school library, anthologies, dictionaries, familiar works of fiction. In the cooking area, there were some staples—coffee, bread, jam, one or two jars of beans and *confit* of duck. No bottles. A man who ate little at home. Any dishes that had been used had been washed, dried and put away. The flat's occupant could have been away from home for weeks.

The only sense of life or living came from the side of the room that was broken by two windows overlooking the street. This part of the room revealed that its occupant had at least one vital spark. Here were Ross's easels, paints and all the apparatus of his vocation. Here were his notebooks and his canvases, some completed, some still in progress. They were piled in stacks against the walls, perhaps ten deep. No paintings were on display. There were no portraits, no photographs. The strong smell of paint and turpentine was underscored by faint odours of herb and oil that must have dated from the time of a more culinarily inclined occupant.

While Ross sat, he heard the girl move around in the room upstairs. Then the sound of the lavatory flushing and of washing. Then silence. After a few more minutes, Ross climbed the stairs. The situation was undeniably exciting, and he sported a reasonably significant erection by the time he reached the bedroom. He was, on the whole, therefore, gratified by what he found. Inez lay on the bed, uncovered and entirely naked. He knew now how the evening was to end.

The electric light was switched off, but there was an uncurtained skylight above the bed, through which some of the illumination of the yellow streetlights shone. Ross stood at the foot of the bed and looked at the girl. Presumably this was what he was entitled to do. She was undoubtedly attractive. Although very slight, almost emaciated, her hips were full and her thighs well formed. Her breasts small but firm, her nipples very dark. Her skin, too, was sallow, almost olive, its smoothness and lack of other blemish emphasised by a circular puncture wound, still livid, just a fraction to the left of a line from her navel to the bush of pubic hair whose darkness contrasted with the fairness of the short hair of her head.

When Ross joined her, he was surprised to see in her eyes neither resignation nor fear, but a laughing smile that seemed almost inquisitive. He felt curiously disarmed. Somehow, their roles were out of kilter. That thought did not detain him for long. He entered her and found her moving against him, not strongly, but insistently. He wondered if she felt that was something she was supposed to do. Then, to his surprise, her mouth sought his and she kissed him hard. She began to make little gasps.

In his brief marriage, Barbara had never achieved an orgasm. Ross's only other lover, his housekeeper in Syria, had brought congress to an end with a business-like grunt, but he had always been aware that this was a signal that time was up, rather than the spontaneous product of pleasure. He wondered if the signs of increasing excitement that emanated from the girl were part of a performance. They culminated in a long, entirely personal sigh that spoke of almost child-like satisfaction. The accompanying spasm brought Ross too to the point of climax. Just in time, he withdrew, depositing a jet of semen from her left hipbone to the base of her right breast, ivory against her dark skin.

They lay side-by-side, both breathless. Then Inez looked at him, again with that kindly mocking smile in her eyes. In some ways, she seemed older than he, rather than twenty years younger.

She said, 'Thank you,' which was not what Ross had expected. In reply, all he could do was to repeat her words.

They lay silently for a moment or two more. Inez saw Ross looking at the arc of semen. 'You don't need to do that next time,' she said, and took his hand and pressed it on the puncture wound. 'He said he wouldn't have a half-Jew baby by me, and that no-one else would either.' Ross wiped away the evidence of his weakness, and drew the sheet over them both.

Inez seemed to go to sleep at once. Ross took a little longer. Now that his excitement was over, he felt vulnerable. He was uncomfortable about the reference to "next time". There would be no next time. It was not for her to presume to tell him about the shape of his life. He was disturbed. There was something in the balance of power in his relationship with this girl which he had not met before.

***

He woke early next morning, little after the first grey light came through the skylight. Inez was still beside him, untroubled and breathing deeply. Her abandoned clothes lay beside the bed. He was softened by the presence of these badges of femininity in his masculine cell. He took his own clothes down to the living room, dressed quickly and quietly, picked up his painting bag and prepared to leave without breakfasting. Normally, he never left as early as this unless he was meeting one of his contacts. It would be hours before the light was right for painting. But this was the way to avoid the consequences of the previous night. There must be none of the complexities that had grown round his last physical relationship.

Shunning the warmth of human contact was achieved with an effort. But for him the alternative was more difficult still, and intimacy had ended in death and pain and humiliation. Running away was preferable to recrimination, protestation and tears, the concomitants of intimacy.

He stopped at the table and thought. On the whole, a thousand francs would be more fitting than five hundred. He left the bank notes and went out into the early morning air, which still carried a slight savour of wood smoke. As he quietly closed the door behind himself, he saw the rat-faced man with the widow's peak slip away down a side street.

21

Part Two:
England, France and the Levant, 1916–1937

Chapter 3
Somerset and Devon, 1916

When is the character of a wife-killer formed? In Alec Ross's case probably long before he was summoned by his housemaster, at the age of sixteen, to be told that his parents had drowned when the ship on which they were returning from India had been torpedoed. But that will do as well as any other date.

He was not invited to sit down. What his housemaster saw was a very ordinary boy, quieter than most, sober and serious. He was of average height for his age, and would remain so as he grew and aged, stocky rather than lithe. His hair was wiry, crinkled, brown with a hint of red through it. When he grew a small moustache a few years later, it would be the same colour. His expression was thoughtful and attentive and his gaze was steady, but not unduly animated.

Apart from the future moustache, his appearance would change very little over the years. At the age of sixteen, he looked older than his years, with already the self-control of an adult, but since his appearance didn't subsequently alter, he was to look progressively younger for his age as the years passed. The schoolteacher was relieved to see that he was taking the news stoically. In the course of this war he had to break the news of parental deaths many times, and some boys had let themselves down quite badly.

'Very sorry, of course. It really is very bad...' (There was a long delay while the man tried to avoid a noun which he was aware might in the circumstances seem inadequate. He gave up.) '...luck.' Alec judged that he'd been dismissed. He turned to leave. As he did so, his housemaster stopped him. Alec was wearing a buttonhole badge of Sir Douglas Haig which his grandfather had given him. He was very proud of it. Lots of boys had cigarette cards of Haig and Allenby and Plumer, but only one other had a lapel badge of a general, and that was of Lord Roberts, who wasn't even in this war. His housemaster pointed at the badge.

'Take that thing out.'

Alec wandered away from the study. He didn't know quite what to do. He'd been given no instructions. Returning to the maths class from which he'd been summoned didn't seem the right thing. He went to the school library and filled the couple of hours before lunch by reading back numbers of *Punch*.

Nothing more was said on the subject for almost a week. He had no friends with whom he wished to share the news. Then he was sent for again, this time by the housemaster's wife, dressed, as always, in grey. Her hair was disposed in two buns, a smaller one on top of a larger one, like a French loaf, and the whole so tightly coiffed that the individual components seemed to have disappeared, fused into a grey helmet. Similarly, her breasts had been tightly combined, their individual characteristics united in a single but substantial prow. Between the prow and the smoke stack, her face was smooth, powerful and uncreased. The whole was suggestive of a dreadnought surging through the waves. She had been working on embroidery. She held a letter in what Alec recognised as his grandfather's handwriting. Alec stood in front of her. He was not invited to sit down.

'You will have been wondering,' she said. Alec did not know what he was thought to have been wondering. 'Well, all has been arranged. I gather that when your parents were on leave, you spent your summer holidays with them at their house in Devon, and the other holidays with your grandparents in the South of France or with your parents' friends in Honiton, the—' (She looked at the letter.) 'Everleys. Well, now you'll go to your grandparents in summers and you'll spend your other holidays with the Everleys.'

Her voice shifted down a tone and she moved to more comfortable matters: 'What will have been worrying you is the question of fees.' She assumed a positive expression. 'There's no need to worry on that score. Your parents have left you well provided for, very well indeed.'

Her expression and delivery changed again to wind up the interview. 'My husband and I are so very sorry. That's why *I* chose to speak to you today,' she explained, as if exposure to a warship bearing down at speed would be a reassuring reminder of womanly warmth and femininity. 'But the great thing is to avoid fuss. Everything will go on much as before.'

***

And things did, to a large extent, go on as before. Alec liked his paternal grandparents, now his only living relatives. He *knew* them better than his parents, who had steadily receded into the shadows since at the age of six he had first made the long voyage to school from what had become increasingly difficult to think of as home. His grandfather had retired at a young age from the Indian Civil Service and had chosen to settle on the Mediterranean coast at Menton, on the French side of the French-Italian border, rather than return to an English climate.

He and Alec's grandmother, who was quite a lot younger, made an easy-going couple. They enjoyed a lively social life, mixing with the local French as well as English and Russian expatriates. Alec had always, truth to tell, felt more relaxed in their company than with his own parents, who had seemed, by contrast, elderly and slow. His grandparents patently enjoyed *his* company. His parents, poor, well-meaning souls, had to fill their brief contacts with him with earnest concern for his moral development. The voyage back from India took six weeks, so between travelling and spending six weeks with him, their trips home meant an absence from India of more than four months which they could only take every three years.

Alec thought that if his parents had truly loved him, they could have arranged things differently. Had he known it, leave as frequent as once every three years cost his father dear in remuneration and promotion. And he had no idea then or later how much both his parents suffered from separation from their only child, a suffering that was made all the sharper by the fact that neither shared it with the other, and a suffering which steadily intensified as they realised their sacrifice was creating a growing gulf that would never be bridged. A brief leave was not nearly long enough to undo the effects of absence and re-establish a warm and natural bond. Each time he saw them, he felt he knew his parents less. His grandparents just had fun with him.

He may conceivably have known that his parents meant well. He was aware that they probably loved him, but he knew that for his part it was his grandmother and grandfather that *he* loved. Poor old (though not all that old—they were in their forties when they died) Mr and Mrs Ross, blameless but blamed. They had little domestic joy to celebrate even before the intervention of that German torpedo.

The Everleys, too, were no strangers. They had been his parents' only friends, and Alec felt at home with them. Mr Everley worked in the city. Mrs Everley, a vague, fair creature who looked as if she had been left out too long in the sun, seemed to spend much of her time resting. There was a son, Hector, seven years older than Alec, whom he scarcely knew. Hector had been on the Western Front since the beginning of the war and had won an MC on the Somme. He had done well. Now he was on General Plumer's staff, presumably to some extent out of danger, although that assumption was never voiced.

And then there were the girls, Barbara, blonde and cool and one year older than Alec, Georgina, one year his junior, dark and unpredictable. Barbara and Georgie were the closest—indeed, in reality, the only—friends that Alec had. He had none at school. But it would be a mistake to imagine that he was essentially cold or incapable of friendship. School was particular. It was designed to stifle sentiment and affection and sensitivity, to foster instead the gentlemanly virtues.

Prep school and public school alike, particularly the minor ones that Alec attended, had been rushed into being as the first stages of the serious matter of training for empire. For most boys, the dehumanising effects of such a system were mitigated by the effects of home and family and siblings, but Alec had none of these influences to soften the austerity of his upbringing. His school friends might have been true friends if he had known them not only in an institutional, barrack-like setting but also against the more relaxed, domestic background of holidays at home. The other boys inhabited this shared hinterland, with its common culture, but quiet, lonely Alec did not. He was accepted. He took care not to look sorry for himself. He was not bullied. But he was entirely alone.

Except when he was with Barbara and Georgie. The atmosphere in their house was as different from that of school as it could have been. To an extent, the nature of that atmosphere was the creation of the girls themselves. Some might have suffered from the distance of their parents and the gap in age between themselves and their brother, but Barbara and Georgie never began to see things that way. They grabbed the space that had been left to them and filled it with fun. No-one pressed plans or ambitions on them. They might have drifted aimlessly, but they didn't. They were well-assorted, Barbara quietly determined and single-minded, Georgie irrepressible, full of vitality. If he had met the girls at his present age, gauche and awkward as he had become, or if there had been lots of other neighbours for them to know, he might not have been accepted, but he had been around with them since they were all little, before he encountered the uncertainties of adolescence and before Barbara resolved to be an ice maiden.

For Alec, his holidays with the Everleys were as close as he'd ever come to family life. Of course, it wasn't quite that. The Everley parents weren't his parents. The adults were even more distant from him than they were from their own children. He was a visitor, even though a very regular one, and always, therefore, just a little apart. And he had developed a shell to protect him from a difficult childhood, in which, without parents, he had had to develop some of the attitudes of an older person. It was not his fault that the result could make what was essentially a sensitive and gentle soul seem distant and unresponsive. But he was at his least distant and unresponsive at Honiton.

There weren't many other young people around. The only two regularly there were Helen, the local doctor's daughter, and Tom, whose father was a farmer in a very big way. Alec didn't feel he knew Helen and Tom particularly, but because he was the Everleys' friend, he was accepted as part of the group. The nucleus of that group was Barbara, Georgie and Alec, and as part of this nucleus, he was actually as happy as he ever had been before and as he would not again be for many years

The girls remained tomboys till well into their teenage years. Their mysteriously frail mother took little interest in what they did, and their freedom was unrestrained by adult supervision. They wandered on the moors, rode their ponies, played on their tennis court. The teasing, the informality, tugged the real Alec Ross out of the carapace. He had a vision of a relaxed existence quite different from the cold conformity and repression of the rest of his life. He could imagine unconstrained relationships that he had never known, openness, affection, even love. Honiton might have given Alec his freedom right at the start of his adulthood. Alas, in the event, it locked him up again for many years to come. But at least these holidays in the Devon air had planted in his mind a vision that his upbringing had denied to him.

Alec was always closer to Georgie. She was more fun than her sister, always a little more imaginative and irresponsible. They constructed fantasies and giggled together while Barbara looked on, sometimes tolerantly, sometimes impatiently. But the distance between her and them imperceptibly grew. They all realised that they were growing up, had grown up. Outward changes had taken place, and there was an awareness of sexuality, expressed only in glances, a new avoiding of ambiguous physical contact, and—so far as Alec and Georgie were concerned—in occasional jokes. Barbara took growing up much more seriously. She felt that she had to become a new person. She cultivated poise and grace and became, the other two agreed, rather too pleased with herself. The dynamics of the group were no longer as simple as they had been.

In the past, Alec, Barbara and Georgie had composed one unit and Tom and Helen another, smaller one. Now, emerged from her chrysalis, the butterfly Barbara fluttered round Tom. She projected her charms at him. She did so very obviously. She touched him more than could have happened by accident. But Alec and Georgie took a malicious pleasure in observing that while Tom responded with perfect politeness, he conspicuously failed to succumb.

Chapter 4
Devon, 1918

The Easter holidays of 1918 were always going to be a watershed, even if the particular drama which unfolded then had never taken place. They were the last which the members of the little group would spend together before dispersing into the adult world—more than that: into the confusion and danger of a world at war.

The education of the three girls, Georgie, Barbara and Helen, would conclude in the summer. There would be no "season" for them. Even in peacetime there would not have been. They were not quite of the class that "came out". They might help at home, do some charity work or, very probably, some patriotic nursing.

Alec, too, would finish at school. His grandfather saw no point in sending him to university, as he would be needed in the army in the following year when he reached the age of eighteen, so he was to pursue an interest in drawing and painting and study art in London for the moment. Hector's long leave implied a return to a correspondingly long spell in France. It remained the unspoken hope that the staff would not be the most dangerous place to be, but one never knew. And poor, brave, foolish, un-succumbing Tom, having defended himself against Barbara's assaults, would face even greater dangers. He had just been called up, and had chosen to volunteer for the Royal Flying Corps. It was common knowledge that there a young officer's life expectancy was calculated in weeks. So this last time that they would all be together was charged with poignancy and heightened feelings.

In retrospect, these holidays seemed to last much more than the fourteen days in which so much happened. The main activity was tennis. A lot of doubles was played, and since there were six of them, there were always two not playing, usually engaged in intense discussion. Hector seemed a little distant, older and more mature, his role in the army complicated and obscure. The others were closer, but a cloud of danger hung over Tom, and Alec had only a year's stay of execution. The girls too knew that their lives were bound to change forever.

What Alec noticed at once was that the glacial Barbara seemed to have thawed towards him. It was now on him, and not Tom, that she directed her formidable charm. She was always at his side, looking into his eyes, her own unnaturally wide. She was at her most demonstrative in company, but when they were sitting out games of tennis, at which neither was very good, she talked about how terrible it was that they would so much apart now. She implied that there would be the end of something he didn't remember ever existing.

'It would be so nice if we were talking of moving on to something new. That would make me so happy. Wouldn't it make you happy Alec?'

Poor Alec Ross's role in all this may seem extraordinarily naive. Indeed, he *was* naïve, but perhaps not, in all the circumstances, extraordinarily so. He was young, inexperienced, an only child—and he was flattered. Even if Barbara hadn't been very pretty, unattainable, too good for him, it was a wonderful experience, completely novel, to find that someone, anyone, valued him. No one had ever wanted him or even seemed much to like him very much before, not his parents, caring and dutiful as they had been, not, in this way, Georgie, and certainly not his school fellows. He wasn't sure of *precisely* what she meant, but he was very pleased to find himself of such interest to her. The hints that had come to him of being close to someone, of having at the centre of his life a warmth that would sustain him even when he was out and abroad in a largely hostile world, had never crystallised into a precise image, but he had now some idea of what it might look like. It would have been asking a lot of such an inexperienced young man to examine closely what appeared to be an escape from his straitened life.

He was naive, but he wasn't stupid. He knew she was talking about romance, indeed marriage, though he didn't know why. Where he can be criticised is in failing to see how foolish it would be to think of any kind of future with this girl. He had never really known her. Georgie, he liked and understood. She was fun to be with. They never lacked things to say to each other. Barbara, on the other hand, had always seemed two-dimensional, indeed cold, even before she became glacial. But her beauty and her unattainability made her a prize to be coveted. The fruit that is out of reach is the one that is desired.

Remember too, before condemning the callow youth, the circumstances that surrounded him. Boys only a year older had been commissioned and had fought and died as officers before their nineteenth birthday. Some of his schoolfellows were among them. Others, equally young, were decorated, battle-scarred warriors. Many of these boys had married girls they hardly knew before they left for France. They may have been ridiculously young but they were too young to know that.

Evidence of impermanence was borne in daily on the little group and reminders of mortality surrounded them as the casualty lists filled the morning papers, U-boats threatened the country with starvation, Zeppelins dropped their bombs on civilians. All six to different degrees affected a maturity, a knowledge of the world, that their years didn't warrant. Tom and Helen seemed stable souls and Hector was a man in his own right, but Alec, with no close family, and Georgie and Barbara, with a father who was generally absent and a mother who was spiritually remote, had no fixed marks by which to navigate. Whatever they thought of themselves, they were far from worldly-wise.

The odd thing was that despite its very public nature, the increasing closeness of Alec and Barbara didn't disconcert Tom, so suddenly excluded from her affections. He seemed very happy to be left with little Helen, and she to be with him. In the past, the overriding impression Helen had given had been of nervousness of Barbara. Now she was much surer of herself, much happier.

The one person who seemed upset by the reversal of alliances was Georgie. She was no longer Alec's giggling confidante. She was the odd one out amongst the younger people, often left with her brother. When she and Alec found themselves in the stable block one evening, putting away tennis gear, she looked at him sadly and said in what was clearly a spirit of kindness, 'You're a fool, you know. At least you're being made a fool of.' Alec may or may not have known what Georgie meant. He certainly didn't ask her.

The climax came just two days before the holiday was to end. Barbara took a route that was not unknown in those days, indeed the only one open to her. There were risks that it might fail, but the degree of compromise that would be needed to manipulate Alec would be mild. In any event, she knew her man.

It was evening, a warm one. The Everley parents were having dinner with friends some miles away, and the six young people, as ever playing at being the adults they thought themselves to be, had decided to have their after-dinner coffee on the gravel terrace outside the house. Barbara made a point of taking Alec out while the others were still clearing the table. She stood very close to him. He could smell her body, not just her perfume.

She looked at him meltingly, said, 'I'm so happy that you've chosen me,' and kissed him. He surrendered himself to the kiss. But more was to come. She did something even more astonishing. With one hand, she opened two buttons on her blouse, while she held Alec slightly away from her with the other, watching his reactions. Then she took his right hand, carefully placed it on her left breast, held him to her and again kissed him deeply. He had never felt anything like that breast. It was simultaneously soft and firm, and at its centre, or, as he discovered, slightly below its centre, was the nipple, also combining strangely a sharp assertiveness with a delicate capacity to yield. The smell of her young flesh, the tactile sensations, the awareness that he was exploring the essence of femininity, overwhelmed him. As they kissed, her eyes were open, but he closed his, and gave himself over to the experience.

Barbara was facing the house, he away from it. He was not unhappy that the embrace continued for quite some moments. His tongue probed and his fingers circled, but Barbara was still, as if she were maintaining a pose for a camera or an invisible audience. Then she stiffened, and broke away.

'We've been seen,' she exclaimed theatrically. Indeed, the others were coming out of the house. But although they continued to approach, Barbara did not turn away or immediately adjust her clothes. 'Alec—you went too far. I think if you *are* going to ask me to marry you, you'd better do so now,' she said. Alec's response and her reply were exactly as she had planned them.

Again, we must be gentle with young Alec. He was *very* inexperienced. But he had always been an outsider, and the experience of being wanted was novel and a delight. He was not a fool. He could see that Barbara had manoeuvred the whole operation. But that was no reason to resist. That she was keen was all the more flattering. And however experienced this vulnerable young man had been, he could never have known what Barbara truly was doing. That he did not know till long afterwards.

Alec made to kiss her again, but the others were approaching, and Barbara turned, and ran towards them.

'We've got the most wonderful news. Alec and I are engaged to be married,' she announced triumphantly. The announcement seemed to be directed towards Tom and Helen, and their reaction was unexpected. They smiled at each other.

Helen shyly said to Tom, 'Well, you'd better make an announcement too.' General amazement followed the news of a second engagement, and that was followed by a mêlée of kissing. In the course of it, Alec received from Georgie not a kiss on the cheek, but a hard kiss on the lips, and then in his ear a clear whisper, 'You chose the wrong sister.'

When the kissing ended, he noticed that there were tears in his fiancée's eyes. But it was not obvious that they were the tears of happiness.

Chapter 5
Devon, Autumn 1918

Helen and Tom wanted to be married before he joined the Royal Flying Corps at the end of August. They did it with a week in hand, he in his new uniform, she looking happy and beautiful, fulfilled, a woman, no longer a girl. The war was expected to last for another two years and they were well aware of the length of a pilot's life over the Western Front. They were determined to be happy together as long as they could. Alec had been surprised by the announcement of their engagement, but he didn't know them well. Their families and other friends saw the wedding as the predestined outcome of a childhood romance.

The engagement that caused more general surprise was that of Alec and Barbara, which no one had expected. In its aftermath, Alec too found it difficult to understand what had happened or why. Although it was technically he who had proposed to Barbara, the initiative had been entirely hers. He was, however, far from unhappy: he welcomed the idea that he had at last acquired an identity, the identity of a soon-to-be-married man. Barbara, on the other hand, seemed far from elated by the success of her initiative. She had abandoned her animated attention to Alec and reverted to the role of the withdrawn ice-maiden. Most fiancés would have been disconcerted, but Alec had never loved Barbara or even particularly liked her. What mattered for him was the status he had acquired. He was triumphant in his emergence from the invisibility of solitude.

When they were alone together, she permitted him to kiss her, but her lips remained firmly together when his tongue made a tentative foray, as Alec understood tongues were meant to do. She didn't restore his hand to its place on her breast, and when he attempted the manoeuvre uninvited, she turned away sharply. But in any event, they rarely were alone together. Barbara seemed to make a point of making sure that Georgie was always with them. She and Georgie were together a great deal in the last weeks of Barbara's spinsterhood, and although Barbara had little to say to Alec, she seemed to have much to confide in her sister. Alec didn't resent Georgie's presence. Far from it: the atmosphere was always livelier when she was around. She carried her sense of fun with her.

The engagement was not protracted: Alec and Barbara were married at the end of November 1918. In the meantime, one great cloud had lifted: The Armistice had been signed on 11 November. The guns were silent. The war to end wars was over.

But another cloud, smaller, but blacker for those below it, had taken its place. Exactly one week before hostilities ceased, and when the war was clearly all but won, Tom was shot through the head as he made his first solo flight. His plane went down over the German lines. He was dead before it hit the ground.

A death on 4 November 1918 is truly no more terrible than a death on 4 November 1914, but the fact that Tom had come so close to surviving added to the poignancy of his widow's brave presence at her friends' wedding. In the circumstances, that wedding was a quiet and small one. Alec, in any event, had no family and no real friends, and the guests at the little wedding breakfast at Honiton were mostly from the Everley side. A surprised school-fellow of Alec's acted as groomsman. Two other contemporaries from school whom Alec would never meet again were pressed to attend for the look of things. His grandparents could not travel from France, but sent a very generous cheque. Barbara's brother, Hector, wearing a very important uniform, gave his sister away. Her mother was so overcome by emotion that she retired to bed immediately after the ceremony.

As Alec kissed his bride, he realised that it was only the sixth time that their lips had met. This time, in public gaze, she allowed the embrace to linger. Alec even felt her lips part; her hands rested on his shoulders. While she was the centre of attention, she bloomed. The ice melted; she reacted to attention as a flower turns to the sun.

There remained something hectic about her until they settled into the train for London. Then the life seemed to go out of her. All the nervous energy drained into collapse. Alec was still stimulated, full of adrenalin, wanting to talk, but Barbara did not engage.

'Just let me rest for a bit. I'm so tired.'

***

The honeymoon was to be spent in Menton with Alec's grandparents. Getting there involved a steamer journey from Southampton, preceded by a night in the Great Southern Hotel. Alec had great hopes for that night. He was a virgin—indeed wholly sexually inexperienced, as he was certain she would be. That brief breastly encounter was not just the most exciting sexual contact he had experienced; it was the only one. Like most of his contemporaries, he had speculated a great deal on the theory of sex, but he had no practical knowledge, and he was uncomfortably aware that some of the theory was based on second-hand lore that might turn out to be very unreliable, anatomically improbable if not impossible.

So, as Barbara prepared herself for bed in the Great Southern Hotel, Southampton, Alec alternated between desire and apprehension, the latter accompanied by a worrying detumescence. When she came to bed, sheathed in substantial body armour, he was almost prepared to acquiesce when she said firmly, 'Not tonight, please, Alec. It's been a long day and I'm not ready for this.'

But of course desire prevailed: after the briefest of pauses, the concurrence of instinct and opportunity was too much for Alec. He knew nothing about the preliminaries, but he knew what the act itself involved, and he pressed on with that. The consequence was painful and quite bloody for Barbara, indeed initially awkward for Alec. But finally, there was exquisite release, and now he understood what all the fuss had been about.

At the same time, he felt a little guilty. The whole thing had so obviously been for his benefit, against her wishes and with no discernible fun for her. By way of apology, and to inject a note of affection into what had been a very animal exercise, he leaned over to kiss her.

She turned her head away in something close to revulsion: 'Not that too. Surely you've done enough?'

***

In the morning, they behaved towards each other with a slightly formal politeness. Neither was quite sure how they were supposed to comport themselves. Were they adults now that they were married? What both were clear about was that they didn't intend to speak about the exertions of the night.

Altogether, this first breakfast was a disappointment for the young husband. Marriage had seemed to him to be about two things. One of them, sex, had certainly been worthwhile, rewarding for him if slightly disappointing in its one-sidedness, the very marked lack of reciprocal ecstasy. But he had also looked forward to finding a whole new aspect to life, a move from a two-dimensional world into one in which there would be a warm, stable centre, in which he and Barbara—and in time no doubt their children—would compose a world within the world, a refuge filled with shared secrets and mutual support. Nothing that he had ever known of Barbara, even in the months that had followed the strange little episode on the terrace at Honiton, had justified him in holding to his dream, and if he had thought about it, as he would much later, he might have found a germ for such a dream more easily in the confiding and open relationship with her sister, but he had all the same expected more than the forced politeness that accompanied the porridge and smoked haddock in the Great Southern Hotel.

***

At noon, they boarded RMS *Corsair* bound for Marseille, and soon afterwards sailed down a Solent that was still busy with warships ready for action. A state of armistice, not peace, existed between Britain and Germany, as in a sense between Alec and Barbara. Their ship sailed with lights doused at night, and protective patrols covered her course until she was in the Bay of Biscay.

After that, she was protected, had she needed to be, by the weather. So was Barbara. She appeared to be laid low, managing only light meals that were brought to their cabin. Alec, still guilty about the one-sided nature of the transaction in the Great Southern Hotel, initially respected her frailty and left her in peace at night, as indeed through much of the day, which she occupied in writing letters and keeping up her diary.

But once the ship had entered the Mediterranean, the seas were calmer and Alec felt entitled to resume his new rights. Barbara did not demur, but if she no longer registered pain, equally she evinced no pleasure. Her mood remained that of the lethargic fatalism that had characterised her behaviour pretty well since their engagement.

For his part, Alec enjoyed the experience of intimacy. Barbara seemed to recognise his right to gratification night and morning, together with his fairly unambitious experiments at procedural variations. Between night and morning, her position in the bed shifted in her sleep, if indeed she was asleep, to close off any attempts at additional congress in the intervening hours.

So, as the last night at sea approached, Alec was on the whole pleased with his new status. He enjoyed the sweaty nights in their cabin. During the day, he and Barbara rarely disagreed. Equally, as they didn't much talk, they rarely agreed. But Alec was no more vociferous than his wife, and he had no experience against which to measure a relationship which others might find hollow and artificial. To the few other passengers on the mail ship, Alec and Barbara must have seemed no more than two children. But for Alec, he was one half of a couple, a married couple, and he felt that, for the first time in his life, he had a public existence. He had to assume that time would furnish the public relationship with the warmth of a private relationship and the support he craved and needed.

Their cabin wasn't large, and the porthole, unnecessarily secured against U-boats which were now corralled in Hamburg, remained shut, screwed tight, its huge handle glossily white with a paint whose odour was powerfully present throughout the ship. To that odour and the essences of two young people in a confined space, the peculiar, oily aroma of the heavy contraceptive sheaths, the sweat and sharp smell of sex, the ammoniac odour of semen, was added on the final morning a new element, the heavy, clinging scent of menstrual blood. Alec was alarmed when he saw the dark stain. But Barbara smiled for perhaps the first time on the voyage.

'It's come,' she said in a tone of unmistakeable relief.

Chapter 6
Menton, Côte d'Azur, December 1918

Alec's grandparents lived in what was rather misleadingly called the Château Barou. In reality, it wasn't a château at all, but a moderately sized villa, built in the Belle Époque style of the Emperor Louis Napoleon in the 1860s. But in comparison with its neighbours, it was set off well, slightly raised from the quiet road which was all that separated it from the Mediterranean, and surrounded by a large garden filled with succulent shrubs, lemon and orange trees and formal lawns. A sweep of gravel led to a paved terrace from which the sea could easily be heard and seen.

The house was in the village of Garavan, in effect a suburb of Menton, nestling on the edge of the Italian border, at the foothills that would climb into the Alps. The main road from Menton rose into these hills to the frontier crossing point. The little road to Garavan continued eastwards along the sea front, going a little beyond the Château Barou before doubling back upwards to join the frontier road.

Menton and its adjoining towns had changed hands between Italy and France many times over the years. It had been Italian only a generation earlier—older residents still called it Mentone—and the atmosphere was more Italian than French. In these early years of the new century, its character was still that of the old one. The streets of the town were cobbled and lit by paraffin lamps. The country roads were unmetalled, and peasants in baggy costumes and wide-brimmed straw hats travelled on them on foot or by donkey. As Barbara and Alec approached Garavan in a light cabriolet drawn by one horse, he felt like a character in a novel by E M Forster. When he said so to Barbara, she looked at him strangely, but didn't reply.

Alec knew the place well, and he always loved coming back. The particular colour of the sea, the indented coastline, the sunlight hitting the outcrops of limestone on the hills, all were very special for him. There was, too, an exotic element. The warmth, even in December, the scent of flowers and aromatic shrubs, mimosa and rosemary, the sight of the lemons and oranges that were heavy on the trees, the smell of dust and smoke, they all reminded him that he was no longer in the sterile north.

As they drove through the Old Town of Menton, he found himself looking directly into a bedroom. He saw a couple, the woman leaning back against the wall, her eyes closed, her lips apart, while the man's hand worked between her legs. The cameo spoke strongly of the sensual, uninhibited south. Alec knew that

Barbara was looking too. He turned to grin at her, but she flushed and looked away.

When they arrived at Château Barou, a gardener was watering the shrubs with a hose. As soon as he heard the cabriolet on the gravel, he ran indoors and by the time they'd drawn up, Alec's grandparents were on the terrace to welcome them.

His grandmother, Alice Ross, a vivacious woman of just sixty years, ran to greet Barbara, seized both her hands, kissed her and embraced her warmly. Then she held her firmly, frankly looked her in the face and said, 'My dear, dear Barbara. How very beautiful you are. How lucky Alec is, and how lucky we are. Welcome to Alec's family.'

Adrian Ross, too, stood on no ceremony. He had acquired French habits. He kissed Barbara on both cheeks before saying, 'We think of Alec as our own child. We're so happy for him and for our new daughter. Welcome.'

Alec stood apart from the others as these endearments were effected. He felt that he'd come home, even if the exchanges slightly embarrassed him: they seemed excessively effusive, and the whole performance was far more emotional and sentimental than his parents would have thought proper. Little more than an adolescent, he suffered an adolescent's embarrassment. But as he watched, even in his embarrassment he was happy. He felt he was watching the materialisation of at least part of his dream. Here were two people who loved him, of that he was in no doubt. In their concern for his happiness, they were truly happy to be welcoming as one of themselves the woman who would be his companion and support through life, a woman who was, it was assumed, united to them in her love for him.

He did not know what Barbara would do. Over these recent months, he had learned that her reactions could never be predicted. But she performed. She performed magnificently. There was no ice. She shone like the Mediterranean sun and sparkled like the sea. Finally, Alec, in his turn, was admitted to the embracing circle, and then all four entered the château and were absorbed in its routines.

***

Over the next few days, Alec showed Barbara the sights of the area. They wandered through the narrow lanes of the old town, climbing steeply through its roughly paved alleys to enter the middle ages and look down on the Golfe de la Paix. They took the electric tram all the way from Garavan to Monte Carlo, returning without getting off. More ambitiously, they hired a horse brake for forty francs and drove to Bordighera on the Italian side. At the Pont St Louis, they crossed the border by an ancient and very slender bridge. Alec watched peasants making their way round on a pedestrian path, no more than a foot wide, that hugged the abyss, bundles on their heads and backs, while the torrent fell in cascades to the rocky bed of the ravine. Barbara was more preoccupied by concern for her safety in the ill-maintained brake, driven by a youth no more than twelve years old.

When they were together alone, the atmosphere between them was much as it had been on board ship, polite but not warm. At breakfast, with Alice or Adrian Ross present, things were different. The act was on: they were charmed, they were dazzled. Then the day's expedition took place. It was followed by a rest for Barbara, when letters were written—mostly to her sister—and the day's entry was made in her diary. In the evening, over dinner, the performance again, though less highly charged than the mornings.

After a week, which Alec, though he was no expert on the matter, judged a discreet delay, he made to resume the activities which he had found so pleasurable on board the *Corsair* but was met with a physical rebuff and glittering eyes:

'My condition! Surely, you remember.' Alec had remembered, and was surprised the 'condition' lasted as long as it apparently did.

***

Menton was not renowned for the gaiety of its entertainments, compared to those of its racier neighbours like Nice and Monte Carlo. It was said that the Museum of Archaeological Curiosities in the Town Hall was the liveliest diversion the town had to offer, but towards the end of their stay, Alec's grandparents invited the young couple to a charity *buffet conversazione* given at the New Casino to raise funds for the Gorbo Sanatorium, which had recently been opened for the consumptive patients whom the local hotels declined to receive.

It was an animated occasion. Most of the guests were English. The lack of French presence was understandable, as the evening was in a sense a reflection on the uncharitable attitude of their hoteliers. But there was quite a number of Americans, led by their vice-consul, and a distinguished group of Russian émigrés, among them some very beautiful and slightly mysterious ladies, and the archpriest from the Orthodox Church, magnificent in his robes, tall stiff hat and flowing beard.

The English community looked to their own honorary vice-consul as their head, and the role was filled by H Humphrey Hill, an unassuming man whose gainful employment was provided by the Banque Isnard, of which he was the local representative. He was also accepted as the local representative of the King-Emperor. The community wanted to have a leader to look to, and he was as good as any other for that purpose.

As the four from the Château Barou moved around the flamboyant room with its mirrors and pillars and gilding, Alec and Barbara were introduced to the leaders of Menton society. There were the Rectors of two Anglican churches and the Minister of the Scottish church, as well as the pastor of the German church, all of whom had remained on the best of terms throughout the war. There was an English solicitor who liaised and interpreted when his fellow-countrymen were obliged to deal with French *notaires* in their property transactions. He was pleased to do so because of the sums he earned from making their wills and winding up their estates.

Indeed, the fact of mortality amongst an elderly community, many of whom had been brought to the south by the delicacy of their constitutions, was emphasised by the medical element of those who sipped their wine and refreshed themselves from the *buffet*. Alec and Barbara were introduced to Miss Beauchamp, the Matron of the English Nurses' home. Miss Beauchamp, who had spent the war as a sister in the British Base Hospital at Boulogne, was notably brisk, clearly efficient. She seemed to see straight into her interlocutor's inner thoughts, but in an entirely frank and kind way. Alec liked her.

From her, they were moved on to a more serious medical colloquium. The director of the new Sanatorium and his assistant were deep in discussion with the English doctors of Menton, of whom there were no less than three. The medical men politely admitted Barbara, Alec and his grandparents to their group. The conversation was widened to bring in the outsiders, but it was clear that they were ready to return to serious matters, and as talk began to turn to the Spanish influenza outbreak and the steps that were being taken to deal with it in the town, Alec's grandmother hastened to move her group on.

It was in Jane McBeth that she found refuge. Jane was the widow of the English interpreter at the principal Railway Station. Alec had already heard of her from his grandmother. The two ladies were close friends. The McBeths' social standing was slightly more elevated than might have been thought. Alasdair McBeth had been a young Scottish lawyer. He had suffered from tuberculosis and couldn't undertake war service. Like so many others, he moved to Menton in the hope, vain as it transpired, that its climate would prolong his life. Unlike most of his countrymen, he had found that reading novels and undertaking the social round did not fulfil him and he was pleased to vary his daily routine by his work at the railway station. It was all, his widow said, that he was physically capable of doing though wholly unworthy of his intellectual capacity.

Jane McBeth was not more than thirty. She didn't wear mourning. She was vivacious, with luxuriant, chestnut-brown hair, and had the same direct and frank style as Miss Beauchamp. Alec's grandmother had told her that one of the English doctors, a bachelor called Terris, had his eye on her, and Alec could understand why.

***

When the party got back to the Château Barou, Alec and his grandmother talked about the evening for a time. Then they followed the others upstairs. As they parted at the top, Mrs Ross kissed her grandson good night on both cheeks, in the French way, rather more formally than usual. She held his shoulders for a moment, looking at him thoughtfully. 'What a remarkable girl Barbara is! What a performer! No wonder you fell for her.'

Alec remembered the little pantomime, because such by now he admitted to himself it had been, contrived by his wife on the gravel terrace at Honiton. He wondered whether falling for Barbara came anywhere close to describing what had happened. It certainly did not—unless his grandmother was using the phrase in a very particular sense. Surely she was not? And yet, she was a wise and observant woman, a good judge of human nature, and experienced in the ways of the world. For the rest of his life, Alec was never sure what she had meant.

***

Throughout the second—and final—week at the château, the quality of Barbara's performance declined. To begin with, the change was only discernible in the evening, but soon it became evident earlier in the day. Alice and Adrian took infinite pains to bring her out of herself—and she made an effort to respond—but she seemed increasingly flat, worn and lethargic. She reminded Alec of her mother, the woman he'd always thought looked as if she'd been left out in the sun too long.

In retrospect, the *conversazione* had been the turning point. Throughout that evening, Barbara had sparkled. As an attractive novelty in the little community, she had been the centre of attention as she was taken round the room. In each group, all eyes were on her. The interest invigorated her. It energised her. She responded to it by directing the full force of her charm on everyone she met. At her shoulder, Alec was reminded of how he had felt when he had been the object of her attention. Barbara was intelligent as well as beautiful. The combination of her sympathy and her breathless enthusiasm left everyone feeling that they had been special for her.

But the performance had been achieved at a cost. When they mounted the horse-drawn taxi to return to the Château, Barbara sank back into the cushions and closed her eyes. When they arrived, she stumbled out and made her way upstairs as if she were drugged.

Already Alec had on several occasions heard his grandmother ask Barbara if she were quite well, if she were overdoing things. Barbara replied, as she did to his own questions, that nothing was wrong, she was just rather tired. On the morning after the *conversazione,* his grandfather, looking very embarrassed, said that his grandmother wondered if perhaps Barbara was in 'a certain condition'. Alec was able to reply in the negative. He knew very little about these matters, but he was aware that the apparently continuing condition indicated by the dark blood he had seen on the *Corsair* precluded what his grandparents had in mind.

But events moved at a quickening pace after that evening at the New Casino. Soon Barbara was running a high fever. A doctor was summoned. Alec's grandparents were very clear that it should be a French one. The English doctors—even Jane's Doctor Terris—were not highly regarded. Doctor Brenot arrived within the hour. The gardener who had been watering the flowerbed when they had arrived held the reins of his horse-drawn fly while the doctor entered the house. He was a large and florid Frenchman, with a rose in his buttonhole. He reminded Alec of a Victorian actor-manager. He left his top hat, kid gloves and silver topped cane on the hall table. Alec had no doubt that he was doing well from treating the hypochondriacs and tubercular refugees from northern Europe and the rich émigrés from the Bolshevik regions of Russia.

Brenot took little time to examine Barbara. When he returned, he announced in perfect English, only slightly accented, 'The young lady has influenza. There is, as you will know, very much of it around. It is a serious form of the disease, but she is young and has resilience. My opinion is that she will be well,' he said in the reassuring tones of professional confidence that endeared him to the infirm of the Riviera. 'A number have died, but none of my patients so far,' he added, the last two words detracting somewhat from the reassurance that had gone before.

By the following morning, Barbara was clearly much worse. The gardener was sent to fetch the doctor. Brenot arrived within minutes. This time, his manner was quite different. There was no flower in his buttonhole, no cane. He wasted no time in pleasantries. He was serious and business-like, and Alec realised he was more than the man he'd taken him for. After forty minutes with Barbara, he left, returning within the hour with an assistant. An oxygen tank was brought in and an electrical device to stimulate the lungs. A trained nurse was required, and it was agreed that Jane McBeth, who had nursed in a war hospital, would be best for this role.

When Jane arrived, quiet and competent, Alec felt relieved; and Barbara too, in her periods of wakefulness, seemed pleased to have her support. But when Brenot returned the following day, he spent a long time with Barbara. He emerged solemn and puzzled.

'She lacks will.' He turned to Alec: 'It is you, young man, who can save her. Medicine can work only if the patient has the will to live. You must give her the will. You are a young couple, newly married—there is every reason for her to wish to live.' Alec would bear the responsibility if influenza claimed its first victim from the ranks of the doctor's patients.

And Alec did his best. For the next twenty-four hours, he and Jane rarely left Barbara's bedside. Jane administered the pills and tonics that the doctor had prescribed. The electric stimulator was soon abandoned as being too aggressive, but the oxygen helped Barbara breathe. Alec sponged her brow, encouraged her to drink. He told her lies. He told her he loved her. She was too close to delirium to say anything intelligible in reply except once, in the early hours of the morning, just as the light of the rising sun was beginning to slant through the louvres of the shutters.

She looked at him and said quite clearly, 'I'm sorry. You never knew.' Jane and Alec were sitting on either side of the bed, holding her hands. Alec didn't know if Jane had heard.

When the doctor returned for his next visit, it was for the formality of signing a death certificate. Alec saw Brenot's face working and realised that he was struggling to hold back tears. The doctor had cared: it was not just that, in Barbara, influenza had scored a victory in a personal and professional duel.

After the doctor had left the room, Alec and Jane continued to sit on either side of the bed. Then Jane came round and sat beside him. She took both his hands in hers.

After a while he said, 'I can't really believe that it's my wife that's died.'

'I understand you,' said Jane quietly and with conviction.

'No, you *don't* understand. I can't take in that she was my wife, that we were married. It was all so brief. I really didn't know her. I don't even know if I loved her.'

'You will know. Sometimes, it takes a lifetime to know what brings you together. But there was something, and finally, you discover it.'

Alec was more curious than bereft. 'But we only had two weeks together, not a lifetime. How will I ever know?'

Jane took some time to answer. She looked down at her lap, the crown of her head, with its wavy chestnut-brown hair, tilted towards Alec as she considered how to reply. 'Maybe it surprises you that my husband, who was a brilliant man, who'd have been a judge or a professor if he'd not been ill, was content to work in the station here as an interpreter. I'll tell you why. I've not told anyone else. He did it to exhaust himself and to forget.'

Alec realised that he was not to interrupt. After a moment, Jane went on. 'He was bitterly ashamed. He couldn't fight in the war. His friends all did, but he couldn't, because he had TB. He felt ashamed.'

'But that was absurd.'

'Of course, it was, and he knew it. But that didn't stop him feeling that he was shamefully weak, and he worked to make himself forget.' Her low voice trembled. 'And then he found that a bottle was even better for that.'

They looked at each other for some moments in silence. Alec felt that he knew Jane far better than he truly did. She continued. 'Not many people know that was how his life ended. Those who did may have thought it a pathetic end. I may have thought so myself once. But in time, I understood. Now I know that he was a brave, proud man who died because he was brave, as brave as if he'd been fighting another kind of war. I know now that's why I married him and I'm proud of him.'

For some moments, Alec thought she had answered his question. Then he realised that she hadn't. 'But Jane, I had no real reason to marry her except that she was available. There was nothing there and I gave her no reason to live. I killed her.'

Jane was thoughtful and for the moment, much more than just a few years older than he. She looked at him with infinite gentleness and said, 'Well, just maybe what you'll know as time passes is that the marriage was a mistake. But you were very young and it wasn't only *your* mistake. If it was a mistake don't make the same one again. Above all, don't feel guilty.'

After some minutes more, Jane got up and led Alec downstairs by the hand. He thought about guilt. How could he not feel guilt if he thought he had killed his wife? The answer must be never to think of her.

What Alec felt in the aftermath of Barbara's death was not so much personal grief as a sense that life had left him. Since his engagement, and particularly since his marriage, he had enjoyed an entirely novel feeling of self-importance, even of purpose. Now he was again reduced to two dimensions. He felt empty. He realised that he had always felt empty, but never as empty as this. He had no experience to guide him on what to feel or what to do.

His grandfather explained that because of the mildness of the climate and the limited facilities of French undertakers, it would be necessary to inter Barbara before any of her family could come out from England. And so, two days later, and less than three weeks after he had married her, Barbara's body was placed in a horse-drawn hearse. The hearse was decorated with black plumes and pulled by two black horses, also beplumed. Their silver bits gleamed against the black leather of their traces and their polished black flanks. The high sides of the hearse were made of glass, through which the dark oak coffin with its gleaming fittings, also of silver, and the lilies that surrounded it could be seen. Alec walked behind it, followed by his grandfather and some of his male friends. Doctor Brenot was there, and also, Alec noticed, Jane's Doctor Terris. He found that touching.

As the cortège made its way up the steep road to the English cemetery, Alec saw a girl of perhaps fifteen walking downhill towards him with her mother. A gust of wind caught her skirt and lifted it above her waist. The girl seemed oblivious. Her mother restored her modesty with a savage sweep of the arm.

After the service, Alec walked back down the hill with his grandfather. The harder he tried to recall Barbara's face, the more difficult it became, and the more clearly he saw the face of the girl whose skirt had been lifted by the wind. He knew that he would not feel guilty.

Chapter 7
London, December 1918

Alec had planned to visit Barbara's parents as soon as he returned to England. In part, he simply felt it was something he should do. He also wanted to give Barbara's diary to her sister. He had hesitated to open it. It didn't seem proper to take advantage of her death to look at something so private that he wouldn't have looked at in her lifetime without her permission.

Eventually, he compromised. They had been united in marriage and there should be no secrets from each other. He opened the page for the day of their marriage. He would read from just that day on. There was one short sentence: 'All wrong. How can I live with it?' The following day's entry was equally brief and disheartening: 'All I imagined. But he has no idea.' It had been a mistake to open the diary, and he read no more.

He wrote to Mrs Everley and proposed a visit, but it was Georgie who replied, saying that it would be better if she called on him in London. So a few days later, he sat in the lounge of the Alington Hotel, waiting for her. The hotel was an old one which his family had used on visits to London. It was quietly situated on the edge of Mayfair, not smart, but solid, comfortable, timeless, patronised by prosperous country families for generations. It was a club-like haven in a city in which they did not entirely feel at home. As Alec had walked across the room to his table over boards which creaked under a fine but worn carpet, he reflected that this was something of what his country had been fighting for, this sense of continuity, this faded elegance, this insular self-confidence that could eschew fashion and modernity.

Soon enough, he saw Georgie hurrying towards him. She carried her air of fresh-faced coltishness with her, and he felt a pang of affection and nostalgia. And yet she looked more grown-up than he remembered. She wore a hat, and a short blue chiffon dress that swung as she walked.

She took both his hands, pecked his cheek and said, 'You poor, poor thing. How good it is to see you, Alec. Let's eat and talk. I'm hungry.'

And they did eat and talk. There was no stiffness. She conveyed sympathy, but dwelt mainly on practical matters. When he handed her the diary, he looked troubled and started to speak, but she stopped him at once:

'I don't think there will be any secrets here for me. She told me everything, you know. And she wrote me the most awfully detailed letters right to the end.'

She sat looking at him for a moment, considering but not speaking. She was the younger of the two, but her attitude was that of an adult assessing a child.

Then she continued, 'Alec, you never understood, and though it may hurt you a little, and though it may seem disloyal to Barbara, I think I owe it to you to tell you why she married you.'

'Well, I never did understand,' he said. 'She always seemed much more interested in Tom.'

Georgie shook her head decisively. 'No, no, no. She was never interested in Tom, and Tom was always going to marry Helen. Everyone knew that. That was the point. It was Helen that Barbara wanted.'

'Helen!'

'Oh, yes. Barbara *loved* Helen. Setting her cap at Tom was supposed to upset the Tom-Helen thing, but of course, it didn't do any good. Tom and Helen just laughed at it. Then Barbara changed her tactics. She loved Helen so much that she assumed that Helen felt to some extent in the same way about her. She was wrong of course, and I doubt if Helen even knew that Barbara wasn't interested in men. But anyway, she thought that getting engaged to you would kindle a spark of jealousy in Helen, and who knows what would happen next.'

'But instead…'

'Yes, instead everything went terribly wrong. Tom and Helen announced their engagement. I didn't know everything about all this till Barbara wrote to me after your wedding. I'd had my suspicions about her interest in Helen, but that was all. But on the night of the two engagements, I could see that something terrible had happened. I had never seen her look so unhappy. I think the moment when she heard Tom's announcement was the moment she started to die.'

'You really do?'

'Yes, poor Barbara. The engagement to you had locked her in to a life she didn't want to live, and it turned out to have been pointless. It was like a Greek tragedy.'

The eating of cakes and drinking of tea had been suspended as reality had been revealed to Alec. Now he and Georgie were glad to return to the camouflage of these activities for some moments, while they took stock of what they had been discussing. Eventually, Georgie asked Alec what he planned to do now that he wasn't required for the war. Would he continue at Art College?

'No. I like painting, but I don't like being taught to paint. I think I'll just go into the army as planned. Not the Regular Army—they don't need officers, but I can take a temporary commission in the Indian Army.'

Georgie looked shocked. 'You're an artist. You don't want to be a soldier.'

'I don't want *not* to be one either. It's not worth thinking of something new. And there's not much else I can do. I can always paint wherever I happen to be.'

For four years, Alec had assumed that he would join the army when he left school. Almost everyone he knew had volunteered or been conscripted. Tom was very far from the first of his friends who had died in the war. His school's 1913 First Fifteen had enlisted together. When the guns fell silent, only four survived, and only one of them uninjured. Was the unimaginative Alec animated by a germ of duty, or was he worked on by guilt?

Georgie looked at Alec for several moments, wondering how well she understood him. Before she came to any conclusion, he broke the silence. He asked how Barbara's family were coping.

Georgie said, 'Mother's taken it very badly. You know she was never strong. Now she's in a deep depression. She scarcely eats and she only sleeps because of the drugs they give her. Father and Hector are angry, bitterly angry with you.'

'Why? Angry with me? What have I done to hurt them?'

'Nothing at all. I know that, but they don't. Barbara wrote all these letters. She was so unhappy and maybe she thought her father and brother would rescue her from what she called your "practices".'

'"Practices!" But that's absurd! I never…' he wasn't sure how to go on, but Georgie rescued him.

'I know, Alec. Barbara wrote me long, detailed letters, and I know *exactly* what you got up to.' She gave an embarrassed smile. 'Not unnatural at all and not, I believe, unusual. But what is entirely natural to you and me,' she coloured slightly, '*was* unnatural to Barbara—and maybe, as I say, she misrepresented a bit in the hope that a white knight—Hector or Father—would ride to her rescue.'

Alec, shocked, looked at her blankly. After a moment, she added, 'Maybe a white knight *would* have ridden to her rescue if she hadn't died. As it is, Father and Hector don't believe she died of Spanish influenza. They say she died because of you.'

Alec began to assimilate what he was being told. He wanted to protest. 'But this is horribly unfair to me!'

'I know it is, Alec, and I'm dreadfully sorry for you, but my first duty is to Barbara's memory and my family, and so I can never tell anyone the truth about Barbara. And neither can you, because you are a gentleman. I know you won't abuse what I've told you today. Only you and I will ever know.'

Georgie and Alec had no more to say to each other. They stood up, and Alec showed Georgie to the front door of the hotel. They stood for a moment, looking at each other, then Georgie moved closer and hugged Alec. He awkwardly returned the embrace.

She kissed him on the cheek and then, with her cheek still against his, said quietly in his ear. 'We'll never meet again, and because of that here's something else that only you and I will ever know. I told you before that you'd chosen the wrong sister, and I'll tell you now that this sister would have been very happy with you and your *practices*.' Then she turned on her heel and walked off quickly on the busy pavement. She never looked back. Her skirt fluttered in the wind.

Alec looked after her. He could still smell her perfume and could still feel the warmth of her cheek on his. In the hour he had spent with Georgie, he had briefly the sense of completeness that had visited him when he and Barbara had been welcomed by his grandparents. He realised he had lost something he had never bothered to see. Now, at last, he felt an acute sense of personal grief flooding in. It was not grief for the sister who lay in the English cemetery at Menton. It was grief for the bright-eyed, auburn-haired girl who had just disappeared into London's traffic. He dealt with his grief in the only way he knew.

He walked slowly into the hotel's reading room and spent some hours with back numbers of *Punch*. The subject of the drawings had changed. Overweight war profiteers and jumped-up businessmen who couldn't pronounce their aitches had replaced cockneys and country bumpkins. But the joke was the same: the elite laughing at the rest.

As he turned over the dusty bound volumes, Alec's mind was not on the words and drawings in front of his eyes. The heavy-handed facetiousness simply kept out other thoughts while he resolved to create a barrier between himself and Barbara and Georgie and between himself and any future Barbaras and Georginas. In that last year, he had allowed the carapace which had surrounded him at school to fracture and that had been a mistake. It had been cold and lonely within his defensive citadel and the world outside had briefly looked warm and tempting. But venturing into it had been a disaster, a weakness and a source of hurt. Withdrawing within his defences, he entered on his army years.

Chapter 8
Mesopotamia, 1919

The army years were not unhappy. The army he was part of wasn't so much a military force as an administrative machine. He wasn't afraid of fighting, and if he'd had to be a soldierly soldier, he might well have been a brave one, but he neither fired a shot in anger nor even heard one fired.

The routine of policing, record keeping and the maintenance of essential services suited him very well, and he was very good at it. Britain found herself at the end of the war in possession of large areas of the Middle East without having planned to acquire them, and without knowing what to do with them now that she had acquired them. The areas that came under British sway were all part of the former Ottoman Empire: Palestine, Jordan, Syria and Iraq. Palestine, with its particular problem in the confrontation between Jews and Arabs, stood slightly apart, the responsibility of London, but Delhi and the Indian army, of which Ross was a part, had to deal with the rest.

The major political issue was which areas would remain in British control, and which would go to France. For centuries, in Napoleon's time and even before that, in the days of the Crusades, France and Britain had competed for influence in the Levant. Through the nineteenth century, the French cultural influence was dominant. There were very many French schools and colleges in the region, and French was widely spoken. But at the outset of the war, Britain consolidated her position in Egypt, a particularly sensitive area of competition, and as the war progressed increasingly became the dominant power militarily and politically. France was unhappy.

And so as the war went on, in order to bind herself to her new ally but old enemy, Britain made promises to France about the spoils they would get in the Middle East, rather in the same way as she made promises to both Jews and Arabs that were difficult to reconcile.

Now, the struggle of war over and with the gains in Mesopotamia won by her own arms, Britain wondered if she had been just a little bit too generous to her Gallic allies. The Entente Cordiale became distinctly uncordial and the relationship degenerated into the squabbles and mistrust with which both sides were familiar. France felt betrayed by perfidious Albion, and Britain felt her position in this oil-rich region, a critical link to her eastern empire, threatened by French ambitions.

Into this standoff, Ross, in his new khaki uniform, was injected. While the politicians in London addressed their minds to the problem, the Indian army and its political officers from Delhi had the day-to-day job of running the new territories. Inevitably it was the machinery of Indian civil government which was imposed through the agency of the army of the Raj. Indian civil and criminal legal codes were applied to areas which were surveyed and mapped according to Indian procedures. Taxes were assessed and levied on the Indian pattern. The new territories had to be run as economically as possible, ideally self-supporting. They had to be secured against the French.

Ross was based at the British Depot in Damascus, in what would later be allocated to France and called Syria, but was still part of Mesopotamia, its future in contention. He had the rank of lieutenant, and he commanded a unit of two platoons which moved out to patrol through the former Ottoman provinces of Syria, Iraq and Jordan, spending a month on patrol followed by a week at base. The extent of his autonomy would have been remarkable in a truly military situation, but made sense in an administrative one. His task was to assist the civil commissioners in policing work, and to compile exhaustive census records on which policy discussions could be taken and which would provide the basis of tax impositions.

The policing function proved to be a minor one, except in Jordan, where the supporters of the Emir Abdullah were running a little wild. But even there, the appearance of an armed patrol was enough to enforce a semblance of order. On the administrative side, with his two clerk-sergeants, Ross ran an efficient little machine, compiling remarkably accurate information very speedily, and sending it back in regular chunks to his superiors in Damascus.

He enjoyed the work, its routine, its system, the sense of dove-tailing into a much larger operation. He took pride in his efficiency and in devising ways of performing what was an entirely novel function. He liked the army, the sense of its size and power. He liked the fact that it was an institution, an entity that was self-providing. Food, equipment, personnel were all delivered without organisation on his part. Having been at boarding schools from the age of six, he'd always been part of an institution, but this was different. There were none of the rivalries of school, the cliques of which he'd never been a member. Here he was left to get on with the job. He rather liked being responsible for his men. The contact was formal. He kept his distance from them, as was proper, but he enjoyed looking after their welfare. They recognised that he did this well, and regarded him with respect, though without affection.

Back in Damascus, at the end of each month's patrol, he was off-duty for most of the week. He had little occasion for contact with his fellow officers. If he had been carrying out a more military role there would have been need for co-ordination with others and for receiving fresh orders. As it was, his job of patrolling, gathering information and reporting was pre-arranged. It was largely left to him to plan his own routine and since he was demonstrably good at his job, he worked away with little interference.

Bachelor officers could choose either to live in barracks or in the town. For the unclubbable Ross, the choice was easy, and he rented a small *beit*, a self-contained eighteenth-century townhouse built round a courtyard with a splashing fountain. At two ends of the courtyard were *liwans,* seating areas, and on the side opposite the entrance doorway was a low range of domestic offices, the kitchen and a shack in which his cleaning man had a room where he kept his equipment. Upstairs, four bedrooms with balconies overlooked the courtyard through lattice windows.

The contrast between the outside and the interior was marked. Outside, the building was plain and without windows, the walls black and white in an uncompromising, unostentatious style. Inside it was quite different. The courtyard was paved with intricately patterned Damascene tiles, the walls composed of striped stone in black, yellow and white. It was lit by elaborate suspended wrought-iron lamps. The bedroom windows looked on to the courtyard through their delicate stone *mushrabiya* tracery and their shutters were decorated in marquetry and mother of pearl.

***

If there were a formal mess dinner during his Damascus week, Ross was expected to attend. Initially, he did so, but found the adolescent high spirits and drinking games tedious, the hilarity forced. He tentatively chanced reducing his attendance record. Nothing was said. At first, he skipped one in three, then one in two. As time passed, his meticulous performance of duty was recognised, his lack of sociability accepted, and by his final year in the army, he was rarely seen in the mess except in the afternoons, when he sometimes looked in to catch up on newspapers, or occasionally for lunch.

Damascus was an ancient city, but not a large one, and the Depot, with its mess, was near the centre and the great Souq al-Hamidiyya. As Ross walked through the town, he passed the entrances to the Souq, with their tantalising glimpses of sights that had changed little in millennia, hardly at all since St Paul recovered his sight nearby in the Via Recta, 'the street that is called Straight'. Camel meat hung above tables that displayed kaleidoscopic arrays of spices, and the air was heavy with the scents that had had been brought there over the Silk Road. There was much to savour. Pyramids of sandy-hued turmeric, darker cumin and terracotta-coloured chilli contrasted with the blue of indigo, along with nameless greens and browns. They composed a palette that should have spoken to the artist in Ross, though his gaze travelled over them fairly mechanically. The stallholders treated their spices as artistic works in progress, restoring their shapes after every sale. To the visual impact of the timeless scene was added the combining scents of the spices, the dried fruit, and the almost narcotic, oily essences of great bunches of lavender and rough squares of Aleppo soap.

All this made little impression on Ross, thinking of his tax schedules and population returns. His mind was unreceptive to the romance of the place, the sense of history, the continuity reflected in the fact that the Omayyad Mosque stood on the site of the Church of St John the Baptist, where the head of the saint is said to be buried. Indeed, before it became a Christian church, the building had been the site of the Temple of Jupiter. Earlier still the God Hadad had been worshipped there. Not far away, Saladin lay buried. Ross walked past his monument without realising who was commemorated.

***

With the *beit,* he inherited its cleaner, Abelcader, a taciturn grandfather who had worked for a French family which had left Damascus to return to metropolitan France. Most of his monosyllables were in their language. Abelcader indicated concisely that his skills did not extend to cooking, and in any event, he understandably chose not to sleep in his room at the *beit*, but with his large family. He did, however, say that his widowed daughter-in-law, Salema, would be prepared to cook for Ross when he was in Damascus. Ross agreed to the arrangement without any questions about Salema's culinary skills.

The first time he met her was on his return to Damascus a month later. He arrived at the *beit* in the early afternoon, washed and went straight to the Orderly Office at the barracks, where one of his sergeants had already deposited the latest volumes of census information. He made his presence known, wrote up the final details of his Report, which he had all but completed already. Habitually, he worked on it at the end of each day's patrol, finding it best to record his impressions while they were still fresh in his memory. In any event, it filled his evenings well, a more congenial occupation than making small talk with any other officers who happened to be at the overnight stopping points.

At six or so in the evening, he returned to the *beit*. Abelcader had left, so he let himself in and climbed to his bedroom to shower again and change for dinner. As he did so, he could smell lamb being grilled, with a strong scent of rosemary and something spicier mingling in the smoke of the charcoal. When he came down to the courtyard to eat, he met Salema for the first time. She was in her middle thirties, plain but not unattractive. She wore western clothes, a widow's black blouse and long dress, her dark hair up but not covered. Her eyes were very black, and lightly outlined in kohl, the only make-up she wore. Her eyes never met his. She introduced herself and gave a slight bow. She didn't shake hands.

As she served the meal, she continued to keep her eyes cast down. Ross was no epicure, but without knowing what he was eating (which was an array of *mezze*, cucumber with yoghurt, minted aubergine and chick pea, followed by the grilled lamb with roast vegetables and aromatic rice, and then a simple pudding of fresh oranges in rosewater, dusted with spice), he realised he had been very lucky with his cook. She brought him a cup of thick sweet coffee and prepared to leave. It didn't occur to him to say how marvellous a cook she was, but he did at least thank her. She acknowledged his thanks, still without meeting his eye.

In the course of the following week, she volunteered a little information about herself. She had been educated at a French convent school. French had been the language of instruction and was her first language. Her husband had been a laboratory assistant at the university. He had been knocked down and

53

killed by a Turkish army lorry when the youngest of her three children was only months old. She lived with his family. They supported her and her children.

By the end of the week she raised her eyes to meet his. He had assumed that the avoidance of eye contact was part of Arab modesty or something she had been taught by the nuns. But now he wondered if she had simply been trying to protect him from their spectacular intensity. As they met his, he realised that he was grinning weakly.

***

While Ross was away on his next patrol, he wondered idly whether he would return to meet averted eyes, but on his return, he found that Salema was continuing from where she'd left off. From the start, she looked straight into him with a wide-eyed gaze that was so steady that he felt his mouth slacken. It must have been obvious, and she knew he had been without the company of women for at least the last month. She gave the slightest of smiles before she left. Ross sat on after his meal, looking out over the town. It was dusk. The sun had just set and the sky was indigo, with a bank of copper on the horizon. In the distance, beyond the minarets and spires he could see against that copper the desert, its curvature broken by occasional palm trees. In the foreground, outside the Souq al-Hamidiyya countless stalls grilled *shawarma* on skewers over charcoal grills. He could see the light of the fires and of the paraffin lamps that lit the stalls. In the still air of evening, the smoke rose in peaceful columns. Ross could smell the smoke, the cooking, the cumin and other less identifiable spices. Even he saw the beauty and thought he understood the point of it all.

On the following night, something had changed. Salema was slightly more business-like, slightly more sure of herself. When she might have been about to leave, her look engaged his longer than it need have, and she raised her hand to the button of her blouse. It might have meant nothing, but there was the faintest suggestion of interrogation in those expressive eyes, and Ross interpreted it correctly.

At the end of the week, he paid her wages. He didn't quite know what to do. It was clear that she found it difficult to have to rely on the bounty of her husband's family to bring up her children, but Ross didn't want to insult her by treating her as a whore. He decided to add a small amount, say two hundred francs, to her pay, as by oversight: thus, he thought, removing the direct financial element from their relationship. He was, however, too fastidious in his processes. Salema looked at the supplement for services rendered and said, in a perfectly kindly way, that that was not enough; the proper figure was five hundred francs.

Both were happy with the arrangement, and things continued on this basis. While they rested on a commercial relationship and on the interplay of supply and demand, Ross liked to think that there was a little more to it than that. Salema hinted that with her convent education, she was of a higher intellectual background than the rest of her late husband's family, and that she appreciated the opportunities which her transactions with Ross afforded for talk of a sort which was beyond the scope of her relatives by marriage.

At the same time, it was clear that neither gratitude for the five hundred francs nor for the intellectual stimulation of which she was able to avail herself would induce her to stray beyond the clear limits she had laid down for their intimacy. For some reason, it was unthinkable that this intimacy should take place in Ross's bed. A couch in the *liwan* that opened on to the courtyard apparently gave it a lesser significance. Her blouse would be opened to the waist, or rather a point slightly above it, and her skirt raised to a point well below it.

What went on in the Free Zones was expected to be limited and to be preceded by meticulous ablution. After only tentative and firmly rebuffed essays at more adventurous activity, Ross accepted the rules with no particular regrets. His affections for Salema were animal ones, and though the power and femininity of those eyes had disconcerted him, they had not wakened an insatiable physical desire for all the delights she might have had to offer. All he truly felt urged to do was regularly to ejaculate into her—or at least into the confines of the cumbrous skin sheaths that the pharmacies of Damascus supplied—and that she allowed him to do.

Chapter 9

And so things continued, and Ross was entirely satisfied with the way they went. The arrangement with Salema provided all he wanted from it—physical release without emotional commitment—and his professional life gave him satisfaction of another sort. He had no doubt that what he was doing was necessary and worthwhile, and he enjoyed the knowledge that he was doing it well. The patrols were physically quite arduous, and it was rewarding to go to bed at the end of the day tired, conscious that something had been achieved.

During the years that he had spent in the army, political decisions were being taken, and the shape of the new Middle East was being formed. Palestine was still riven by clashes between the two communities, but it was now clear that Jordan and Iraq would be controlled by Britain, through the agency of puppet rulers assisted by British advisors maintained in position by British arms. Syria and Lebanon would go to France, despite the wishes of the British and the Arabs.

So as Ross's temporary commission was coming to an end, he faced the certainty that the British military presence in Damascus would be replaced by direct French rule. On the other hand, he could be realistically confident that his life in the army in the Levant would continue. The British would be needed in Jordan and Iraq and Palestine, and his annual reports had revealed that his superiors thought well of him. The warmth of these reports was reflected in his promotion to captain, a higher rank than most temporary officers attained.

He was, accordingly, in a confident frame of mind when he made his way to the Depot for a meeting with his Commanding Officer just before his final leave prior to the expiry of his commission. The meeting had been arranged a week before, and was to deal with his future on his return from leave, when he could expect his commission to be confirmed on a regular basis, resulting in a long-term career in the army.

He arrived at the Orderly Office and was told to go straight in to the Colonel's office. Lieutenant Colonel O'Neil was well-known to Ross. He had served under him from the start and liked him. O'Neil was tall, thin and very bronzed. He had been a cavalry man and had the cavalry man's slightly bowed legs. Although he hadn't ridden a horse for years, he still wore breeches and highly polished boots. They twinkled and winked, and his Sam Browne belt seemed to conduct the twinkles up to his brown, leathery face, which transmitted them anew.

He greeted Ross and got up from behind his desk, but only to turn his chair round, and remount it, placing his hands on its back, over which he looked at

Ross. He looked at him for a little too long before speaking. Quite suddenly, Ross realised that his confidence was misplaced. Something was amiss.

Eventually, O'Neil spoke, 'This is all rather strange and sudden, and I don't know quite what to say. When I told you a few days ago that I wanted to see you, it was to congratulate you on a difficult job well done and to tell you that when you come back from leave it would be to a regular commission and the rank of major.'

He stopped, as if inviting a question. He picked up a pair of tortoise-shell half-lens spectacles and rotated them skilfully, a leg in his ear. He examined the leg and wiped it on a red silk handkerchief which he kept in his cuff.

Ross could think of no intelligent question to put, so the Colonel continued, 'Then, out of the blue, I received fresh instructions from the War Office just yesterday. I've been trying to find an easy way to tell you this, Alec, but I'm blowed if I can think of one. The long and short of it, I'm afraid, is that your commission isn't to be renewed.'

'But why, sir? You told me that you thought I was doing a good job and rather hinted that a regular commission was in the bag.'

'I did, Alec, and I'm bitterly sorry if I misled you. All I can say is that I believed it. I thought you'd make a first-rate regular officer. I recommended that, and this is the first time that my advice has not been acted on.'

'But why, sir?' Ross repeated.

'Just don't know, Alec. I sometimes forget myself enough to imagine I'm a slightly important person out here, but the fact is that I've a very small part to play in a very big army. All I can say from experience is that when a promotion's blocked, it's usually because someone's made an enemy in the War House. But you're too young to have done that, so it's perhaps part of the economies or just the usual army cock-up.'

He thought for a moment. 'Some much less able people than you are being renewed, so, yes, probably it is just a cock-up. But I'm afraid I can't do anything about it. I've tried already, and it did no good. As I say, I'm a very small part of a great big army.'

He rose from his mount and started to come round his desk. Then he checked himself. 'But this isn't the time for farewells. You go off and enjoy your leave. We'll say goodbye when you come back, and I'll give you the best reference I've ever written.'

As Ross was about to salute, the Colonel recalled something. 'Nearly forgot, a Johnny called Perry-Plumb would like to see you in the Indian Artillery Column mess at Inkerman Barracks this evening at 7:30.'

'What's that about, sir?'

'No idea, Alec. I'm just the messenger, but the message comes from on high, wearing cloaks and daggers and with red tabs instead of tits. Perry-Plumb I've heard of, but never met. Full colonel, not just a half-jack like me. Very able, I believe. Enjoy your evening with him. Remember, when one door closes…you know. Back in 1914, I was a major on half pay. Thought my career was over. Had three children to educate. I…' he coughed and decided not to communicate an intimacy. 'Well, anyway, a Serbian student shot an Austrian arch-duke and here we are. So you never know what the future holds. All the best, Alec.'

***

Ross had heard about the Indian Artillery Column. They had started as irregulars during the Mutiny, when they were known as Sewell's Column. Long since, they'd been assimilated into the Indian army, where they were an elite and rather exclusive unit, very efficient but very informal, and usually known as Sewell's Swells.

When Ross arrived at the Column's Brigade Headquarters, he was not greatly surprised to find the Arab mess staff wearing Indian turbans and addressed in Hindi. The British officers were wearing the Indian army khaki drill shorts in which they had endured three bitter winters on the Western Front.

The exterior of the mess was composed of a heterogeneous mosaic of plywood, canvas and metal sheeting, but within there was a completely convincing impression of solidity, age and tradition. All was panelled in dark mahogany and draped with heavy curtains. In the ante-room, sallow portraits of whiskered commanding officers and mess presidents from the Mutiny onwards looked down on a rich red carpet surrounded by highly polished wood. The carpet was covered by small tables and chairs, the table tops resting on feet of elephant and rhinoceros and less easily identifiable mammals. On the polished wood floor surrounding the well-worn carpet were brass shell cases and more elephants' feet, hollowed to contain selections of trout rods, tennis rackets, cricket bats and billiard cues.

In the centre of the room stood a long, ancient table. Its magnificent patina of wax and lavender served to emphasise, rather than disguise, a craze of scratches and fissures. On it lay a selection of English periodicals that reflected the interests of sporting gentlemen.

On one side of the table was a fireplace, in which a log fire burned. It was protected by a club fender, and above it on a wooden over-mantel hung a portrait of the Queen-Empress, surrounded at a respectful distance by a number of her more exotic subjects, heavily armed and in a state of undress which she would surely have found disconcerting.

At the other side of the room was a table laden with bottles of whisky, liqueurs and beer, over which presided a magnificently moustached and bearded havildar, garbed entirely in white silk from the top of his jewelled turban until it disappeared into the black boots in each of which a silver dagger had been inserted. His Ashoka emblem was worn on a silver bracelet on his wrist. It was to him that Ross directed himself and asked where he might find Colonel Perry-Plumb. Before the havildar could reply, the only other visible occupant of the room rose from the fender. He was very tall. His face was bronzed, with a deep scar that ran diagonally from the middle of his forehead to the right cheek. He was bald, such hair as remained ginger. He came across the room quickly, despite a distinct limp.

'Ashley Perry-Plumb,' he said. 'P-P will do. You're Ross. Good of you to come. You must meet Asquith and Bonar Law.' He led the way back to the fireplace. In front of it sat two leather armchairs. Their high backs concealed their occupants.

'Asquith farts appallingly,' said Perry-Plumb. 'It's best to say nothing.' They had now reached the fireplace and Ross saw that the armchair which P-P indicated contained a large and elderly Afghan hound. Asquith did nothing to acknowledge Ross, continuing instead to fix an interested and kindly eye on Bonar Law. Bonar Law was a Jack Russell terrier.

'Didn't know what to call him,' said P-P, 'till Lloyd George said the House of Lords was Mr Balfour's poodle.' Ross did not follow. P-P received unordered whiskies from the havildar. 'Asquith was easy, though. Extraordinary farting.' Ross and P-P sat on low elephants' feet placed between Asquith and Bonar Law and rather below the level of their earnest but silent communion.

It became clear that there was much more to P-P than his initial appearance suggested. Behind a self-deprecating style, there was confidence and authority. Ross knew he was being appraised.

'Want you to meet someone,' said the colonel. 'Chap called Cantley. Frightfully clever fellow. I'm just a farmer who's found himself obliged to do some rough stuff.' Ross could see the worn and unobtrusive medal ribbons. 'But Cantley's one of the chaps who knows what to tell us to do. On the staff from start to finish, but I'm sure he'd have been a good soldier if he'd had the chance.'

'Why does he want to see me?' asked Ross. 'I'm not a real soldier. Just a temporary commission, and that's almost over.'

'No idea, my boy,' said P-P, suavely and unconvincingly. 'He operates at a different level from me. Politics, the future, balance of power, that kind of stuff. Listen to what he's got to say. Don't react till you've heard him out.' A pause, then levelly, 'Don't be ruled by your first impression.'

As they'd talked, the room was filling with young officers. They smiled quickly to P-P and formed in small groups around the room, talking quietly. After some time, a lieutenant colonel wearing a different uniform and a staff officer's red tabs entered. Unlike the others, who were relaxed and genial, he carried himself stiffly and with a forced military bearing. After a word with the havildar, he walked quickly across the room and stopped, unsmilingly, in front of P-P.

For his part, P-P smiled broadly at the new arrival, though perhaps with private amusement rather than pleasure. 'Ah, Cantley, I want you to meet Alec Ross. And now that you're here, I think we can proceed to dinner.' He gathered the company behind him with a sweep of his eyes, and led them from the ante-room to dinner.

***

It wasn't a mess night, and dinner was taken at separate tables. P-P, Ross and Cantley were alone at a long table, attended by an Arab waiter, Ali. The others were at small tables, in groups of three or four. There they ate fairly rapidly,

59

managing to drink copiously without becoming particularly noisy. There was a discernible respectful deference to the three at the top table.

At that table, P-P did his best to promote the civilised clubbability that pervaded the rest of the room. Ross tried to reciprocate, though he was conscious that he had little knowledge of the field sports and political gossip on which to build small talk. Cantley made no such effort and seemed unaware of longueurs. The other two followed their whiskies with a half bottle of Meursault and a bottle of claret, but Cantley nursed a single glass of India Pale Ale. His little mouth was pursed, and his smooth pink cheeks and his full and well-brushed head of hair combined to present an appearance of complacent self-confidence. He resolutely eschewed addressing the Colonel as 'P-P', insisting on a gratingly formal 'sir'. There was a hint of awkwardness in his habit of tugging at the cuffs of his tunic, as if to draw them down over the cuffs of his shirt. Ross wondered if it was designed to draw attention to his badges of rank, which Cantley's unit still wore on their sleeves rather than their shoulders.

Sooner than it seemed to Ross, aware of the sticky atmosphere at his table and aware also of his lack of capacity to remedy it, the meal had finished. P-P rose to his feet: 'Gentlemen, only a brief recital tonight.' He banged on the table with his gavel and three Indians filed in and sat on the carpet in front of the high table. P-P leaned towards Ross: 'You're going to hear something really special,' he said with the grin of a schoolboy. Then he closed his eyes, and for the next few minutes, the room was full of the dreadful sound of sitar and drums, balanced as by a bagpipe drone and a sustained yowl from Asquith (or perhaps Bonar Law).

Whether P-P's eyes were closed in silent rapture or in sleep was not clear, but at last they opened. He banged his gavel again. The performance stopped and the musicians withdrew. He then intoned some words in Hindi. The younger officers rose, responded in the same language, bowed and retired to the ante-room, followed by their waiters, leaving just Ali, or Mustapha Drink, as P-P addressed him, to hand a decanter to those on the top table.

P-P and Ross had by now consumed enough drink to enable them to talk in easy relaxation, although Cantley remained primly silent, but their conversation was disturbed by an increasing uproar from the ante-room. Ross wanted to know what was going on, and in particular what caused the shrill screams of real pain that were occasionally uttered. His opportunity came when the double doors of the ante-room were knocked open and two young officers barged through, one on the other's shoulders, and wielding a billiard cue.

'Pig-sticking,' said P-P in insufficient explanation. 'The Arabs love it.' He noticed that Ross still looked blank. 'They're the pigs, of course.' When even that seemed not to have resolved Ross's surprise, a look of comprehension broke over P-P's kindly, battle-scarred face. 'Ah, see what you mean. No, we tell them they're sheep.'

The pig-sticking soon gave way to another game. Ross heard barked commands, 'Front Rank, fire! Back Rank, fire!' followed by volleys of glass breaking against a wall.

'Firing Squad,' explained P-P. 'Nowadays, we get the Arabs to wear blindfolds. It adds to the atmosphere. Anyhow, I imagine it must be quite unnerving to see twenty-four liqueur glasses coming your way. And it protects their eyes. But they're well looked after if anything goes wrong. The chaps see the families right. 'Well, now,' he added looking at his watch, 'it's getting late and I'm getting old, and I don't want to play Cannonballs.'

'What's that?' asked Ross despairingly.

P-P looked at him in surprise. 'Cannonballs? Well, you wrap a chap in a blanket and slide him off the mess table. He's got to strike a match before he hits the ground, otherwise it's a miss-fire and he's shot off again. The chaps like to do it to senior officers. Old Plumer was a great sport, but Haig wouldn't play. Dignity of the office, he said. Stuffed shirt. Our French friends didn't know how to play. Their schools are different. But they pick it up. Joffre was surprisingly good once he understood. One of his chaps badly concussed, I'm afraid. Invalided out. Runs a post office now.

'Well, I'm off. Taking Asquith and Bonar Law back to England tomorrow. I shan't see you again, Ross. Listen to what this chap has to say. It's a different world now and we have to change with it.' He thought for a moment. Then, as if referring to something they'd already been discussing, he observed quietly, 'Sometimes, it's better to do the easiest thing. I've never been very good at that. Tend to see things as black and white. There's a lot of grey around these days. You younger men seem to emerge from the womb carrying an embryo of doubt with you.'

He nodded briefly to Cantley and smiled gently at Ross. Then, without warning he turned fast in his chair and hurled his port glass at Ali. It was clearly rehearsed. Ali, reacting with equal speed, caught the glass and placed it on the table.

'Well done, Mustapha. We'll have you in the slips for England,' called P-P as he left the room, spinning a half-crown in the air. Ali caught it in his teeth, grinning broadly all the time.

Chapter 10

Cantley had been detached and remote for some time. Now he came to life and switched on. 'Well, that's the end of the entertainment.'

Ross bridled, to his own surprise. He felt that the older man was being unfairly treated. 'I thought there was much more to P-P than that. Wasn't he wearing ribbons—an MC and DSO? As he asked the question his eyes innocently and unintentionally took in Cantley's virgin tunic.

Cantley, whose cheeks looked as if they had first been closely shaved and then rubbed down with fine sandpaper, became even pinker. 'Oh, of course he's a fine soldier, good regimental officer and so on, but that's not enough. I was at a dress dinner last week. Unlike Field Marshal Haig, I wasn't invited to play Cannon Balls. I imagine they thought that I had gone to the wrong school like the French. But I met P-P and lots of little P-Ps. All fine soldiers, and good eggs, but amateurs, yesterday's men. The war's changed the world and there are new forces at play. These old fools don't realise that. Asquith and Bonar Law are only the start of their menagerie. I met Hopeless, Moggs and Hardwicke, and heard all about The Rat, which had once belonged to Kitchener. We're being pushed out of Syria by the French, of all people, and the eggs are only interested in jackal hunts in the morning and polo in the afternoon.'

Ross felt that something had to be said for the Column. 'All the same, none of that does any harm,' he said.

'No harm and no good either,' said Cantley, his voice increasingly nasal and harsh as he embraced his theme. 'We only just won the war, and we did so because the German army was stabbed in the back by the civilians. P-P and his type are a danger. For all his jokes about forgetting the servants' names, he loves these fellows, and they love him.'

'Surely that's a good thing?'

'Oh no, it's not,' said Cantley smugly. Ross had fallen into a trap. 'At heart, he and his good eggs don't really believe that we Anglo-Saxons are any better than the wogs and the Indians. They're delighted to hand over Syria to the Frogs, and they'd be perfectly happy to hand over India to the Indians.'

'And that's where I come in,' he continued, looking even more self-satisfied. 'I'm in Political Intelligence, which is why I haven't got a chestful of medal ribbons. My masters and I have to supply the professionalism that England needs if we are to continue in our destiny. Winning the war wasn't enough. But we're off to a good start. Despite the amateurs, the men I work for have managed to extend our Empire here in the Levant, and it will be the basis of a belt that will circle the globe through India, linking England to the Dominions.'

Ross was neither interested nor impressed by the world-vision by which Cantley was so inspired. The latter now folded his hands together, dropped them heavily on the table and looked Ross directly in the eyes with what was a rather unconvincing man-to-man gaze. 'And that's why I wanted to speak to you. For reasons which I understand but don't approve of, France is to be allowed to take over Syria, which we very reasonably occupied by virtue of the fact that it was taken by a British feat of arms. France is our enemy.'

'I rather thought France was our ally,' interrupted Ross.

'*Was* our ally, during the war, of necessity. *Has been* our rival in the Levant for centuries. *Will be* our enemy again. The alliance was an aberration. Germany is and has been a reliable friend. France is and will be our competitor. While we will remain in Mesopotamia and Palestine, France will be our neighbour here in Damascus. We need to know what she's up to, and I want you to remain here to keep us advised.'

Ross could not believe what he was hearing. 'Why on earth would I do that?'

'Because of your duty to your country of course.'

'What do I owe my country? I've got no family, no friends and when I offer to serve in my country's army, I'm told I'm no longer needed.'

Cantley looked smug again. 'I'd be a fool to come here without learning something about you, and I am aware that you're a man without ties. I rather liked that, to be frank. I also am a man who suspects emotion. But you need an occupation.'

'My occupation will be to return to England and to paint. I have a little income and I hope to sell some of my work.'

'Not an ambitious plan.'

'Perhaps not, but other doors have closed. I've been married. I've tried an army career. I think I can quietly amuse myself now.'

'Are you saying you will not consider my proposal?' said Cantley sharply.

'Nothing could interest me less.'

Cantley separated his hands and sat back and upright in his chair, like a judge about to pronounce his sentence. 'Then I must suggest that it will be harder to amuse yourself quietly than you imagine. The circumstances of your wife's death are far from forgotten in certain quarters.'

'She died of influenza. What the hell are you talking about?'

'Finally, perhaps of influenza, but only, her family tell me, when she had already been brought low. There is talk of...' (He hesitated for effect.) '...unacceptable demands.'

Ross felt as if he'd received a physical blow. He remembered what Georgie had said in London, a passage he had worked to dismiss from his mind. He felt his stomach turn at the thought of what was being said. He sat silent for a moment and then said quietly, 'That's a lie, an allegation made in grief. Absolutely nothing more.'

Cantley could not disguise his satisfaction. He pursed his little mouth and raised his hands, palms in front, deprecatingly. 'Oh, no doubt, no doubt. Probably not a word of truth, and for myself I care not at all what people choose to get up to.'

Ross briefly tried to imagine what Cantley got up to, but after a momentary image that was pink and shiny and far from pleasing, he replied, 'But I got up to nothing. At least nothing in the least unusual.'

Cantley was enjoying himself. 'Well, of course, what's usual for one man…may not be usual for a delicate girl, fresh from school. But you're missing the point. What matters isn't what you did or didn't do, but what people think happened. All they know is that there are rumours, that they finished Mrs Everley. The family is distraught.'

'Is Mrs Everley dead?'

'Not dead, no. It might have been better if she were. No, she's alive. The body is, anyway. Mentally, she's reduced to a stupor by chloral. Deadens the pain. The Everleys need someone to blame, and you, my dear Ross, are that someone.'

'But that's grossly unfair.'

'Unfair it may be, but that's how it works in our "right little, tight little island" as someone called it.'

'Thomas Dibdin,' said Ross automatically.

Cantley looked irritated. 'Impressive,' he said, 'and you didn't even go to the university. But *your* school made you a poet and a painter and P-P's school made him a gentleman who rides to hounds. My background is different, but I may turn out to be of more value to my country.'

Ross was confused and tired, 'Look what is the point of all this?'

'The point, Ross, is that *you* have choices and *I* have some power. Your wife's brother, Hector, is now in government. He's a junior minister at the War Office. That's why your commission wasn't renewed. If you choose not to help your country, my masters will give Hector—what shall I say?—' he tugged at his cuffs for several moments, '—a favouring wind. You'll come home, but you'll find yourself unwelcome here and there, your existence a little *attenuated*.' He looked pleased by his choice of word.

'You exaggerate what you can do, Cantley. I'm a man of little importance. You can't do much to hurt me.'

'I think we can do enough. In our "right, little, tight little island" you know. There's the matter of living with your Arab bint, for example.'

Ross realised Cantley was watching him carefully in case he'd gone too far this time, but he was too sickened to react. Reassured, Cantley continued, 'Quite a lot could be made of that, you know, a practised oriental mistress, more ready than an English schoolgirl to satisfy your exotic requirements.'

Despite himself, Ross was amused to hear such a description of the convent-educated Salema, and her fastidious modesty. Only the day before he had reflected that despite their nightly congress, between eighty and eighty-five per cent of her body remained *terra incognita*. And although the Free Zones were regularly visited, detailed surveys and scientific investigations of anything further afield were prudishly discouraged.

'You're smiling,' said Cantley, 'but just think about the practicalities. I know you've got *some* money, but it won't go as far as you think in England today. Prices have gone up, and I know just what your income amounts to. You'll have to find a pretty desperate prep school to supplement it. Parents won't like the rumours. You'll need to sell an awful lot of daubs.'

'You really are a little shit, Cantley. I can now see why you feel you're an outsider.'

'The point is, I'm not an outsider any longer. Very much an insider now, actually. And I'm prepared to be a shit if I have to be. But there is an easy alternative. Reconsider my proposal. You stay out here with your accommodating Arab friend. The living will be *commodious*.' Again, he looked pleased at his choice of words. 'You'll receive a salary to add to that private income of yours. You won't have much to do to earn it. You'll be attached to the French as a Political Liaison Officer—just like me.' He smiled generously at the compliment his words implied. 'All you've got to do is keep us in the picture about our French friends and what they're up to. Plenty of time for your painting.'

Cantley looked up brightly as a new idea came to him. 'In fact, I can put you in touch with just the chap to help you in your artistic career. Now all I'm asking is that you think it all over and come and see me in London. That's not a lot to ask, is it?'

It was a very long time since Ross and P-P had finished their port, and its stimulus had worked off long since. He was tired by Cantley's remorseless whine, his cynical self-assurance and his nervous energy. Sometimes, the easiest thing seemed best.

'All right, I'll come and see you,' he said.

As he walked across the parade-ground to leave by the Orderly Office, he could see in the light of the moon pairs of young officers, one carried on the shoulders of the other, whooping and running and stabbing with billiard cues at two fleeing Arabs, one of them quite certainly Ali.

Chapter 11
Menton and London, 1921

Ross travelled back to England via Marseille and visited his grandmother, Alice Ross, in Menton. His grandfather had died two years earlier. His grandmother, still not an elderly woman, was coping with the loss of a greatly loved partner by throwing herself into charitable work. She and Miss Beauchamp had joined other members of the English expatriate community in helping in the running of one of the many *Résidences des Mutilés* which France had set up for disabled ex-servicemen.

Ross visited it with the two ladies. They were full of brisk conversation with the men they met. Some were learning the use of new limbs and prosthetic devices and could expect to be discharged—to subsist on miserable pensions eked out by begging. Others, some lacking all four limbs, could hope for little more than a lifetime of institutional life, interspersed by occasional visits until their families forgot them.

In the company of his defiantly cheerful grandmother and the efficient Miss Beauchamp, Ross would have been ashamed to show any emotion. He did, though, find himself challenged in the last room they visited. Here the patients were victims of shell shock. They were without outward injury, but they were quite unable to speak. The two ladies addressed them kindly on every-day topics. Some of the men opened and closed their mouths in an attempt to respond, but only uttered inarticulate yowls. Worse still was the plight of the others. They were closed to the world, looking vacantly at the ladies, seeing them but not truly observing them, not even trying to respond. When Ross and the others left the building, the ladies started discussing their various committees and commitments, but Ross stood aside, his mind wholly absorbed by the tableau he'd just left—those men in this world, but not of it.

When Miss Beauchamp was about to go off, she turned to Ross for a last word. 'Will it be difficult for you to visit Barbara's grave, Alec? We look after the English cemetery carefully and I think you'll find it very peaceful.'

'Don't know if I'll have time for that,' said Ross, taken aback.

***

On his last night in Menton, Ross and his grandmother were invited to have dinner with Jane McBeth and her new husband, her doctor Terris. Jane had not been a weeping widow when Ross had last met her. She had been full of life then, but she seemed an even more vital life-force now, confident and reinforced by her domestic status. And Terris, whom Ross remembered, to the extent he recalled him at all, as a shy and self-conscious presence in the shadows, had also enlarged as a personality. He was a confident and self-assured host and he and Jane were full of concerned attention for Mrs Ross.

They were no less thoughtful towards Ross. He didn't find it easy to respond. Things had changed. When he had last met Jane, he had thought of her as an adult, himself not much more than a boy. Now the few years' difference in their ages was insignificant: they were contemporaries. And yet he felt further from her than before. He noticed the little signs of affection between her and Terris, the small, shared jokes. He rather resented these intimacies. He could see that marriage was more than the sum of two individuals. Something had happened to them that had injected vitality into both of them. He, on the other hand, felt contracted rather than expanded by what life had done to him, particularly by the unnerving interview with Cantley from which he had learned how little control he had over his own life.

When he and his grandmother were about to leave, he suddenly remembered Miss Beauchamp's question and his surprised reply. He confided to Jane, 'I hadn't planned to visit Barbara's grave.' A moment passed.

'I quite understand,' she said.

She gave Ross's hand an unnecessary squeeze as she said goodbye. Then she turned to Terris, smiled into his eyes, took his hand, and went indoors. Ross felt an absurd sense of jealousy.

On the following morning, Ross said goodbye to his grandmother. The visit hadn't been a successful one. The army years had made him less direct with Mrs Ross; the spontaneity of the warmest relationship he'd known had gone. She, too, had withdrawn. Throwing herself into a routine which kept grief at bay had changed her.

The gardener who'd been watering the garden when Ross arrived with Barbara drove him to the station where Jane's alcoholic husband had interpreted for the English valetudinarians and the Russian refugees. Ross could not imagine that he would return to Menton.

***

Back in London, he stayed again at the Alington. Even as he stepped out of his taxi, he was vividly drawn back to his parting from Georgie. He had thought of her increasingly rarely as the years had passed, but here, where he had been allowed a moment of seismic insight, he was struck by an almost physical sense of loss. He found his eyes drawn across the road where she had disappeared into the crowd five years ago. He realised he was seriously looking for her as though time had stood still for these years.

As he dined alone in the same dining room, perhaps at the table they had shared, he thought of her freshness, her enthusiasm, her almost gauche directness. He felt himself relax in the warmth of complete recall, and although he tried to banish a memory that could only be fruitless, in the course of his few days in London he repeatedly found himself scanning the crowds for a tall girl in a blue chiffon dress that fluttered round her knees.

He was disturbed. His coupling with Salema was purely functional, but his memories of Georgie evoked a reminder of feelings that were much more than physical, of a dimension to life which he had vowed to put out of reach. It was difficult to put such thoughts aside. In any event, he found little pleasure in London. He had never really known the city or felt at home in it, and now it was far more foreign than Damascus. Not only had he changed, so had his country. He couldn't have been expected to know that his absence had seen the death of Edwardian England, with its moral certainties and a still-Victorian pace of life. In its place was a new society, choked by the costs of war and the privations of the peace. In Parliament, the whiskery old men who governed to maintain a system of stability and privilege had been replaced by men of push and go. It was too early for Ross to understand all this. Indeed, even as time passed, he was too uncritical to understand fully what had happened. But he found the atmosphere uncongenial.

* * *

And so it was after just two days, rather than the week he'd planned, that he phoned the War Office, asking for Colonel Cantley. '*Brigadier* Cantley' he was told was on permanent secondment to the Colonial Office, and it was there that he went to see the man he had so greatly disliked on their last meeting.

Cantley was in a large room, behind a desk of imposing size. He was not wearing a uniform. The other civil servants Ross had seen in the building were for the most part wearing dark lounge suits, but Cantley had chosen to affect the pre-war garb of black jacket, striped trousers and a wing collar that was high, tight and very stiff. The effect of this almost archaic attire was to make the small, pink head that emerged from the collar seem absurdly young.

Apart from the civilian clothes, little had changed about Cantley. His skin was smooth and well-scrubbed, his hair very full and carefully oiled and dressed. His impeccably groomed moustache looked even more military than it had done when he was in uniform.

He rose to shake hands with Ross and then nodded to seat him. Without preamble, he began in his grating voice: 'I'm glad you're prepared to continue our discussion.'

'I'm not here to continue any discussion. I've come to say that I shall go back to Syria in the role you offered me.'

Cantley was silent for a moment. He had clearly expected a more difficult interview. 'In that case, I'm even more pleased that you were persuaded by my arguments.'

Ross had been determined not to be affected by Cantley's unsubtle offensiveness, but he couldn't let this go. 'My decision has nothing to do with what you said to me in Damascus. It's based entirely on my own convenience.'

'Be that as it may, and rationalise as you will, it's actions that interest me.'

This time, Ross managed to remain silent.

Cantley, as they say, visibly relaxed. He clearly thought he had won, and without the fight he'd expected. He looked increasingly smug and self-satisfied, which is to say very smug and self-satisfied indeed. His pleasure in his status and surroundings was evident, and he settled into that pleasure. His manner was more assured than it had been in Damascus. His voice, though still harsh and nasal, attempted the accents of the ascendancy. He wore a signet ring on his little finger and a tie which might have been a club tie. But he still tugged nervously at his cuffs as he spoke.

The remainder of the meeting was largely a monologue by Cantley. Ross was told that on reflection he'd not be in a military role. 'You and the government mustn't be too close.' Instead he would receive a retainer from the hands of an art dealer with official connections.

The details would be sorted out by this versatile connoisseur; 'I shall be there in the background directing and observing, and we may meet from time to time, but Digby will be your principal contact.' The condescension amused Ross more than it irritated him, and he waited for a phrase about bigger fish to fry. What arrived was even better. 'I shall have my eyes beyond the horizon.'

Chapter 12

The meeting place chosen by Hugh Digby, man of art, to emphasise his bohemian persona rather than his more prosaic functions on behalf of the Colonial Office didn't surprise Ross. The dark, slightly dingy Italian restaurant was just as a theatrical designer would have visualised the gathering places of intellectuals, artists, and assorted demimondaine subversives.

Decoration was limited to portraits of Garibaldi and D'Annunzio, and details like the ribbon in Italian colours twisted round the latter's frame. Candles burning in empty bottles on checked tablecloths were the only means by which the shadows of the interior were dissipated. They revealed diners who were, for the most part, again as the director would have imagined: mainly male, slightly scruffy, earnest and quite possibly artistic.

What was quite out of character was Hugh Digby himself. He had managed the setting for meeting his new protégé perfectly, but there was nothing he could do about his own appearance. He was large, red in face and loud in speech, and he wore a checked tweed suit. He had been careful to arrive first, and as Ross was led to the table, he thought the man he was meeting looked more than anything else like a prosperous rural auctioneer or land agent. The impression was wonderfully enhanced by the happy accident that the copy of the *Morning Post* that lay on the table was open at a page that reported the previous day's Hereford fat-stock prices.

As they worked through introductory commonplaces, Ross was slightly disappointed that Digby was bucolic rather than Bloomsbury. This reaction was checked to an extent by the reflection that his own brogues and thorn-proof tweed suit were hardly the uniform of a starving artist in Montmartre. In any case, he found himself warming to Digby as soon as the jolly auctioneer opened up serious conversation:

'Ross, I want your informed opinion on an important point. Has Cantley become even more of a shit since he moved to the Colonial Office?'

Ross said that he had thought Cantley so shitty on his first meeting him that he couldn't get worse.

'I respect your opinion, of course. You have the artist's gift for observation. But I'm bound to say that in my view you under-rate the man. Shitty he may have been, but shittier he has become. He was a shit in uniform, but plain clothes have brought out another dimension to his faecal offensiveness. Maybe it's something to do with the world of diplomacy. Talleyrand was a diplomat for much longer than most, and he was known as the turd in silk stockings. Cantley's a turd in a wing collar.'

After this Ross began to approve of the jolly auctioneer, and their conversation went well. His life in Syria would be that of a gentleman painter. It would be a comfortable one. He would receive from Digby a monthly remittance made up in part by Talleyrand's retainer, which would amount to exactly what his army salary had been, and in part by what seemed a generous price for a number of paintings which the jolly auctioneer undertook to take from him.

Ross wanted to know what he had to do to earn Talleyrand's shilling. Not a lot, it seemed. Digby would communicate Cantley's requirements along with the monthly remittances, but essentially what was wanted was a report on French military movements and dispositions. In addition to verbal information, Ross's role as a topographical artist would allow him to roam the country, sketching installations. He would have to be sensibly prudent, but communications to him would be by the diplomatic bag, which is how he would return his reports, sketches and paintings.

Despite Digby's genial bonhomie—even to an extent because of it—Ross's professional vanity was pricked. The art dealer had said nothing about Ross's art.

'In all this set-up, it seems my paintings don't amount to very much. I don't imagine I'm the greatest painter in the world, but I do take my art, if I may call it that, seriously. I've been selling my paintings quite successfully over the last year or two, and I hope the market for them will increase as I develop.'

The jolly auctioneer was no longer jolly. He was concerned, sympathetic, even hurt that Ross had felt slighted. 'My dear Alec, I thought it went without saying that I have the highest respect for your art. I buy for various collectors and I've watched your technique evolving with great interest.' He was silent for a moment, frowning. 'I hadn't intended to mention this, but to show my respect for your work I must tell you that almost everything—no, I think I may say absolutely everything—you've sold in the last three years was bought by my gallery. I just want to formalise that arrangement, so that we are your sole agents.'

Ross was shaken by this revelation. He had little sense of self-importance, but in his limited, lonely life it had gratified him to think that he had a skill that the world valued. Not in anger so much as in sadness he said to Digby on a dying note, 'So all this time I've been deluding myself. I'm not an artist, I'm just Cantley's prostitute. Tart, not art.'

Digby's ruddy countenance flushed darker in his concern. 'Alec, Alec, you're seeing the whole thing back to front. Have confidence in yourself, you're an outstanding painter of this generation. This lot…' he waved disparagingly at their fellow diners, 'are nothing, but if John or Brangwyn were here today, they'd tell you how much they admire your work. They've often told me.'

He continued to reassure. 'Look, the point is this. I bought you long before Talleyrand stuck his nose in. I had been buying you and selling you on because—purely because—I think highly of you. Cantley came to me because I was already buying you—on your merits—as much as because of some connection we have with his department.'

Ross felt a little reassured, and, sensing that, Digby changed gear, back into the jolly auctioneer. 'And nothing wrong with taking the government's money when we can,' he grinned conspiratorially. 'Fat lot these philistines care about art. We've got to look after ourselves when we can, haven't we?'

Despite the force of his extrovert good humour, and despite a remarkable amount of alcohol that accompanied it, the meal ended on a less boisterous note than it had begun. But Ross accepted his benefactor's reassurances. It was simpler to do so.

Chapter 13

The next few years tell us little of the humanising of Ross. He returned to the functional embraces with Salema and a routine in Syria not hugely different in his new role from what it had been earlier. Instead of moving across the country with his soldiers, making inventories for administrators, he walked or drove on his own with his painting materials. More of his trips were just day expeditions from Damascus. That was the essence of the change.

He painted and drew; he sketched many a French fort and gun emplacement. His canvases and his reports went back to Britain in the diplomatic bag, the latter to the shitty Talleyrand, the former to the jolly auctioneer. He enjoyed painting. Since he had a guaranteed market, he felt himself liberated and able to experiment as he could not otherwise have done. The results were not disappointing and he felt cautiously pleased with his work. On the whole, the disillusionment of London, the sense that his vocation was no more than a fig-leaf for his true employment, dissipated: Digby, he thought, was getting reasonable value for his money.

On the other hand, he felt something he could never have imagined in regard to Cantley. Much as he despised and disliked Cantley, Ross was a decent man, a fair man, and Cantley's money, he felt was not truly being earned.

This reaction was interesting. Ross was motivated not by self-interest, not by his appetites, but by something almost altruistic. Too much should not be made of it, but it reflected a sense of guilt, and guilt is at least the lowest form of duty, perhaps even the germ of idealism.

So, in addition to the sketches of barracks designed in Paris and implanted in the desert like illustrations from *Beau Geste*, the estimates of military strength, the reports of troop movements, he took to sending back appreciations of the political situation. This he found infinitely more congenial, and it was no labour to him to take stock of the way in which French colonial presence was regarded by the native population.

France's idea of how a mandate should be run was very different from Britain's. For France, a mandate was just an old-fashioned colony. Its resources were there to be exploited, to be drained off to metropolitan France. As for the policy of the League of Nations, the idea that the mandates were being prepared for early independence, the response was a cynical shrug. In the British mandates, attempts were made to set up representative bodies to take over government. Not so in Syria, where democratic institutions were strangled and independence movements put down harshly by torture and arbitrary detention. Ross found all this hugely interesting. For the first time, he began to be absorbed by the theatre of human interaction. He observed the way the nationalist flame flickered here and established itself there and how the French authorities moved to extinguish it.

The motives of the French were obvious, but Ross found himself intrigued by the aspirations of the Syrians. What did they really hope for? Did they simply want their children to be taught their own history and in their own language, for instance, or did they want more? Did they just want seats on a Consultative Assembly, or did they aspire to rule themselves? Some certainly did, but how many? Were the more extreme views shared by both Bedouins and the urban professional classes? The only way to find out was to talk to people. Those who are interested in the evolution of the man Ross may find it significant that to satisfy his curiosity he spent time in the coffee houses and often forsook the culinary and other pleasures of the *beit* for an evening, to eat with the local people in their restaurants or at long communal trestle tables in the market square.

Because he was interested in them, those to whom he spoke responded to him. He came to be on friendly terms with middle-class enthusiasts who were delighted to expatiate on their views. He was invited into their homes and moved easily among them. No one would yet call him clubbable, but he was a very different man from the withdrawn figure who avoided the mess whenever he could—indeed would have paid to do so, had that been necessary.

***

Things might have gone on like this indefinitely, but for the concurrence of two factors: a geopolitical development, and Salema's desire for status and security.

In the early years, the border between French Syria and British Jordan was ill-defined, and patrols of different nationalities confronted each other repeatedly. France considered she had been cheated by Britain of much that had been agreed during the war when Mark Sykes and François-Georges Picot agreed on the distribution of the Ottoman spoils. The Syrian notables, on the other hand, voted not to give in to France, and to be ruled instead by Britain's protégé and Lawrence's friend, the Emir Feisal.

France would have none of this and brusquely expelled him. Between France and Britain there was a *rupture diplomatique*, just one notch on the scale below a state of war.

But time passed and the frontiers stabilised; Britain found a throne for Feisal in Iraq and for his brother Abdullah in Jordan, and the temperature fell. The two western nations were now looking less to the consequences of the last war than at the prelude to the next. In 1933, the Nazi party took power in Berlin. Germany reoccupied the Rhineland. Italy was already governed by the Fascists, and there were powerful forces of the right reaching for power in Austria, Spain, even France itself. London and Paris, close to war in the 1920s came together again in the 1930s, threatened by a common enemy.

In June, 1937, Ross received the following letter from the jolly auctioneer:

My dear Ross,

How are you? I always picture you reading on a divan, being fed dates by dusky handmaidens. I do hope I have the picture right—a scene from the Arabian Nights, *or perhaps the* Rubaiyat: *"A jug of wine, a loaf of bread…"*

This scribble is to deal with two things. First of all, I have to admit that I'm doing quite shamefully well out of our business relationship. Your works sell like good old hot cakes; your stylistic developments tickle the artistic fancy wonderfully. Your move to oils was a great success. Pile on the pigments. The paying public love to get a thick layer of paint for their money.

As you know, we've had you on show in the gallery every two years or so, and they've been pretty well sell-outs. The only regret is that you can't bring yourself along. Don't blame you—it's all pretty grim here just now. First, the national strike, then this series of bastard coalition governments, now a stock market slump.

Anyway, that brings me back to the old res. *What with shareholdings being worth no more than the paper of the certificates, my clients are piling in to things—stuff that'll weather the storm. And what better than the paintings of the highly regarded Alec Ross? Net result: in all fairness, I must revise the terms of our agreement, and that I do, forthwith, herewith and so forth. From now, a 2% reduction in my commission and a 10% increase in your retainer.*

I hope that brought a blush of maidenly happiness to your rosy cheeks, but now stiffen the sinews, brace yourself and take a stiff peg of raki *or other suitable restorative, for I have to tell you to expect an imminent visit from the great Talleyrand—greater than ever, indeed, because his ultimate dream has been achieved. He is now at the heart of government, in the Foreign Office, formulating policy at the highest level on behalf of the King-Emperor. He has many distinguished suffixes after his nasty little name, and will soon, I'm sure, have a prefix as well. As a consequence, his shittiness has reached new heights.*

So, be warned, he will shortly deign to descend from the clouds, as Jove from Olympus, though in this case in a heavier-than-air flying machine. He will bring with him a proposal. I know only that it involves a change of scene. That I'm in favour of—fresh fields and pastures new would be stimulating for the growing lad and good for your work.

So all best wishes dear fellow. Back to the handmaidens and apologies for interrupting their attentions.

Best wishes and ila-liquaa.

Hugh Digby.

Within a few weeks, Cantley did, indeed, appear. The meeting was as distasteful for Ross as the others had been. He sought to anaesthetise himself against the crass aspects of Cantley's manner, and focus only on the matter of what he had to say. That was, first of all and surprisingly, that Cantley and his masters and minions (there seemed to be few of the former and many of the latter) were finding Ross's situation and intelligence reports very useful ('the very stuff on which we base policy'). They wanted more of the same. But they didn't want it from Syria. Concern now was about a possible German war. It needn't happen ('Cadogan and Henderson and I don't think it's necessary. We see our future in an Anglo-Saxon alliance with Germany, even if we're not too fond of Herr Hitler and some of his associates'), but she had to be prepared.

In the event of a war, Britain would ('regrettably, in my view') be dependent on France, and there was much that gave concern about France. There was a significant fascist element within the country, pro-German and very anti-Semitic. Moreover, if Spain, now fascist and ruled by the Generalissimo Franco, sided with Germany, France would face a war on two sides. She would be a weak ally.

So what was wanted was that Ross should go to France, to Perpignan, on the Mediterranean border with Spain, and provide the sort of assessments from there that had been so helpful from Damascus. Correspondence to and from London would be via Spain, unless that country became a belligerent. To minimise difficulties in case of a German invasion, Ross would be provided with French nationality.

**

How Ross would have reacted to Cantley's request in isolation can't be known, though history suggests he would have complied rather than fight. But he was ready for a change. The complexities of the political scene had subsided, and he found the coercion, torture and imprisonment by which French rule was maintained distasteful. French policy was to integrate Syria and France. The French language and French institutions were intended to create cohesion where there had been a colourful mosaic of tribes and traditions.

There was also a domestic dimension. Salema was a proud woman. She considered herself socially and educationally superior to her late husband's family. Her status as their dependant was a matter of shame, and her relationship with Ross, she was convinced, a matter of common knowledge which compounded that shame. She wanted to be made an honest woman of, and she couldn't see why Ross wouldn't take the appropriate steps, unless, as she suspected, he intended to be off, leaving her unprovided for in her old age.

Ross assured her not of undying love—neither side had ever professed that—but that he would never think of abandoning her. Of course, he would see her provided for, whatever happened. His assurances cut no ice with Salema, whose view of life was informed by cunning and suspicion. Their exchanges became frequently heated and very wearing.

For Salema, the end of Ross's marriage had been a precedent, an abandonment that might be repeated. Yes, Barbara had died, but for one from Salema's cultural background that didn't begin to justify turning his back on her family. Indeed, with her death his obligation to support and sustain her family became paramount '—but you, look at you, you leave her mother to starve.'

However often Ross tried to explain his mother-in-law's financial and social circumstances, Salema never accepted that the *mores* of an upper-class English family were not those of the Bedouin camp. Perhaps Ross was unfair in expecting anything else. At any rate, far from mollifying Salema, Ross's explanations only served to increase an unbearable emotional tension. Salema's attack widened. Ross was a strange kind of man, if, indeed, a real man at all. What kind of man showed no grief for a dead wife? Where are the photographs, the mementoes? And, turning from the dead Barbara to her own situation, what kind of man did not want a wife, a family? Ross was no better than a dog looking for a bitch in heat.

Ross, at last, could take this no longer. He named a day, exactly a month ahead, when Salema would move in to live with him as man and wife. A formal wedding would take place. The month's delay was justified by the formalities of acquiring French citizenship, which would entitle Salema to a pension on Ross's death.

On the appointed day, Salema, accompanied by her father-in-law, Abelcader, who carried her worldly goods, arrived at the *beit*. They found it empty of Ross and his few possessions, for he was on board a train, on the long journey to Perpignan, reading for the moment Berenson's *Aesthetics and History*, but with Edgar Wallace's *The Four Just Men* to fall back on. He had left money—quite a lot of money—in the *beit* for Salema. He went with no sense of guilt. He had never been weak enough to engage with Salema, to commit himself to her in any way. She had satisfied urges which he acknowledged but of which he was not proud, and her culinary skills had made his bachelor life more commodious, as Cantley would have put it, than it might have been, but he had not been interested in her nor had he particularly liked her, and there had been no danger of his emerging from the carapace into which he had consciously withdrawn as he leafed through *Punch* in the Alington after Georgie had disappeared into the crowds.

Salema was broken. The shock together with the blow to her self-esteem was total. But Cantley and Digby would not have been surprised. Ross had communicated his decision to them exactly one month earlier.

Part Three:
Perpignan Before Inez

Chapter 14

Ross felt more at home in Perpignan than he had ever done in Damascus. French culture was familiar to him from his visits to his grandparents in Menton. But it wasn't just French culture that appealed to him. Perpignan was consciously Catalan before it was French: French Catalan rather than Spanish Catalan, but Catalan first and always. The Treaty of the Pyrenees, which had transferred the region to France centuries before, seemed to have had little impact on the local population.

Since the Great War, there had been a conscious effort by the central government to stamp out local differences and languages other than French. French, not Catalan, was the language of instruction in school. Parents sometimes encouraged their children to speak it to improve their chances in life. But while teachers and administrators and some of the young who wanted to advertise their cosmopolitanism spoke the national language, the mass of the people retained their traditional tongue and spoke the French form of Catalan, guttural and initially impenetrable to Ross.

They retained too the attributes of people of the land. Even those who lived in the town were bound to the soil by powerful roots. These town-dwellers were a minority: most of their families still lived on the plain of Roussillon and in the narrow valleys that climbed from it into the mountains. Roads had come late to Roussillon and only half of the hill villages were accessible to four-wheeled vehicles. The peasants made their way by foot and on mules to and from their inaccessible homes, living a precarious life without the benefits of running water, electricity or modern sanitation.

They and their urban cousins retained the ways of those who scrape a living from the land, taciturn, suspicious and withdrawn. Ross and other incomers found it difficult to establish connections with them. So although he continued to spend time in cafés and eating places in order to glean information as he had done in Syria, it tended to be with the French-speaking minority and incomers of other nationalities that he talked.

There were many such incomers. Europeans and Americans who had been fighting in Spain drifted north to Perpignan. Others came to provide help for the Spanish refugees who were increasingly propelled north by the conflict of the Civil War. Not yet confined in camps along the coast, the refugees found what shelter they could, with little to protect them from the heat and sun of the summer or the bitter cold of the winter, sharpened by the biting wind from the north, the Tramontane. There was no medical provision for them, and women delivered their own babies and cared for their children with no more protection than a sheet of canvas.

If some of the visitors may initially have come more through curiosity than humanity, they were moved by what they found. As well as organised volunteers, there were distinguished individuals like Nancy Mitford and her husband, Peter Rodd. Mitford was horrified by the deprivation. She and others, like Humphrey Hare, a South of France playboy who had fought in the International Brigades, worked sixteen hours a day along with other society figures, like General Murgatroyd. Nancy Mitford reported that the General 'speaks no French or Spanish but bursts into fluent Hindustani at the sight of a foreigner'. The most notable element among the volunteers were the Quakers. They had done notable relief work during the Great War, and after it they had continued to work in the chaos of post-war Eastern Europe. Now they gravitated west to Perpignan and the Spanish border.

***

As the months and then a year passed, Ross became familiar with the level, fertile plain of Roussillon faced by the Mediterranean and its brackish lagoons, and surrounded by the ranges of hills that fused into the *massif* of the Canigou, and behind that the Pyrenees. On the coastal hills were ancient forts and citadels, supplemented by more modern concrete gun emplacements designed to meet challenges in the war that all expected. Ross came to know well the tracks that led up to them from the valleys of the three rivers, the Tech, the Têt and the Agly, which flowed down from the hills to water the plain.

He grew to love the warm, dry airs that he met as he climbed. In the open places the air was moved by a welcome breeze. In the sheltered gullies where it didn't move, it was heavily scented by the flowers that grew through all but the hottest months of the year: Pyrenean azaleas, wild fennel, mimosas, gentian and towering, exotic agaves. Beneath the canopies of oak and beech forests, by contrast, the air was cool, almost cold, and here he saw ancient ice-houses that had been filled in the past with snow and ice from the summit of the Canigou.

Over the Albères, separating France from Spain, ran an intricate network of narrow paths that had been used for thousands of years to move from village to village and country to country, a witness to the timeless need for food and fornication.

Some of them were open and evident to all. They had been carefully constructed in a manner that spoke of an unmeasured view of time when seen by a poor society rooted in a subsistence existence that had gone on unchanged for centuries past and that would so continue for centuries to come. It was a peasant life very different from that of the gentlemen farmers Ross had known in Devon.

To construct these routes, boulders had been chosen for their shape and painstakingly fitted together. At intervals, these stones were braced by longer narrow stones that ran laterally or diagonally across the line of the path. Where the track ran through terraces, gutters formed by smoother river stones allowed surface water to run downhill without eroding cultivable soil. Some of the terraces were long and expansive. Here the earliest agriculture had taken place, when the plain was still undrained marsh, infested by mosquitoes. But others were no more than pitiful pockets of soil. While some tracks were not unlike those Ross had known as a child in villages like Salham or Tafton, broad enough for mules to pass, most consisted of no more than the traces of previous passage.

The paths snaked through impenetrable scrub and could only be detected by those who knew them well. They were intersected by the tracks of goats and wild boar, and a casual walker would soon be lost. The consequence could well be death by cold or starvation even if the travellers could see the lights of a village: such was the nature of the rugged ground and the dense scrub. In the summer months, a traveller could sleep comfortably in the open, but during the winter in these high hills, it would be difficult to survive the night even in a shepherd's *cabane* without fire and a heavy coat.

Local people knew these routes which their ancestors had traced and they used them daily. They could read the ground and recognised secret signals, a broken branch, tiny cairns, no more than one stone on top of another, which a townsman would pass by, but countryman knew to be placed artificially. Now, in addition to their traditional licit and illicit purposes, mountain guides, *passeurs*, piloted those who needed to escape to Spain: Jews, those who were politically unacceptable and, when the war came, British soldiers and airmen. In the other direction, contraband came as it always had done to evade the customs officer.

As he walked on the hill tracks, listening to the racket from the cigales, and observing the lizards and geckos scuttling out of his way, dusty grit alternating with sand over the exposed roots of umbrella pines, Ross looked over an arid landscape that could have been on the slopes of the Beqaa Valley back in the Levant. When he saw the timeless blue of the Mediterranean, or the white-washed chapel, Notre Dame de la Salette, above Banyuls, he could imagine himself in Crete. And indeed, why not? The first sea-visitors to the generous splayed buttocks of the two bays of Banyuls had been the Phoenicians. The massive remains of the Greek city of Empuries lay just over the border in Spain. The Roman Via Domitia had bound the region together long before it became part of that Carolingian Empire of which so many Romanesque churches were evidence.

On one of his trips over the border he visited the Cathedral of Tarragona, and saw the High Altar which stands on a Roman temple-pavement, a Muslim *Mihràb* still standing in the cloister. All this was no more than evidence of that continuing civilisation to which he had been indifferent when he had seen it in the Omayyaad Mosque in Damascus, but here it affected him while there it had not. Partly that was because he was no longer looking through an exotic prism. But there was more to it than that. Having moved to the west, he was conscious of the approaching western war. He saw the shared values of a common civilisation threatened by fascist ambitions and fascist values, values which repelled him increasingly as they were progressively revealed.

***

In the early evenings, Ross and other incomers tended to drift towards the Place Jean Jaurès, to sit outside the Café de la Loge, flick through the pages of *L'Indépendant* or *La Malicieuse*, two of the local papers, or listen to the news taken from the third, *L'Intransigéant,* broadcast over loudspeakers.

On an evening some months after his arrival in Perpignan, Ross made his way there as usual. He saw three women he knew at a table near the front of the terrace, drinking glasses of rough, red Catalan wine. In the heightened atmosphere of these months, as the detritus of the ending Spanish war washed over the French border, and another, larger and even more horrible conflict seemed unavoidable, the incomers felt themselves unconstrained by convention. The women, unlike Frenchwomen, felt quite able to sit in a café with other women, or even alone, and men who only knew them by sight would join them.

Ross knew the three, and not just by sight. Two of them were Quakers who had been working with refugees since 1916: Edith Pye, a small, solid nurse and midwife of enormous energy, and her friend Hilda Clark, also small, but spare, a doctor. They were obviously very close, as they had been for almost thirty years, and they made no attempt to hide their affection for each other. The third woman was younger, tall, blonde, with tight curls. Her name was Veronica Harrington. She was dressed, as she almost always was, in a tight-waisted black leather jerkin and fawn slacks that emphasised her long legs. She too had worked with refugees in the Balkans. She appeared to have independent means and wasn't, like Edith and Hilda, employed by agencies such as the Women's International League.

Ross joined them and ordered a carafe of the red wine. Veronica didn't talk much. She and Ross listened to the other two. They talked fast and purposefully. Edith was much concerned about the children in the camps. She told the others that earlier in the day she'd seen no less than two mothers nursing babies that were obviously dead. Her concern was that the children were vulnerable not just to disease and malnutrition, but also aerial bombardment. Occasional Francoist planes had already over-flown the camps and dropped bombs.

'Imagine what the Germans may do,' she said. 'I've told the Child Refugee Commission what's happening, but they do nothing.'

The failure of the international bodies to grasp the seriousness of the situation was accepted without debate.

'But Edith won't knuckle down,' said Hilda approvingly. 'She's persuaded the Quakers to take on some of the empty spa hotels in the hills.'

Edith nodded. 'I remembered something we did in the war. I had set up a maternity hospital near the Marne. In 1917, the fighting got too close. I hated the idea of sending the babies and their mothers back to villages that could be shelled and overrun without warning. Meanwhile, the hotels on the coast were deserted. Not many holidaymakers while Third Ypres was in progress. So we just took over one of them.'

84

At the next table sat two men whom Ross did not properly know. He had seen them around for just a day or two. Both were communist intellectuals. Both were Jewish, and both were, therefore, bound to be on the run, not welcome, heading for Spain. Otherwise, they were far from alike. One was confident, good-looking and extroverted, already popular with the regular expatriates. The other was intense, his hair *en brosse*, gold-rimmed spectacles on his nose, a bushy moustache below it. Ross and he were almost brushing elbows. They talked.

The man was no conversationalist and asked nothing of Ross. He did, however, talk a lot about himself. His name was Walter Benjamin. He clearly thought that Ross might have heard of him, but they came from very different backgrounds, and Ross knew nothing of the world of which Benjamin spoke, and understood only a small part of the ideas that informed that world.

Benjamin came from a rich family of integrated Jews of the Kaiser's Germany. He was highly educated in the literature and culture of nineteenth-century central Europe and would have enjoyed the standing of the intellectual elite in that *ancien régime*. As it was, he was without status as a result of Nazism, stripped of his German nationality. He had already been imprisoned by the French, and with a warrant out for his arrest by the Germans, he seemed, unlike his buoyant companion, disheartened and defeated. He told Ross that just a few days earlier he had seriously weighed up suicide as an alternative to flight. It was clear that his decision had been made very much on balance, and might yet be reversed.

All the same, his opinion of himself was considerable. Even if he had no social skills, he had an intellectual *amour propre* and a readiness to assert his views that was unusual in Ross's limited experience. He talked at length about his concept of what he called 'cultural Zionism', which seemed to mean that his Jewishness was expressed in the furtherance of European culture. This he regarded as infinitely superior to the crass values of Hitler's gang. His inner confidence in his own values seemed so unquestioned that Ross discounted his outer defeatism and talk of suicide. He certainly hoped he was right to discount them. Though he could never inhabit Benjamin's intellectual hinterland, he envied the man his resources.

After a little, Edith and Hilda went off, back to the camps, where they'd set up 'the University of the Sands' to teach French to the Spaniards. They went out talking intently, uncaring of anything but each other and their projects.

'They're very fond of each other,' said Ross.

'They're very much in love,' said Veronica, in a spirit of correction, 'and we need more of that and less hate.'

Ross felt that he had been rebuked for a lack of sympathy, for having seemed to criticise the saintly couple for their lifestyle. That hadn't been his intention. Veronica sensed his reaction and broke the tension by asking him with a grin, 'Well, we know who they love, but what about you, Mr Alexander Ross?'

Ross's usual reaction would have been to evade an intrusive question, but the wine had relaxed him and her smile disarmed him. He found himself telling her about his brief marriage, the Spanish flu, and Barbara's death. Veronica's manner changed. She looked grave, and even more disturbed than Ross's narrative warranted. He felt fraudulent to be receiving sympathy for a loss which had troubled him so little, and hastened on to say in honesty how little he had known Barbara, and how little, frankly, he missed her.

Veronica's silent reception of his candour incommoded him, and he felt the need to tell her more about his cold, friendless childhood. The gap between them closed a little.

'And since then,' she asked, 'has there not been anyone else?'

He told her about Damascus, and Salema. She seemed pleased that Ross had found a partner. Again he felt he was being credited with something bogus. He ended his story lamely but thoughtfully, by saying that Salema had wanted more than he was prepared to give and so he'd left and here he was in Perpignan.

Veronica shook her head, puzzled and sad. Ross perceived that she saw reprehensible failings in relationships with Barbara and Salema which seemed to him quite unreasonable. Very soon she got up.

'It's time for us to go home. But tomorrow, come for me at nine o'clock and drive me in your car. I shall show you why we must love as well as live.' They had both drunk a good deal of wine. She slipped her arm in his and they walked unsteadily across the Place Jean Jaurès.

Chapter 15

Ross was anxious when he drew up outside Veronica's flat next morning. Her confidence and self-assurance, her comfort with herself, had inspired respect and he wanted her to think well of him. He was aware that he'd told her much more about himself than he felt appropriate. He believed he had little to be proud of in the life he'd lived, and he was equally aware that her reaction to his self-exposure had not been of unqualified approval. He was accordingly relieved when she came through her door as soon as he stopped: she was smiling and clearly looking forward to the day.

Ross had bought a two-seater Citroën when he arrived at Perpignan. The roof was down and as they drove in the strong morning sun, Veronica's red scarf blew back like a pennant. Her hair was confined by a black beret. In her leather jacket, she looked to Ross rather like an early aviatrix.

She directed him south from Perpignan, across the river Tech and up towards the Spanish border, where the Albères hills ran from the coast to the high Pyrenees. They met some other cars, but most of the traffic was on two or four legs. The further they left Perpignan behind, the more they saw of the ordinary Catalans. A typical man wore his red cap, his *barretina*; his trousers and blouse were made of moleskin, with a scarlet sash across his shoulders. On his feet, he wore rope-soled espadrilles. Over one shoulder hung a leather *bota* filled with wine. Over the other he carried a satchel containing a hunk of bread and a piece of sausage. His woman followed him. Unless she was a young bride, she looked prematurely old, her face lined by the strains of her hard life, her figure bulky and covered to her espadrilles by a voluminous black costume. Most of the women carried kindling faggots or other burdens on their heads, which were covered by hoods, again of black. The occasional shepherd was on the road, leading small flocks of long-legged sheep and carrying over his shoulder a blanket in which he would wrap himself beside his fire on the mountainside.

Here and there at the roadside—sometimes even on the road itself—were little family groups of charcoal makers, *charbonniers,* painstakingly collecting fallen timber and reducing it to charcoal in smouldering heaps covered in turf. They were witnesses to the production of iron from the ore in the hills, an occupation that went back to the Iron Age itself. It had almost withered away as ore came to be mined more efficiently in Alsace, revived when the north-eastern provinces were lost to France in 1870, and then declined again with their recovery in 1918. Charcoal was needed to process the iron. The *charbonniers* were small, thick-set and swarthy, reputedly remnants of the Balearic peoples who had inhabited the region when the Kings of Mallorca reigned from their

Palace in Perpignan. Ross suspected however that they were the inbred products of tribes who had lived on the mountains when the ore first began to be exploited.

If Ross and Veronica could have ignored two extraneous elements, the pitiful ragged groups of starving refugees coming north, and the steady stream of soldiers who harried the exiles, and had seen only the peasants and their animals, they could have thought themselves surrounded by scenes and a way of life that had remained entirely unchanged for centuries.

This sense of continuity with the past was enhanced by the fact that they were following the route of the Via Domitia. Indeed, at places where the road consisted of bedrock, they could see the ruts dug by Roman chariot wheels. Ross and Veronica were driving towards the distant cleft in hills for which travellers had headed for millennia, and through which Hannibal had come with his elephants when he waged war on the young Roman republic. At this gap in the hills lay the frontier village of Le Perthus, and through it proud armies and poor travellers round the Mediterranean basin had moved since the dawn of civilisation. Today, the detritus of republican Spain was flushed through it by Franco. It was here that Veronica had brought Ross.

The border between France and Spain ran up the middle of the unmetalled track that led from one country to the other. One side of Le Perthus was in Spain, and one in France. Ross parked the car and they walked along this divided street. On the one side, French *paysans* lived in huts, shacks and cabins, crossing the road to buy cheap tobacco and wine and the occasional piece of ham from the stalls of their even poorer Spanish cousins.

In a few hundred yards, Ross and Veronica reached the frontier. The weighted pole that could close the road had been swung up. Unwelcoming French soldiers grudgingly admitted members of an immense crowd, group by group, pent up like a flood contained behind a narrowly breached dam.

When the mass of refugees had first reached the border in the early weeks of the *Retirada* they found it closed, and no welcome awaited them. Even before the Civil War, Spanish immigrants had been seen as illiterate peasants who had come ostensibly to work for almost nothing as seasonal agricultural workers, but in reality to scavenge and steal. In their new manifestation they attracted little more goodwill. Their political and democratic aspirations were ignored: they were feared as anti-clerical communists who would overturn church and state, dirty, lazy, a burden on the hardworking peasants of the region. The stability of that region was threatened by their sheer mass.

Hounded to the border by African troops fighting for Franco, the immigrants were dismayed to find themselves confronted at it by Senegalese soldiers, stationed in Perpignan. Even refugees had their colour prejudices. Hard on their heels Franco's troops arrived. They blew their bugles and the *Indépendant* published pictures of the French and Spanish generals shaking hands. The Spaniards saluted with their version of the Fascist salute, displaying their open palms. The French establishment rather liked Franco and his ideas. When Pétain was appointed French ambassador to Spain he had described Franco, el Caudillo, as 'the cleanest sword in the western world'.

For weeks, the destitute mass had been held at the border crossings. They faced bayonets and some were shot. The border guards were brutal. In the early spring of 1939, the refugees, in their hundreds of thousands, faced the cold of the mountains. Many died if not of the cold then of starvation or disease. Those who could make their way through the dense *maquis* or over the rocks did so, but few were able to do so, and the numbers grew. Women gave birth, but death was more common than birth. Franco's planes flew overhead, bombing the pathetic columns.

Matters could not go on like this for long. The threat of epidemic, which would not respect a frontier, was a real one; in addition, France faced condemnation from the world's press. Those countries which were far enough from the tragedy to feel free from doing anything about it were quick to criticise. Finally, the border was opened—but only enough to allow the victims to come through in a controlled flow.

***

Ross had often seen the refugees in their camps on the coast. There the inmates had become, as they were no doubt meant to be, dehumanised and institutionalised. Here he saw individuals, individuals at a turning point in their lives and with no control over what would happen to them. There were men, women and children, but young able-bodied men were scarce. *They* did not leave Spain. The faces Ross looked at were dirty and coarsened by exposure to frost and sun, their cheeks hollowed by the malnutrition which left them with sores and ulcers. Their eyes were staring, dead. Ross understood now why so few had come over the open mountains: almost none had serviceable footwear and many had bare and bloody feet.

The refugees were funnelled between two posts that marked the frontier, where they were searched by the French soldiers. Ross saw a woman carrying a baby that was clearly dead. It was roughly prised from her hands and thrown to the ground. She was prodded with the butt of a rifle and propelled into democratic, libertarian France.

Those Spaniards who had weapons handed them over willingly enough, and the machine guns, armoured cars and cavalry that greeted them were palpably unnecessary. From time to time, the soldiers arbitrarily stopped the flow to clear the road down which the Spaniards trickled; they had still many miles to walk before they reached le Boulou, and the barren inhospitality of the camps. On their way, they were harried by cavalry charges from time to time to keep them from straying.

Ross and Veronica stood watching for well over an hour. From time to time, Veronica left him to speak to one of the handful of volunteers who handed bread to some of those who passed. Ross gazed at the flow. He had seen poverty in Syria, even starvation and death, but there the people had been quite unlike his own. Here he was looking at Europeans, less fortunate than he, but still recognisably beings with whom he could identify. The suddenness, the arbitrariness, of the reverse of their fortunes shocked Ross. He was horrified that so much suffering was caused not by natural catastrophes, but by the deliberate contrivance of man. His certainty about the state of things and the solid order of events was challenged by the evidence in this human flotsam of the chaos that human intervention could cause. If he had been a man who wept, he might well have done that. He felt shaken and weak from the swirl of tragedy that swept round him and from gazing into so many empty eyes.

At last, Veronica came back. 'Come on,' she said, 'you've seen enough.' They made their way to the Spanish side of the road. She took him to an open-fronted shop which smelt strongly of the goats which were tethered outside. There was no sign to indicate that food and drink could be had, but Veronica seemed to know her way and led him up a narrow staircase to the first floor and into a large room. In one corner, an old man was cooking over a wooden fire and in a corner some men played cards.

When the old man saw them, he called loudly into a back room, 'Infanta.' A girl in her late teens appeared, her blonde hair plaited at the back. She took their orders.

'Infanta?' said Ross.

'That's an old tradition,' replied Veronica, 'the Spanish princesses who were sent to Perpignan to marry the Kings of Majorca were all blonde. Now any young girl with yellow hair is called Infanta.' Infanta brought them a bottle of *pastis*, two glasses and a jug of water. Ross poured them each a large measure. He needed to be settled.

'Well, was the dilettante shaken by what he saw?' asked Veronica with a smile.

Ross stiffened.

'I'm sorry,' she said, 'that was unfair. No one could fail to respond to what you've just seen. You told me a lot about yourself last night.' Ross made to demur, but she continued, 'No, you did and I valued your honesty. I felt that I must respond in kind. The purpose of this rather brutal little trip was to show you what motivates me, what makes me alive. When I see the kind of thing we saw this morning—and I've seen a lot of it in countless refugee camps—I feel that I must engage, that something must be done. I feel a duty to try to improve things.'

'You mean a religious duty like Hilda and Edith?' asked Ross.

'No, not religious in the conventional sense—although Hilda and Edith are not entirely conventional as you discovered last night.' She hesitated and considered for a little time what she would say next. She made a decision. She leant forward and spoke very directly to Ross. 'You probably saw my reaction last night when you told me that your wife had died from Spanish flu. My husband, Frank, and Terry, my brother, died of the same thing, probably at much the same time as your wife, just after the end of the war. Terry was my twin. Our mother died in childbirth and our father brought us up until *he* died. We were just eighteen and now there were only the two of us. We lived together. We were very close.

90

'I met Frank when I was twenty. Marriage didn't mean that Terry and I were apart. It simply enlarged us—now we were three. Life was fuller. Frank was a submariner. After our honeymoon I went back to the flat and he joined us when he was on leave. He was demobilised in 1919. He'd come through the war without a scratch, but within a week of taking off his uniform he felt unwell. He was dead in a matter of days, and Terry died six hours later.'

Ross was going to intervene with some conventional words of sympathy, but Veronica motioned his interruption aside. 'I was desolate at first, of course. We'd made such plans together. Frank and Terry were all I had in life. I couldn't see any future for myself. But after a while, I thought about everything very hard. Apart from losing *my* men, I was thinking about *all* the men who had died in the war, many of my friends and family amongst them. I thought too about the millions more who died of the influenza. It seemed to me that there were just two options. Maybe life is entirely meaningless and we're just like swarms of insects with no control over our destinies. Some of us get stamped on, some of us die for other reasons. We move around purposefully, as it appears to us, but truly we're entirely without purpose or point or control over our destinies. *Or* we try to take control of our destinies. We have a duty to improve, as far as we can, to save lives and mitigate suffering and try to order things for the better. We may never fully succeed, but we can improve things to a degree and that is what gives our lives purpose and point.'

Infanta had brought food, a meagre bean stew that contained some Catalan sausage. They ate and they drank a bottle of red wine. Veronica talked as she ate. Ross understood that he wasn't meant to interrupt.

Then he asked, 'Is all this an expression of love, love for your husband and Terry?'

'No, not really. Of course, I loved them both hugely and still do, but what I'm doing for them isn't expressing love, whatever that means. I'm trying to make their lives and deaths more than meaningless. I'm trying to find a sense in their lives and deaths. I'm trying to find sense in my own life. I'm trying to see a reason for human existence—if that doesn't sound preposterously pretentious. I'm trying to say that life isn't purposeless, but something nobler than that, in which the tragedy is balanced by an endeavour to improve things.'

They sat for a while without talking. Infanta brought another bottle of wine. As Ross poured it, Veronica, more relaxed as the alcohol filled her veins, went on, 'Of course individual love is important. When Frank died, I took off my wedding ring. I sold it along with my other jewellery, and the proceeds together with money I inherited are enough for me to live on so that I can live the kind of life I decided to embark on. If I find love again then so much the better, but it's not what I'm looking for.'

Because it was cold, Ross and Veronica sat close together in their corner. They warmed to each other, both figuratively and literally, as the wine entered their blood. They warmed also because of the effectiveness of the peculiarly Catalan charcoal heater that sat under the table, emitting gentle warmth that was contained by the thick tablecloth which fell to the ground. In a poor community in a part of the world that felt the chill of the winter in substantially unheated buildings, this little invention was very effective—though Ross had on occasions seen women rushing from the tables, their petticoats in flames.

'Are you afraid that surrendering to love reduces you to one of these insects that you want to feel superior to?' he asked, feeling that he was possibly going further than he should, but Veronica replied with a grin.

'Well, it's certainly got to be more than lust otherwise we're just like rutting dogs, and I certainly couldn't marry a man who didn't have the same sort of views as me. If *I'm* more than a dog, I don't want to be married to someone who isn't.' Ross wondered if there was an element of challenge in this, but her grey eyes were level and her tone dispassionate.

It was late when they left the café and the sun had long gone down. The one street of le Perthus was quiet now. The barrier had come down and the frontier guards faced the Spaniards with loaded rifles. The huge crowd of refugees, waiting now for the morning and the deaths that would occur before the dawn, was quiet. The children were too weak and exhausted to cry. Some fires had been lit and people crowded as close to them as they could. Most carried a blanket and tried to wrap themselves against the cold. Gas lamps flickered weakly along the French side of the street, their flames flaring up and dying back as the supply faltered.

The moon was fairly full and lit the majestic bulk of the Canigou and the road on which Ross drove back to Perpignan. For two nights running, he and Veronica had drunk a lot. Veronica soon fell asleep, her head on Ross's shoulder. Alec enjoyed the physical intimacy, as he'd enjoyed the moral intimacy of their closeness and confessions. Veronica was attractive in appearance and in the frankness and vivacity of her manner. He could be drawn to her, but his ingrained instinct was to resist the desire before he was even aware of it. In any event, she seemed stronger than he, more disciplined. That he knew very well. He drove carefully and his mind was perfectly clear in the cold air. He was struck by the cliché of their image, she the frail female, resting against the strong capable male. How different the reality.

Chapter 16

In the months after that visit to the frontier, the political and military situation grew dramatically worse. When Ross and the others gathered at the Café de la Loge in the evenings, the headlines from *L'Intransigéant* that were broadcast from the loudspeakers were daily more pessimistic.

Despite that, he enjoyed the conviviality of these meetings. During the day all the participants had separately witnessed grim aspects of life. They had tasks to perform that brought them into contact of some sort with human suffering or the baser aspects of human nature. In the evenings they shut an imaginary door behind themselves and settled to relax. They drank a lot—even Edith and Hilda—and the atmosphere was convivial. As they broke up at the end of an evening, one or other of the group very often said, 'That was fun'. And Ross frequently thought that these gatherings *were* indeed fun. This was something new. In the past, he had *existed*: sometimes happily enough, sometimes unhappily, but life for him had been no more than a matter of coping. Now a part of it at least was, positively, fun, and that fact made the rest of his life not just tolerable, but worthwhile. The drudgery of spying was invested with a sense of purpose which legitimised the totality.

It was novel for him to find himself not an outsider, an observer, but a participant. He was not the centre of the little group of expatriates, but he was certainly within it. Since he was not given to introspection, he did not analyse the dynamics of the group or consider his place in its currents. If he had thought about himself, he would have avowed that his was not a strong character. In truth, it was stronger than he would have thought—and capable of being stronger still—but there were more obvious leaders in the café. Some of the military men who appeared from nowhere and equally mysteriously disappeared on missions of espionage were clear-cut leaders of men—who usually, Ross noted, needed to do nothing to emphasise their toughness. Their self-assurance was inviolable and quiet.

Of the resident members of the group, it was probably Veronica who came closest at this time to being its leader. She, too, did nothing to advertise her qualities—she didn't talk more than the others or trumpet her opinions—but in her quiet confidence in what she was doing, these qualities were evident. Ross and she spent much of their free time together. She shared all her thoughts with him, and he shared more of his with her than he had ever done with another person, and he was flattered that she considered him worth her confidence.

Meanwhile, developments in politics and war were increasingly alarming. First came the news of Germany's attack on Poland, and France's declaration of war on Germany. The atmosphere in the town became charged. Blackout intensified the sense of anxiety in the darkened streets. Beyond that, little happened to remind the town that they were at war until Germany turned her attention to the west.

This Phoney War, the *Drôle de Guerre*, ended in May 1940 when Germany finally did that. The little band of expatriates sitting outside the café heard that the government had abandoned Paris. First, it moved to Tours, then to Bordeaux. The French and their British allies retreated in disarray and were finally separated. It was now that the aged hero of the First World War, Maréchal Pétain, became Prime Minister. Veronica and Edith and Hilda were clear that he was much more sympathetic to the Spanish Fascists than to the miserable prisoners, but most of the public who gathered to see him visit Perpignan gave him a warm reception.

For millions of French, Pétain was the man who had listened to the *poilus* in the First World War and brought an end to the mutinies amongst the soldiers in 1917. He was a father-figure, a representative of an older, traditional way of life, a man who would shelter France from her eternal schisms and all the tensions of an industrial society that seemed brutal and barbarous compared to a rural age, idyllic and imaginary. Pétain understood what people wanted. He promised to take France back to its dream of a stable, old-fashioned society, a hierarchical world with the church and the aristocracy maintaining the ancient values. He signed an armistice with the Germans. Defeat had been due to decadence and France would be redeemed by hard work and discipline. *Travail, Famille, Patrie* replaced *Liberté, Fraternité* and *Égalité*. His image was everywhere. Demoralised, infantilistic France surrendered itself to the cult of Papa Pétain. Even the Canigou was defiled. One of its peaks was named Pic Pétain. Later, a group of boy scouts climbed the mountain, some barefoot, in atonement for France's decadence, dragging a huge cross to be planted in cement at the summit.

France's humiliation was marked by the scale of the concessions Pétain made to the Germans in his armistice settlement. The French army was halved in size. Her fleet was locked up in home ports. The country was divided and the north-western half of the country was occupied by the Germans.

So Perpignan was in the Unoccupied Zone, notionally still governed by Pétain's government, now installed at Vichy. In many ways, however, the Unoccupied Zone was more Germanic than the Occupied Zone. Pétain abandoned the democratic institutions of France and governed as an absolute ruler. He invented the word *collaboration* which was without any pejorative sense. Collaboration was a virtue, not a vice. He shared many of the German objectives as did very many of his supporters. They desired a New Order as fervently as the Nazis. They embarked on the harrying and deportation of the Jews with an enthusiasm that sometimes embarrassed their German associates.

So the distinction between the Occupied and Unoccupied Zones was pretty nebulous, a sop to French self-respect. German troops were increasingly stationed within the Unoccupied Zone and soon Vichy had followed Germany's instructions and declared that all border areas had to be cleared of foreigners.

With this Vichy decree, the atmosphere changed almost overnight. The more exotic elements disappeared. Those who remained became more clandestine. The mood became tenser.

***

These developments impinged on Perpignan and Ross's circle in different ways. Rationing began almost as soon as war was declared. The rationing of meat was particularly savage—but of little consequence as there was almost no meat to be had and what there was commanded prices that were out of the range of the ordinary person. The staples of life like bread, milk and coffee were only sold on pre-announced days. On those days there were long queues; queuing before five in the morning had to be forbidden. Wine, and perhaps milk, was watered. Coffee was made from acorns, and cafés had no sugar to sweeten the bitterness of the repellent dark brown juice. People carried their own sugar tin with them if they had been able to get hold of any, in the same way as they carried a tin, a *mégotorium*, containing cigarette stubs which might have enough shreds of tobacco attached to form the basis for a short hand-rolled cigarette.

Increasingly, Ross found the city strangely quiet. There was none of the vibrancy and bustle of Damascus. It took him a while to put his finger on what it was. Damascus had been a city built for pedestrians, and its narrow streets were full of people rushing around on foot or with donkeys and, above all, handcarts. Perpignan, apart from the warren of tiny concentric *ruelles* that formed the centre of the old town, had evolved into a town designed for modern traffic, but since Ross's arrival, cars had all but disappeared from the broad streets, and with them the noise and clamour of a modern conurbation.

There were broken-down horse carriages where taxis had plied, many bicycles, some with two-wheeled trailers for passengers and goods. Many of those cars which were still to be seen had been converted into *gazogènes*, fuelled by gas generated from charcoal rather than petrol (though a hoarded pint of petrol sometimes had to be used to get the vehicle started on a cold morning). Donkeys, which had been an important part of the city scene, had been converted into protein to eke out restaurant dishes of swede or sweet potato as an alternative to what was always referred to as 'pigeon', whatever find it might originally have been.

On the country roads outside the town, donkeys were, however, still frequently seen. Their peasant owners were able to supplement their diets from the fields in the way that their town cousins could not. In any event, in the countryside, a donkey was not a luxury but the only means of cultivating the land and getting around.

And so in the towns, the pedestrians, other than the privileged little community of which Ross was a part, increasingly lived grey lives, shabby and disheartened, shuffling on wooden-soled shoes, trying to exist on paltry rations.

Ross and the others observed these increasing privations, but as they assembled for an aperitif outside the Café de la Loge and then moved on to the

Café Gambetta to eat, they were largely protected from them. Because they were known at both places, where their tips were appreciated, they received favourable treatment, and black-market supplies were often available. The effect of rationing on the Café Gambetta was less dramatic than its effect on ordinary householders. All the same, the quality of food and wine markedly deteriorated. The banning of *pastis* was more of a blow than the proscription of the manufacture of *croissants*, but in the event something that looked and tasted very like *pastis* but cost twice as much continued to be available.

***

The composition of the little expatriate community was changing. As soon as France entered the war and long before the fall of France, it had begun to shrink. The English civilian community left at once. Major-General Rawston Davidson, CB, was not exactly a civilian, but he had retired from the army on half pay in 1903 after a distinguished war in South Africa. He had been too old to fight in the First World War and lived through that war and up to the beginning of the second in Perpignan, latterly as a widower. When the camps on the coast filled with refugees, the call of duty took him there. He was far too old and infirm to be of the slightest practical use to anyone, but he was delighted to find himself at the centre of the unofficial mess that had established itself in the Café Gambetta. There he presided with great geniality, making the most of the role of Senior British Officer, entertaining the others with rambling stories of long-forgotten colonial wars and taking great pains as a host to ensure that no-one felt shy or was left out of the conversation. When war was declared, he returned to England to fade away in the house of an elderly spinster daughter in the Mendip Hills. He was accompanied by most of the other genteel, elderly foreign residents, the Perpignan equivalent of Ross's grandparents and their friends in Menton. With the fall of France, any remaining elements of the long-time expatriates, the casual volunteers and the inquisitive spectators disappeared at once.

Ross and Veronica missed them greatly. They had been people of character and courage who had contributed to the gaiety of daily life.

***

But coming and going continued. In the early days, immediately after the fall of France, it was possible to pass quite openly from France to Spain, and Ross saw some distinguished visitors reach Perpignan. The Duke of Windsor and his consort made their way over the border. Jean Cocteau turned up in Perpignan with a large supply of opium and spent some time there until he decided that it would be more fun in Paris. The cellist, Pablo Casals, arrived in Prades, in the valley of the Têt. Spain was no place for him to flee to, and he remained in Prades throughout the war. Thomas Mann's brother and son escaped, and the elderly Alma Mahler, Gustav's widow, clambered over the frontier while the train she'd left carried twelve suitcases containing the original scores of all her husband's music as well as her clothes and made its way to Spain through the tunnel to Portbou. Many of these people were helped on their way by the American vice-consul at Marseille, Hiram Bingham whose policy was to 'issue all the visas you want, but not for people who had asked for them'. All this coming and going created a cosmopolitan atmosphere in Perpignan. It still had the feel of an international city.

Alongside these itinerants, others arrived, not civilians but military men, some of them servicemen struggling to make their way back to Britain, some of them there to assist others in that endeavour, setting up escape routes and trying at the same time to do as much damage as they could to the German war effort.

***

Almost the first of these to arrive was Peter Graham, an infantryman who had been left behind at Dunkirk. He would also be the last to leave; he became an essential part of the expatriate scene. At an early stage in the war, he had been able to make his way on his own through a France that was not yet divided into Occupied and Unoccupied Zones. He had fought in the First World War. He said nothing about either of his wars, First or Second, but he walked with a slight limp which it was assumed was the result of a wound from one conflict or the other. He had fair, slightly greying hair, a blond moustache, was tall and self-contained and carried a sense of authority. The fact that he spoke very little was rightly assumed to be the consequence of being a strong, silent type and not because he had nothing useful to say. Graham had the habit of looking not at his interlocutor, but rather allowing his eyes to roam away in a preoccupied way as if scanning the horizon for a sail or a distant hill for signs of movement.

Peter was soon at home with the group, Edith, Hilda, Veronica and Ross and its other more transient members. It was clear that he knew something of Ross and what he was doing. He and Veronica, rather than Veronica alone, were now looked to as the leaders of the little community in the Café Gambetta. There had never been an emotional link between Veronica and Ross, Nor, initially at least, was there between her and Peter. But Ross found himself slightly awkward in Peter's presence all the same. He was aware of the fact, but didn't analyse the reasons for it.

Others came, but unlike Peter Graham they did not stay. They were birds of passage and they passed and some of them were pretty exotic. Perhaps the most distinguished was an Air Chief Marshal who managed to get shot down over France. He was helped to escape by a famous Resistance heroine from Marseille, Nancy Wake, known to her enemies as the White Mouse because of her capacity to escape them.

Another arrival, who did not disappear, and whose activities were to intertwine with those of Ross and Peter, was Pat O'Leary. O'Leary came ashore at Collioure, a picture-perfect little harbour between Perpignan and Port Vendres which had been home to Picasso, Derain and the Fauve painters thirty years earlier. He arrived on HMS *Fidelity*, a Royal Naval ship disguised as a cargo vessel. He had escaped Dunkirk and was returning to France to establish one of the most important escape lines in the war which ran through Marseille to Spain and would take his name, the Pat Line.

A frequent visitor to Perpignan, when he came to consult with Peter, was Ian Garrow. Like Peter, he was a very tall man. Unlike him, he had a strong Scottish accent. He had been in the Seaforth Highlanders and was left behind at the fall of France. Like Peter, he had chosen to stay behind rather than escape. He worked on O'Leary's Pat Line, mostly on the section from the north to Marseille. From Marseille, the line split into two final routes. The northern line ran through Toulouse towards the west of the Pyrenees chain. This line was run on a hands-off basis by Donald Darling, the vice-consul in Lisbon and later an MI9 agent in Gibraltar. The southern line ran through Perpignan, over the Albères mountains and into Spain. This was the line for which Peter was responsible, and its existence increasingly affected Ross and affected the direction of his life.

Chapter 17

By degrees, the nature of Ross's work, and the way he performed it, changed. The idea that he was an artist was increasingly a fiction, though he went through the motions of continuing to draw and paint to provide the excuse for ranging around the area and observing, but his contact was no longer with the jolly auctioneer. His instructions came from an anonymous hand which may have been that of Cantley, and Ross reported to he knew not whom at an address that meant nothing to him. Corresponding via Spain had been deemed to be incautious and had been replaced with cloak and dagger techniques. His instructions were secreted in condoms within tubes of oil paint, and for his replies, he laboriously glued messages on the back of canvasses on which he had painted what he increasingly regarded as his worthless art. He rather enjoyed this introduction to the world of Sapper and Bulldog Drummond.

The rocky, indented coast of the Côte Vermeille had received contraband for centuries. Now it was patrolled and defended more diligently than it ever had been, but legitimate ships sometimes carried illegitimate cargo. Just twenty miles from Perpignan lay Port Vendres, used by navigators since the Phoenicians came to what the Romans, much later, called Portus Veneris, the Port of Venus. It was a major port, outranked on the Mediterranean coast only by Marseille and Toulon, and the nearest point for a crossing to North Africa. Two packet boats, *El Kantara* and *El Mansour* plied between Port Vendres and Oran and Algiers, as well as numerous freighters carrying cork, wine and vegetables. Captains and crew did very well out of the supplies they brought to feed the Catalan black market. Ross's communications inward and outward went through the hands of the purser of the *El Kantara* which arrived in Port Vendres twice a week.

His trips to Port Vendres were always agreeable jaunts. The roads were empty and he enjoyed driving down to the town between hedges in which the golden flowers of the mimosas dripped like molten gold. He often took Veronica with him and they drove slowly in the open car smelling the wild thyme mixing with the salt of the sea. Port Vendres had the attraction of being a bustling port, still animated in a way in which wartime Perpignan was not. Little fishing boats emptied their cargos, particularly huge catches of anchovy and sardines. There was a lively fish market in the early morning and in a little restaurant beside it, La Crie, the freshest of fish could be eaten and the white wine seemed to escape the rigours of rationing. Larger ships unloaded cargos of vegetables and oranges destined for the Reich. Such exotic fruits were never seen in Perpignan, but there was always some with which to end the fishy meal in Port Vendres.

Veronica was pleased to join Ross on these excursions. On the way, she visited the huge refugee camps to the south of Perpignan where she talked to officials, and on which she reported to the International Committee of the Red Cross in Geneva. She seemed happy with Ross's company and he enjoyed hers. She always talked with animation and frequently squeezed his hand or pressed his arm to make a point. Ross would have liked to think that there was an element of sexual attraction in all of this, but he was too realistic to delude himself. Ever since their confidences at Le Perthus, and on the preceding night, there had been an openness in their relationship which he had never known with another woman, but it was perfectly clear to him that this was without significance. As an only child, he could only wonder if their relationship was like that of a brother and sister.

He had the feeling on the other hand that Veronica and Peter Graham were becoming closer. In his reaction to that, there was the tiniest element of disappointment: not more than that and not jealousy. He had always been aware that Veronica needed a bigger man than he was and he had no doubts that Peter was such a man.

His own relationship with Peter developed. They got on well together but although they were very much the same age, Ross felt distinctly the junior. Peter continued to say very little, but what he said was always to the point, and rarely required correction. His way through life had given him a confidence and judgement that reinforced his opinions.

***

Ross's instructions were frequently to meet agents who appeared on the coast in the middle of the night. A motor torpedo boat appeared off a narrow creek at Paulilles, a deserted beach a mile or so beyond Port Vendres, with a narrow stretch of shingle above which ran steep cliffs. A light flashed from the motor torpedo boat which Ross had to acknowledge. Soon, a surf-boat landed, often containing the Commander of the MTB, a very large Lieutenant with a splendid bushy beard and a booming voice.

'I'm Hairy, Hairy Watson,' he bellowed, ignoring the possibility that the beach might be surrounded by aggressive *Milices*. The purpose of the visit was usually to pick up or land agents or to give instructions to Ross and others who were already in place: sometimes a conference took place. On one occasion, by the time the discussions had ended, the MTB had cleared off, presumably under the impression that it had been sighted. After paddling around the bay for an hour or so, the surf-boat was carefully sunk and Ross had to secrete the agents wherever he could hide them until Hairy's next visit.

There were other cloak and dagger figures who came ashore on the coast from clandestine vessels or submarines. They hugely enjoyed themselves, though their contribution to the war effort was doubtful. They were often poorly trained, poorly equipped and of little value as agents. They tended to land in the wrong places, get lost and frequently got arrested.

But what surprised Ross—at this stage in the war—was how many of them *didn't* get arrested. It was true that a high percentage of those who got over the frontier were taken prisoner by the Spanish Carabiñeros and were put in jail or one of the camps like that at Miranda. But while it could be a long wait, the British Consul was advised and once the men were vouched for, they would eventually be released and moved on towards Britain.

Most of the *évadés*, the escaping British servicemen, originated in Marseille, where the flow was directed by a remarkable Scots Minister. Donald Caskie ran the Seamen's Mission there. Caskie had been the Minister of the Scots Kirk in Paris. He had been an outspoken critic of Hitler and when the armistice was signed, he moved south to the Vieux Port of Marseille, where he felt called to help the military wanderers who had congregated there as the German flail swept south.

What Ross found extraordinary was the openness of the arrangement. Caskie apparently wore his kilt and was allowed to run the mission as a seamen's refuge. He was a civilian, but a high-profile activist. The Vichy authorities knew perfectly well what he was up to. He was supposed only to provide succour to civilians and merchant sailors, but the Marseille authorities were well aware that the mission was full of fleeing soldiers, and that others were secreted around the town. Security at the mission was laughable. Soldiers on the run knew that all they had to do was knock on the door three times and ask for Donald Duck.

With Veronica and Peter one evening, Ross raised the question of the remarkable toleration that seemed to be afforded to Donald Caskie and his charges. Did the authorities choose to turn a blind eye because they were cunningly obtaining valuable intelligence about the British?

Peter reacted more spontaneously than usual and laughed uproariously, 'Oh no. It's not nearly as subtle as that. Don't conjure up conspiracies—accept cock-ups. It never does to underestimate the lack of drive in the south of Europe. They just can't be bothered to get off their arses. They do occasionally raid the mission and take British servicemen into the prison which is almost next door, but the following day they let them out again and back they go to Donald.' Not for the first time, Ross felt he had a lot to learn about people.

But before he had time to analyse the variety of human nature in all its disparities, he was reminded of another specimen he had briefly contemplated. Veronica interrupted Peter—very much in passing because only she and Ross had met him—to say that Walter Benjamin was no more. He had safely reached Portbou, on the Spanish side of the border. There, just as escape to America seemed certain, he had learned that the Franco government had cancelled transit visas. He and his travelling companion, who turned out to have been a writer called Arthur Koestler, of whom Ross had not heard, had been told that they would be deported to France.

Benjamin had panicked at the thought of falling into Nazi hands and had killed himself with an overdose of morphine tablets. Ross remembered Benjamin's dispassionate talk of suicide. Koestler had also tried to kill himself. He had not taken enough tablets. Ross had the impression on his brief meeting that the man was a survivor. To compound the irony, Koestler *wasn't* returned to France, and was now on his way to England. Poor Walter Benjamin had died unnecessarily.

Ross remembered listening to Benjamin talking of life in Berlin before the Great War. He had not particularly warmed to him, but he had been intrigued by his talk of the intellectual life in *Mitteleuropa* and of a civilisation that spanned nationalities and cultures. He sensed a further crumbling away of that civilisation.

***

The allied soldiers who made their way through Perpignan were often wearing items from their old service uniforms. They looked suspicious and talked English fairly audibly among themselves. They waited for several days in Perpignan while their escorts across the Albères were arranged and it was difficult to keep them out of sight. If they got into the cafés, and they often did, they drank too much and could become spectacularly indiscreet. On his Wednesday evenings, when Ross played draughts with his friend, the burly *brigadier de gendarmerie*, Georges Cadot, the policeman often overheard snatches of English, even quickly silenced bursts of soldiers' marching songs. He raised his eyebrows and winked at Ross, who was careful to make no response. He wondered, however, how the authorities could be so lax or tolerant.

These soldiers and airmen were taken back through Spain and Lisbon to Britain, shepherded by agents and *passeurs*, some of whom were brave and some of whom were ready to betray their guests for German money. On the various escape lines, a lot of time was spent in trying to establish which *passeurs* could be trusted—and indeed which agents: the Germans had been quick to infiltrate the escape lines with double agents. They proved very difficult to identify. They spoke English perfectly and they were provided with genuine papers and documents taken from captured RAF officers. By finding their way into the escape system and travelling on it they could accumulate a devastating amount of information. Accordingly, anyone who sought to join the underground was subjected to close questioning about details of life in England, their bomber station, routines in the RAF and finally, very often, about cricket; if they could explain what a *silly mid-off*, or a *maiden-over* was, they were usually accepted.

When Ross looked back, later in the war, these early days seemed childishly safe and straightforward. A train took the escapers from Perpignan to Banyuls, the sleepy resort and fishing port just on the French side of the border. The aim was to arrive there as the light was going and the little party climbed up the railway embankment and followed, more or less, the railway lines heading south.

Care was, of course, needed to the extent that at bridges and when roads were being crossed the *evadés* crawled on their hands and knees, and once the railway reached the hills, sticking to it would have confined the escapers to an obvious route. At this stage, they climbed until they reached a disused pigsty in the early hours of the morning. Here, they were joined by escapers approaching from other routes.

The climb continued as soon as dawn broke. By noon, the border would have been passed. By late afternoon, they came off the slopes on the Spanish side and hid till dark. After dusk, they continued till they reached the railway. Again, they hid up until it was time for the early morning train. The guides got them on to that and continued with them right into the middle of Barcelona. There they walked, as nonchalantly as they could, to a café near the British Consulate. This was about as risky as any moment in the journey, as the Falangist Guards were keeping a close look out for *evadés*. Once the guides were sure that the coast was clear they parted, the guide to return to France, the escapers to be welcomed by the consul, in a study decorated with prints of Oxford.

Chapter 18

As they left the café one evening in these days between the fall of France and the Germans' entry into the Unoccupied Zone, Peter asked Ross to accompany him on the following day on a trip to Marseille. Peter's manner was, for him, slightly awkward, and it wasn't immediately clear why he wanted Ross with him.

'Just a routine jaunt—I'm bringing back a new man.' Then slightly more explanation: 'Thought you should get involved a bit more in the bigger picture.' Ross was irritated to feel flattered by this initiation or probation—a demeaning reaction for a mature man.

Everyone in Perpignan knew that the Catalan artist, Salvador Dalí, had called their railway station the Centre of the Universe', although there was no unanimity on why he had done so. Ross and Peter departed from the Centre of the Universe early on the following morning and reached Marseille before lunch. Donald Caskie was away but they'd been told anyway not to come to the Mission.

'Can't imagine why,' said Peter, 'the dogs in the street, not to mention every Gestapo agent in France, know what it is.'

They met their contacts in a little restaurant near the Vieux Port, where bouillabaisse was available. The traditional Marseillaise fish stew was made up of such ill-considered bits of the contents of the ocean that it escaped proscription. Ross reflected that it was odd that some of the most delectable foods the world over could be looked down on just because the ingredients were readily available. He wondered whether eels in London or herring in Scotland had swum through the net of rationing.

There were two men to meet them, one the Seaforth Highlander, Ian Garrow, whom Peter knew well and Ross had of course frequently met. The other was a man they hadn't met before and who was introduced as John Miller, a slender, younger man of middle height with fair hair. The two tall ex-soldiers, Peter and Ian were similar in demeanour. They met regularly to liaise on the operation of the Pat Line and understood each other well. They spoke the same language.

John Miller was to move from Marseille to Perpignan to help Peter. He was quiet and less extroverted than the other two, but wholly relaxed, almost dreamy, and Ross found him sympathetic. The two of them contributed little to the conversation. Peter and Ian Garrow brought each other up-to-date on news from their different parts of the line. Their main worry was about security. There was concern about penetration of the different lines by Germans and French collaborators. One British man in particular, known it seemed as Harold Cole, was a particular cause for concern. Ross wondered if all the detail was being spelled out at length as part of his education.

Ian Garrow was well known in the restaurant, and the proprietrix, a buxom lady of middle age wearing a red head scarf and red sash around her waist, who looked as if she could have come out of the pages of *The Count of Monte Cristo*, produced a bottle of whisky which appeared to be kept purely for him and which she described as '*le vin de votre pays*', 'the wine of your country'. The men emerged happily into the Mediterranean sunshine, Garrow heading back to his secret world and the other three for the train back to Perpignan.

For the first half of their journey, replete, happy and warm, the three dosed. It was prudent in any event not to talk too much, although the other two occupants of the compartment, an elderly couple who struggled to subdue the chicken which was in their charge, looked unlikely to be in the confidence of the Gestapo. In a flurry of feathers, they got off at Sète, an hour or so short of Perpignan, and in the empty compartment John Miller introduced himself. He talked slowly and smiled ruminatively as he outlined his history. He'd been at Cambridge before being called up and had got detached from his unit as it fell back on the Channel ports. The Resistance had put him in touch with the Pat Line and, like Garrow, he'd chosen to stay with it and work on the line, rather than go back to England.

'I don't think there was anything wrong with deciding that, do you? I don't want to shoot a line, but I imagine it's at least as dangerous as defending a seaside resort on the south coast of England.' He seemed to be looking for reassurance. Ross, the civilian dilettante, least qualified to give it, did so nonetheless. Peter, as usual, said nothing.

When they reached the Centre of the Universe, which, like many French railway stations stands slightly apart from the centre of the town, they took the little electric tram, the only one in the town, which plied from the railway station, up the Avenue de Grande Bretagne directly to the Place Jean Jaurès and the Café de la Loge. The gas lighting had become increasingly unreliable, almost non-existent, and had been supplemented by paraffin flares which burned erratically and smokily, casting wild shadows across the street and impregnating the air with an oily flavour which did at least keep the mosquitoes at bay. They arrived at the café just as the broadcast of the day's news ended. The three women were already there, and after John had been introduced to them, they brought the men up-to-date with the news of the day.

John was easily accepted as a welcome addition to the group. He was less military in bearing than Peter or Ian or the other soldiers who came and went, less military, indeed, than Ross had become. While he wasn't in the least diffident, he was sensitive, understated, a gentle man. Veronica found him easy to confide in.

Chapter 19

After the trip to Marseille, the relationship between Ross and Peter changed by a tiny, but perceptible degree. He must have eaten his bouillabaisse like a true spy, because Peter now tended to treat him more as a fellow-agent than as an artist who only dabbled in the black arts. His opinion was sought and sensitive information was confided to him.

In response, the tiny chip which had rested on Ross's shoulder in relation to Peter Graham fell away, and so he experienced no demeaning sense of gratitude when, a few weeks later, Peter asked him to accompany him on another trip to Marseille. They were now colleagues, and equal, more or less anyway, in status.

'I'd very much value your judgement. There's a suspicion that one of the agents on the line that our chaps come in on is a German agent.' He was talking about the man Cole, whose name had been mentioned on the last trip to Marseille. 'We're bound to have some people getting caught, but there's too much of a pattern here, and it looks as if the line's been infiltrated. There's no hard evidence, but eventually we may have to eliminate an agent on the basis of our feelings. They want me to come along so that there's no question of personalities or grievances getting into it. It's not my idea of fun and it won't be yours, but I'd be glad if you would share the responsibility with me.' Ross knew that he had been accepted as part of the community of resistance. The acceptance was implicit but clear.

Early on the morning of the day of their trip, Ross and Peter met at the top of the Avenue Grande Bretagne. Their meeting point was where the concentric pedestrian streets of the old town met the rectilinear outline of the twentieth-century new town. The Avenue Grande Bretagne was as busy as any street in Perpignan was these days, as Peter and Ross pushed towards the station.

It was a bright day with a brisk Tramontane which blew the fumes from a swarm of beetle-like *gazogènes* into clothes and nostrils. As they passed the gendarmerie, Ross looked up at the windows to see if there was a sign of Cadot, but there was not. Most days there was a German soldier on guard outside the gendarmerie. Ross was amused to wonder who guarded the guards.

As usual, the two expatriates were not bothered by the plain-clothes policemen who guarded the platforms at the Centre of the Universe. Their interests seemed always to be concentrated on those who looked vulnerable and clearly unthreatening.

They walked along Platform One to reach the steps that would take them over to Platform Two, from which their train would depart. They passed a stationary train. Ross was assailed by a foul smell, unmistakeably of urine and excreta. The train was composed entirely of goods wagons. The sliding door of each wagon was slightly open and a soldier stood close to it, his bayonet keeping the occupants inside. Ross walked up to one of the soldiers and looked into the interior. It was difficult to see much as very little daylight came through the partially opened door.

It was full of Jews, men, women and children. They were packed tight. Some lay on the ground. It was not obvious at first whether they were alive or dead. Those who stood up could not move without walking on those who lay. Everyone was covered in ordure. Those who could get close to the gap held out tin cans or even their cupped hands desperate for a drink. A nun was making her way from wagon to wagon pouring out water, but it was a tiny contribution to an insatiable need. Some of the guards had vomited in response to the stench. Ross felt his own gorge rising and hastened to catch up with Peter, and be on and away.

They shared their compartment with four taciturn peasants, and there was no opportunity for talking. An old copy of L'Intransigéant lay on the bare wooden bench between the two Englishmen. Peter split it in two and they turned over pages they had read days before as the train trundled through the outskirts of the town into the plain of Roussillon and towards the Corbières hills to the north. For the first forty minutes of its journey, the train served as a local means of communication to hamlets that lay round the periphery of the town. Thereafter, it stopped only at the larger towns that lay between Perpignan and Marseille, Narbonne (Narbo to the Romans, first daughter of Rome), Sète, from which the galleys had set forth on the Mediterranean, and Arles, like Port Vendres a Phoenician trading settlement.

Ross and Peter were left alone at the last of the local stops, Salses, where their companions all got off, probably embarked on a common purpose, although they had not felt obliged to share their thoughts on it—or indeed on anything else. They had all opened their mégotoriums and rolled very small cigarettes which filled the compartment with a strong and not unpleasant aroma. Once they had left, Peter took out and lit a cigarette of his own, a Senior Service Full Strength. He always had a supply of these exotic products, although for a number of reasons he would not have thought it appropriate to smoke them in front of the Frenchmen with their inferior supplies. He did not offer a cigarette to the non-smoking Ross.

Both men put down their sundered newspaper. Peter sat up straight and became self-evidently the man of action, decisive and efficient. Ross had not often seen him in this mode before. In the café he was charming, considerate, exquisitely well-mannered, but slightly withdrawn, on standby. But he had always known intuitively that there was very much more than that to Peter, and so, he thought, had everyone else. As Peter started to brief him, Ross remembered that the man who was talking had been an effective and distinguished officer in the previous war.

'Right, we're going to see some people in Marseille. You will have heard of Donald Caskie?'

Ross confirmed he did, indeed, know something about him. 'A Scottish minister who came down from Paris and runs a mission for merchant seaman under the noses of Vichy and the Germans?'

'More or less. I'll fill in a bit. It's better for you to have a little too much information, at the risk of my boring you, than not enough. Caskie had been quite outspoken when he was Scots Minister in Paris, so he was a marked man when the Germans arrived and he left in 1940 as part of what he called 'the great exodus'. He trekked south. Had an exciting time. Started off on foot, throwing himself into ditches as patrols passed. He bought himself a bicycle at Tours. He had quite a tough time—and, remember, he isn't a soldier. He's a man of the cloth. He slept alongside cows in byres and all that sort of stuff. At one stage, he even had the indignity of being arrested by partisans who thought he was a German because there was a swastika on his bike. He was almost torn apart and only escaped because in his pack he had a bible and his kilt. He credits the kilt with saving his life and as often as not that's what he wears in Marseille. Eventually, he got to Bordeaux and the British Consul offered him a place on the last boat to the UK. He's a brave man. He decided that his duty was to stay in France. While he was in Bordeaux, Pétain made his peace with the Germans.'

Ross understood that this was an instructional lecturette and that he was not expected to intervene.

'Eventually, Caskie made his way down to Marseille,' Peter continued. 'There he received instructions from Britain. He took over the old British Seaman's Mission, and Vichy allowed him to help distressed British civilians— but not military personnel. In theory all he does is to give shelter to non-combatant civilian seamen. There are lots of them around as a result of naval engagements in the Mediterranean. But of course, he's doing very much more than that. He's at the centre of two escape lines, and all British soldiers and downed airmen making their way south go through his hands. This, soon enough, became pretty obvious, and when he came under suspicion, he was again given the chance to get back to Britain. He declined it. His activities have got him sentenced to two years in prison. It's deferred and he's only on conditional release. He's actually been thrown into a pretty nasty prison in Marseille on a number of occasions.'

'But—' Ross found all this too difficult to accept in silence '—why does this happen? How does he get away with it?'

'Just because of the man he is. He is self-evidently *good*. He's got a beatific indifference to his captors, and his accusers don't know how to react to him. I'd say he had a simplicity, and so he has in a sense, an evident and total faith, a belief that the right thing is the only thing to do—but don't confuse that kind of simplicity with stupidity. He's a highly educated man who studied divinity at Edinburgh University.'

Peter turned his thoughts over for a moment or two in silence. His face wrinkled as he tried to get at the essence of the man he was describing. He continued. 'It's not surprising that the French, and particularly the Germans, don't know what to make of him. He is not remotely an Anglo-Saxon and I can't pretend that I fully understand him either. He's a highlander from one of the islands—Islay I think. He speaks Gaelic. He's fey. He believes he has second sight. At any rate, he and his activities are perfectly well understood in Marseille, but he's tolerated. The authorities, to maintain a semblance of authority, so to speak, play a sort of cat and mouse game with him. They do it as a matter of form. They always come at exactly six o'clock in the morning so Caskie knows when to expect them. He's kitted out the Seamen's Mission with all sorts of hidey-holes, spaces behind cupboards and up on the roof, that sort of thing, and they rarely come upon anyone without papers or in uniform. He has a cosy relationship with the American vice-consul in Marseille who is responsible for handling British affairs and gets a steady supply of identity cards. From time to time, the Vichy people haul a few suspicious characters away, but they let them out the next morning and they come straight back to the mission. It's all incredibly relaxed. If men on the run appear at his door, and he can't take them in immediately he sends them to a café nearby, Dupont's Café, and tells them to say "Donald Le Pasteur" or "Donald Duck". Dupont keeps the men in his wine cellar and sends them back when it is dark and the coast's clear.'

Ross had become increasingly confused. He shifted in his seat and shook his head. Eventually, he had to interrupt. 'I'm sorry—I just can't understand all this. You're saying that the Vichy authorities—and even the Germans—are turning a blind eye on an active enemy agent who is right under their noses and that they know all about? That they're just going through the motions and making no real effort to prosecute their war?' He was irritated by the sloppiness. 'I mean, this is just a pretend war. What about the total war we keep being told that's going on? Are we just fighting a make-believe war?'

Peter wasn't amused. 'Politicians talk about total war. Perhaps they have to. But people are people, not machines, whether they are English or French or German and I hope we never submit to totalitarian directions. It is only that which allows us to keep our faith in humanity.'

He stretched his shoulders and tilted his head back and looked out of the train window at the high sky above the edge of the Mediterranean and its coastal lagoons. More reflectively: 'I hope total war isn't totally total. You were too young to experience it, but the last one certainly wasn't.'

Ross couldn't accept that. 'Come on, what about the trenches?'

'Oh, I know a bit about the trenches,' said Peter. 'I was on the Western Front for three years and it was horrible. All the same, there were good things too, examples of good human nature—the prisoners who *weren't* shot, the times when a soldier *didn't* pull a trigger, the times when you *didn't* bayonet a man because he looked like a sad little cur that had never had a chance in life. There was a beauty, too, in the way that men, even the toughest, least sensitive fellows you could imagine, would look after each other—no show of sentimentality, just practical help, carrying little chaps' loads or sharing rations. You know, in the years between the wars I used to work in a university settlement in the east end and for some of the ex-servicemen I saw, the war years had been the high point in miserable lives. The camaraderie, the reciprocal support they had given and enjoyed, made their war years stand out from the selfish squalid years of unemployment in peace time.'

Ross waited as Peter reflected for a moment or two and then continued in an even more philosophical tone. 'I lectured at Oxford on Medieval Literature as seen in the eighteenth century, the idea of romantic chivalry and the code of bravery along with restraint, and of fighting along with courtesy and respect, of gallantry. You can argue, indeed that's what we spent our days doing, about how far it really existed and how far it was an idealised notion, but it's an ideal that I do believe we have to hang on to.'

Ross felt that the conversation had been one-sided, and that he should interject something, perhaps also of a literary nature, so he said, 'I see. You're not a Little Englander. Not for you a "right little, tight little island".'

Peter looked at him. 'What?'

Ross wished he hadn't spoken. 'It's a poem...' He ran out of steam. 'A poem,' he repeated.

'Well, so I suppose is "The harp that once in Tara's halls", but so what?'

Ross didn't reply and Peter went on mercifully, 'Well, at any rate, we obviously had to fight in 1914 and we have to fight again now, but if we do so without hanging on to these ideals then men are no more than animals.'

Ross remembered what Veronica had said about men and insects. He recognised that she and Peter saw life in variegated tones, where he tended to see it in black and white. *He* would have been embarrassed after such a spiritual declaration, and expected Peter to be. But he was not and after just a moment continued in the same tone as before.

'So there you have Donald Caskie and the British Seamen's Mission. At 46 Rue de Forbin he receives a constant stream of British soldiers and airmen along with a handful of *bona fide* merchant seaman. The soldiers and airmen are kitted out with fresh papers and civilian clothes, fed and housed and then processed on to the escape lines that take them to Spain and then Lisbon and Gibraltar. Some of them as you know come on our line. Others go to Toulouse. He also gets a lot of information about enemy agents and enemy activities and agents in German-occupied France. Some of this he communicates back to London via SOE operators, but he also sends scores of telegrams with lists of escapees and so on, all *en clair*, not in code, by telegrams routed through the Church of Scotland Offices in Edinburgh.'

Peter lit himself a fresh cigarette. Ross confined himself to a long, disbelieving shake of his head, as he looked out of the window while they speeded through unbroken acres of vines unpruned and untended.

'Now I turn,' said Peter in the style of the university lecturer which he had been, 'to the other men you are going to meet, Captain Ian Garrow and Pat O'Leary. You've met Garrow. O'Leary you've heard of. He is a most unusual man, probably the bravest man I have ever met. Like Donald Caskie, he isn't what he seems. Indeed, even Caskie doesn't know the truth about O'Leary so what I am telling you is in confidence. As far as Donald Caskie or any other civilian is concerned, O'Leary's a lieutenant commander in the Royal Navy, an

Irishman from County Cork. But I will tell you a little more because you're one of us, a cloak and dagger man.'

Ross felt as if Peter had physically touched him when he said these words. It was a rare explicit acknowledgment of his status.

Peter seemed to sense his reaction. He smiled slightly as he continued, 'In fact, O'Leary is a Belgian, real name Albert Guérisse, not Lieutenant Commander Pat O'Leary, RN. His *nom de guerre* provides the "Pat" of the name of the escape line which he and Ian Garrow have established from Lille or thereabouts to Marseille. At Marseille Donald Caskie takes over and organises the route via Narbonne and Perpignan to the Pyrenees.'

Peter, reticent in a social setting, was fluent as a lecturer. 'He was a doctor before the war and then he joined the Belgian army and fought till May 1940 when he escaped to England through Dunkirk. He took the name of O'Leary from a Canadian friend and volunteered for the Royal Navy and when he was putting two SOE Agents ashore near Collioure in April 1941, his skiff was overturned. He swam ashore and here he's been ever since. He was taken prisoner by the French and pretended to be an escaping Canadian airman. He had a bit of difficulty convincing British agents of his identity and was still locked up and under a degree of suspicion when he was pulled out of prison by Ian Garrow. Garrow, as you know, is a captain in the Seaforth Highlanders. He's in Marseille to help evaders and escapers. He took O'Leary to Marseille with him and managed to get London to broadcast a code message to vouch for him— *"Adolfe doit rester"* or some improbable words to that effect.'

He paused for a breath, was not interrupted, and continued, 'So at that stage, we have Caskie, O'Leary and Garrow all working together in Marseille. Unfortunately, Garrow finally got arrested and was sentenced to ten years in a concentration camp at Mauzac. But O'Leary's not the man to turn his back on his friends. Garrow had got *him* out of prison and now *he* got Garrow out. O'Leary got a guard's uniform smuggled in to him and now Garrow's out and about again. He's not around today, but you'll meet Donald Caskie and Pat O'Leary and you won't meet many more remarkable men than that pair. Their qualities are the sort of things that maintain the belief in human nature that I was trying to tell you about a little while back. You'll see that O'Leary has the most extraordinarily deformed right hand. It's the result of an accident he had a year ago and I once made the mistake of asking him why, as a doctor, he hadn't been able to get things sorted out better. I shouldn't have been such a fool. He explained he was afraid if he had gone to a doctor with it, he couldn't have failed to disclose his own medical knowledge. The doctor he would have gone to was a member of the resistance and he didn't want to risk compromising the man. As I say, O'Leary or Guérisse or whatever you want to call him is a brave, brave man.'

By now, they were only an hour or so distant from Marseille. Peter said he had work to do. He left Ross to digest what he now knew. He himself opened his notebook and immersed himself in its details. Ross, from force of habit, picked up the sketching pad which he always had with him for cover, and recorded the

Mediterranean defences they passed as they moved towards Marseille and its naval facilities.

**

The train pulled into Marseille station close to one o'clock. Ross and Peter headed straight for the Vieux Port. The Mission was in this quarter of the town but they didn't directly go there. Caskie would be out and about. He and about a half dozen of his assistants got up at four every morning and went off foraging. Despite rationing, they were generously supported, particularly by the Greek and Cypriot merchants in the harbour. Between what they were given and what they were able to buy with their own funds, some of them donated by wealthy patriots on the Côte d'Azur, he always succeeded in feeding those who depended on him, bringing back sacks of supplies in the late afternoon.

The Vieux Port was a state within a state. Long before the war, it had been a refuge for outlaws and those on the run, criminals, drug dealers, smugglers, those who manipulated the sex trade, those who dealt in currency and goods that weren't scrutinised.

Vichy was good for criminals. The Gendarmerie and the Gestapo—because already the Gestapo was present in the Unoccupied Zone—were more interested in escapees and the Resistance and Jews than in professional criminals. Indeed, the organs of the state were heavily complicit in corruption.

More than ever, therefore, the Vieux Port was beyond the law. An occasional attempt at penetration was made by an armoured vehicle, but in practice soldiers, Gestapo and even the Vichy police ventured into the labyrinth rarely and at a cost. A knife in the back or a bullet from a window put an end to patrols. Sometimes, the victims would be found floating in the harbour but on many occasions, bodies were laid out on the pavements as a message to the morning patrols, just as a gamekeeper hangs a row of dead crows on a fence as a warning to others.

As Ross and Peter walked through the red-light district of the Rue Bouterie, the dangers of the town were not evident. Women lolled in doorways, uninviting in full daylight, possibly off-duty. Some equally unprepossessing potential customers watched them dispassionately from tables outside Basso's, a working-man's eating place, but there was little sense of threat. Ross remembered something Walter Benjamin had said to them at their only meeting, something about the women of the Rue Bouterie deriving their colour from the only garment they wore, their pink shifts.

A man out of uniform and peaceably inclined could safely walk through the winding street, watching browned, lithe street urchins playing, residents talking together and ordinary people going about business which was not evidently more criminal than that carried out in the financial district of the city proper.

Ross quite liked the uncompromising, practical lack of hypocrisy of the place. After he had heard of Benjamin's death and had learned something of the man's reputation, he had read in a newspaper what he had written about

Marseille. He had described it as the mouth of a seal, with yellow teeth through which the salt water flowed. 'When this gullet opens it exhales a stink of oil, urine and printer's ink.'

The city proper could have been in another country. The two men had walked through it on their way from the station before exploring the Vieux Port. Here were wide streets and monumental buildings. As in Perpignan, these streets were essentially empty of traffic. A cluster of German staff cars came and went from the old offices of the Sûreté Nationale, now the Gestapo Headquarters. Swastikas fluttered outside the building and Ross noticed that peopled tended to stop talking and quicken their pace as they passed it.

He remembered Cadot telling him of the Gestapo motto, 'Don't shoot them in the head. They don't talk after that.' He strained his ears for the sound of thuds or screams, the sound effects of the regime's *Nacht und Nebel*, Night and Fog.

They stopped for a late lunch outside a café where the daylight of the town proper gave way to the moral twilight of the Vieux Port. Peter talked about the two major escape lines, the *Comète* Line, concentrating on the north of the Pyrenees at Bayonne, and the Pat Line. Most of the *Comète* evaders made their way south on the western side of France, while the Pat Line men came via Marseille. As the war had gone on, German surveillance had increased and French collaborators, usually from the *Milice*, had infiltrated the lines as double agents. Although Peter and Pat O'Leary guessed that scores of thousands of *évadés* had reached freedom by this stage in the war, several hundred had been arrested, many of them shot out of hand.

In particular, as allied air activity had built up over France, the Germans had cranked up their efforts to target the escape routes. The aim was not usually to close down a line. In that case, a fresh line of which the authorities knew nothing would simply take its place. It was better to maintain a level of attrition that was high enough to damage the flow of escapers but not high enough to endanger the double agent.

Comète had been compromised in just this way by a double agent called Jean Masson. He supervised the transfer of many escapees, while he built up almost enough evidence to engineer a coup. Even then he had managed to preserve his cover for quite some time.

Pat Line's problems concerned the Captain Harold Cole of whom Ross had already heard. He worked the part of the line from northern France to Marseille. He had appeared as a soldier on the run himself, escaping from the defeat of May 1940. Peter and Donald Caskie had not the slightest doubts about Cole. They were convinced that he was a traitor, and, left to himself, Peter would have put a bullet in the back of his head long ago. As Ross heard the evidence against Cole, he too was easily convinced of his guilt. Army records revealed no Captain Harold Cole, though Scotland Yard was aware of a criminal of that name who had deserted from the British Expeditionary Force after embezzling mess funds. That wasn't conclusive, but the evidence continued to add up against him. Additionally, Donald Caskie's second sight satisfied him of the man's guilt.

Cole was suspected of reverting to his old habits of embezzlement, taking funds now from the Line itself. O'Leary had ordered Cole to Marseille for investigation. There he more or less confessed to misappropriating funds, although nothing more. Peter had been with O'Leary and Donald Caskie at this little commission of enquiry. They had locked Cole in the bathroom while they decided what to do with him, when they heard a noise. They went to investigate just in time to see Cole disappearing through the window. He was chased but not caught, and now he was believed to be in Lille. The purpose of the meeting later in the day with Garrow and Donald Le Pasteur was to decide what to do.

***

Towards the end of the afternoon, after Donald Caskie would be back from foraging, Ross and Peter walked the short distance to the Seamen's Mission at 46 Rue Forbin. The building was a large one on a corner with, conveniently, doors on both the streets it faced. It was of two storeys. It had formerly housed a building company, and the company name was still painted on the splayed corner of the building.

Their knock on the door was answered promptly by Caskie himself. He was middle height with a schoolboy haircut and an amused but inquisitive expression. He was wearing his kilt, as Ross had rather assumed he would be, and his appearance was initially rather that of a Highland Chieftain. The warmth of his welcome, however, ('Come in, come in. Peter, it's good to see you. And you of course are Alexander.'), was very much that of a minister welcoming visitors to the manse. There was nothing furtive about his manner. He had flung the door wide open to receive them, and as they entered, he had a good look around the street to see if anyone else was on their way to visit him.

The hall opened on to the kitchen area. Ross could see eight to ten men, some preparing a meal, others sitting around reading. He wondered if he would have seen them as so obviously British escapers if he hadn't been forewarned. He thought so: even those who were not wearing army boots or bits and pieces of battle dress looked inescapably like British service men.

Caskie was surprisingly genial for the president of a court martial. He ushered his two guests upstairs and into what clearly doubled as his bedroom and study. A single bed lay along one wall. On the table beside it was a bible and a volume of the metrical psalms, a candle and a photograph of a homely woman and her husband, presumably Caskie's parents. Three heavy wood-framed chairs with worn cushions were ranged round a table on which there stood a bottle of malt whisky, two glasses, a jug of water and a paraffin lamp. A desk and a bentwood chair completed the furnishings of the room. Heavy curtains had already been drawn although it was broad daylight outside. The room was lit by the paraffin lamp.

'Come in boys and install yourselves,' said Caskie in the soft, lilting voice of the Highlands and Islands. 'O'Leary is here already. He is helping with the meal downstairs. I'll fetch him.' He went out to the landing and called loudly,

114

'Pat, come away up here. Peter Graham's here and he's brought Mr Ross with him.'

Pat O'Leary, known to Ross and Graham, but not to Caskie, to be Dr Albert Guérisse, very quickly came upstairs and entered the room. Ross's first impression was of a slight man. As he studied him in the course of the evening, he came to see that this insubstantial impression derived mostly from the grace and agility with which he moved. It was the movement of a ballet dancer, and like a ballet dancer, he had, as Ross realised, muscular legs and shoulders. The feline impression was enhanced by the delicacy, precision and economy of his movements. He handled workaday objects like his knife and fork as if they were surgical instruments.

His face was an attractive one with almost film star good looks, a slightly beaky nose, very black, well-formed eyebrows and a wide mouth from which he frequently flashed very white-toothed smiles. Ross was aware that he and Caskie were very unremarkable compared to the other two, he himself neither tall not short, neither fat nor thin, with a moustache rather like Anthony Eden's and curly brown hair, Caskie very much a schoolboy, though probably the school captain. Peter, tall, thin with his fair hair and blond moustache, a natural leader, was also an obvious school captain and probably captain of the rugby team too, but in his case from an English public school rather than Oban High School or wherever bright pupils from Islay were sent.

Caskie produced two more glasses and without asking, poured out whisky for everyone. He, the Scottish connoisseur, added an equal measure of water to his whisky; the ignorant Sassenachs did not.

'*Sláinte Mhath*!' he said, raising his glass in a jovial toast which Ross thought slightly inappropriate in view of the gravity of the proceedings. But Caskie quickly explained. 'I've brought you here, I'm afraid,' he said, 'on slightly false pretences. I'm sorry about that. I should have known better—I had a feeling, things were going to work out like this.' Speaking directly to Ross, he said confidingly, 'I have the second sight, you see.' Ross nodded. He saw the other two exchanging smiles.

Pat O'Leary, who, it transpired, had only returned to Marseille one day earlier, filled in the story for the Perpignan men. Even after Cole had so evidently run away to Lille, there had been an unaccountable resistance to accept that an Englishman—because it was clear that he was an Englishman—would have been treacherous. But there was more. One of those he had betrayed, and who was now in Loos Prison awaiting execution, the Abbé Carpentier, had managed to smuggle out of prison a detailed account, thirty pages long, no less, of the extent of Cole's betrayal of the O'Leary line, complete with names and addresses of his victims. The Abbé's evidence was supported by that of another agent in the prison.

O'Leary explained that he himself had been extracted through his own escape line to a meeting in Gibraltar. There the evidence had been reviewed, and Cole's guilt agreed on. He was to be executed on sight and every step that was possible had been taken to minimise the damage he had done.

'So, as Donald says, this meeting is strictly speaking unnecessary, and I am sorry, chaps, if you've been inconvenienced.' O'Leary concluded with a courtly inclination of his head to Ross and Peter. He had spoken in perfect English and in the unlikely event that anyone had thought his vowel quantities unusual, the County Cork story would have disposed of any suspicions.

'But a day away from Perpignan will be good for you both,' said Donald Caskie, full of goodwill and a disarming host. 'It's good for us all to get together from time to time and I want Alexander to see something of this end of the operations.'

They soon moved downstairs and had a copious and enjoyable meal, accompanied by a more than adequate volume of rough Marseille rouge. Caskie and the other three sat at a table by themselves, and the rest of the inmates at a large communal table. Ross was a little surprised by this segregation, but Caskie explained that all of the men would be moving out over the course of the next few days. They were too keyed up not to talk about the arrangements. Caskie himself knew all about them, but it was better that the others should not, 'in case you came under any untoward pressure'. In fact, the men did not talk much amongst themselves. They looked strained. All of them were victims of reverses in war of one sort or another and had not reached the South of France without privation. They were now within sight of deliverance, but only after getting over some very real hurdles.

After dinner, Peter and Pat O'Leary withdrew to talk together about operational matters. Again, it was good practice that information should be confined to the minimum number of people. Ross and Donald Caskie returned to the Minister's study. The better he got to know Caskie the more Ross warmed to him. As Peter had told him, Caskie was certainly no fool, but he was utterly without pretention. He talked about his childhood in Islay. His background was very important to him, and he enjoyed talking about the simple way of life and the sense of values it had engendered. His experiences, including the treatment he had had at the hands of the Germans, had generated no bitterness. On the contrary, he was full of wonderment at the goodness of people and the kindness he met with in Marseille.

When Ross complemented him on the quality of the dinner they had just enjoyed, Caskie nodded enthusiastically, 'And do you know,' he said in gratified amazement, 'just what the monthly ration is here?' Ross did, in fact, have a pretty good idea of what it was, and was thankful he could supplement it from the black market. Caskie did not, however, wait for his reply. 'One kilo of potatoes, a cup of cooking oil, 200 grams of sugar, when it is available, and 100 grams of coffee, which is never available. Do you know, when the people here buy rotten lentils, they sort out the stones but leave in the worms. They say that a little protein helps. We get so much assistance,' he went on. 'There are good people who give us money, and there are some very bad people here in the Vieux Port who give us food—so they can't be entirely bad. Anyway,' he added, 'who are we to know who's good and who's bad and how good would you or I be if we had been born in the Vieux Port?'

This rhetorical question created a moment or two of silence, but silence was not part of Donald Caskie's stock in trade, and he filled it quickly. 'You might be surprised,' he said, 'that even those Vichy detective men can be very humane. I always feel they're looking for us to say something that they can accept so that they don't have to pursue matters. They really do the least that they possibly could to bother us. Another man who is awfully good to us is the United States vice-consul, the man Bingham. The consul too, Mr MacFarlane. With a name like that, I've always wondered if he has a soft spot for a Highlander like me.'

The only time his supply of goodwill seemed to falter was when the talk turned to Cole. He had never had any doubt of his guilt. 'I was uneasy from the start. It's because of my Celtic gift. I saw through him. This second sight is a spiritual faculty. Highlanders of my generation and those who went before us live simple lives. We are not great ones for mechanical pleasures or pastimes—they blunt the faculties. Our vision remains fresh. We can sense a wicked man. He has an existence, among his other lives, that is evil and egotistical. And Cole did bad things. He betrayed better men than he was. But all men are both good and evil.' He looked as if he felt he had been too hard on Cole. 'I believe he may have been forced to do it by the Germans, and he is very fond of his wife. No one is entirely evil.'

It grew late and after Ross and Caskie were joined by the other two they separated, Caskie to sleep in his Spartan cell and the others to look for beds and blankets in the dormitories.

***

On their return to the Centre of the Universe, Peter walked off to his lodgings. Ross caught the electric tram back to the middle of the town. On its way, it passed the Commissariat de Gendarmerie. As they approached it, something caught his attention. The man with the widow's peak, whom he now knew to be called Hulot, was entering the Commissariat. That didn't surprise him; the Widow, as Ross thought of Hulot, was so frequently in Cadot's company. What he did notice was a man of middle height who accompanied him. He saw him only from behind and there was nothing unusual about his clothing. Ross noticed that as he squared himself up to enter the building, he nervously tugged at the sleeves of his jacket.

Ross jumped off the tram at the next stop and made his way back to the Commissariat, and asked for the *brigadier*. He was taken up to Georges Cadot's room. As he approached it, he passed Hulot, coming out. There was no one else in the room apart from Cadot.

'My dear Alec, this is, indeed, a pleasure. This is the first time you have visited me in my place of work. I am honoured that you should interrupt your artistic endeavours to visit a philistine.'

'I saw someone come in, who was it?'

'Why, little Hulot, he passed you a moment ago. Surely you know him well?'

'Yes, but apart from him there was another man.'

'Another man?' replied Cadot, his eyebrows rising in theatrical surprise, 'no, not at all, just little Hulot.'

Ross felt there was prevarication going on. 'I know Hulot. He works for you. I'm not talking about him.'

The gendarme interrupted, 'He wouldn't wish it to be said that he works for the police. He is not my employee. He makes himself useful, as we all must do my dear Alec. We here are simple people, we are engaged in barter, giving and taking, you must remember that. We only survive by making ourselves useful.'

'Yes, yes,' said Ross, not wishing to be diverted into a discussion of the workings of the Catalan economy. 'But I saw, quite clearly, a man with him. They came in together. A little man who tugged at his sleeves.'

'No, Alec,' said Georges, laughing tolerantly. 'No sleeve tugging has gone on here today I assure you.' Ross started to wonder if he was making more of what he had seen than it deserved, but he was quite clear that he'd seen a man with a mannerism that was very familiar. 'Are you saying, Georges, as my friend, that there was not another man with Hulot?'

'That is exactly what I'm saying, Alec.'

'Do you promise that that's the truth?'

'Of course it is the truth my dear fellow. Would I lie to my old friend who has defeated me so often at draughts?'

Ross had to leave the matter there, but he remembered the Catalan saying that was recounted to all visitors to Perpignan: 'The truth is as real as a handful of wine.'

He got up to leave, but Cadot detained him for a moment, 'Alec, it is time that I admitted you, whose company has become such a pleasure to me, into my wider domestic circle. As you know, I am not a married man, and for the delights of Venus must have recourse to the unfortunately hirsute *veuve* Lagrande, but I am not entirely a solitary fellow. At the weekend, I stay with my sister at her little *mas* outside the town. Her husband, alas, is in our navy, possibly fighting your brave countrymen at this very moment, but she and her children are there and I should like it very much if you would join us for a little *cargolade* not on this Sunday, but on the one after it, when I shall tell you exactly what a *cargolade* is.'

The details were fixed, and Ross continued up the Avenue de Grande Bretagne and then walked along beside the little river which runs through the middle of the town, the Quai Vauban, whose name commemorated the great engineer.

When he reached the Castillet, he walked across the Place. And there he came on a group of thugs from the *Milice*, who were attacking a gamine, Spanish girl whose name, he would learn, was Inez.

Part Four:
After the Meeting

Chapter 20

Ross's early start on the morning after Inez had come into his life meant that he caught the first train of the day to Port Vendres where he had to exchange packages with the purser on the *El Kantara*. The boat had got in late the previous night and there was no stirring aboard, so Ross sat at the bar of la Frégate and looked across the horseshoe basin of the harbour, sipping a hot but repelling cup of acorn coffee and thumbing through the previous day's copy of *L'Intransigéant* which as usual contained a photograph of the whiskery Maréchal and an extract from yet another of his speeches in which the old man said that France was suffering to make up for abandoning her standards after the great victory of 1918. He, the Maréchal, regarded himself as making greater sacrifices than anyone else for *la Patrie*.

Hard news was, as always, thin on the ground, and news of the war particularly so. The common cause between the decadent regimes of Britain and the United States was deplored. These corrupt countries, infiltrated by the world-wide Jewish-Communist conspiracy, would attempt to interfere with the new World Order which France and her German ally was establishing, but wherever they struck, they would be thrown back into the sea choking in their own blood. Churchill, a friend of Zionism, was known to be courting the Jew, Roosevelt, attended by the traitors, Giraud and De Gaulle. De Gaulle was already under sentence of death and he and other enemies of France would not escape their just fate.

Ross walked the long way round to *El Kantara*, via the fish market where the little boats that had been out all night had unloaded their cargo. He walked past the ninety-eight feet obelisk decorated with reliefs that celebrated the achievements of Louis XIV and then back to the opposite tip of the horseshoe, passing the Hôtel de Commerce, where a Scottish architect and his wife had spent the 1930s, he painting and she counting out their francs so that they could avoid penury in England. Looking across the calm waters of the harbour at the white horses, as he called them, or the white sheep, as they were to the French, which rolled across the exposed Gulf of Lyon, he wondered again at the skill of the Phoenicians who had first found the harbour without maps or instruments thousands of years earlier, by studying the eternal pattern of the stars.

When he reached the ship, the purser was up and about. He took Ross down into the twilight of the stuffy crew's fo'c'sle with its smells of sour bilge water, engine oil and turpentine. There they had a cup of much better coffee than had been available in la Frégate, together with the usual glass of fiery liquor from an unlabelled bottle. Despite his time in Syria, Ross had no more than a couple of dozen words of Arabic, and the purser had about as many words of French, but with good will and some garbled pidgin language they got on well enough. Ross handed over the notes and drawings that were the fruit of his week's work, and he received in exchange a slim envelope from London. They parted, under the influence of the liquor, on cordial terms.

Ross was in no hurry to get back to Perpignan. He was taken aback by what had happened on the previous night. It was the first time he had intervened—and physically, and perhaps at some personal risk—for the sake of another person. His motives for doing so were not clear to him, but he had done it all the same. He wondered if he would have done it if it had not been for what he had learned from Veronica, and from Edith and Hilda, Garrow, Peter and John. They, all of them, lived their lives on an assumption which divided them from Ross's detachment: the assumption that it went without saying that one did things for other people. He felt uncomfortably rewarded not just by the night with Inez. Indeed, enjoyable as that had been, it seemed in a way less significant than the fact that she had accepted his intervention by giving herself to him, not in a sexual way, but by following him like a child from le Castillet to the café. Whatever he had done and whyever he had done it, her response had been to adopt him. He wondered what would have happened if they had come together in different circumstances and not as they had done, never to meet again.

He spent a long afternoon walking in the deserted lanes that lay beyond Port Vendres, smelling the thyme, the wild fennel and the iodine odour of goat piss on the dry grass, thinking of these things and conscious of an emptiness at the heart of his existence.

Late in the afternoon, he caught the train back to Perpignan and, ignoring the tram, walked in a vacant state of mind back to the Castillet where the events of yesterday had taken place. As on the previous day, too, the Widow was there, although he disappeared as soon as he saw Ross, and there was again a gaggle of refugees near the base of the Castillet. In his detachment, he paid little attention to his surroundings.

The blow of a leaded cosh to his shoulder came as a complete surprise. He blacked out for an instant but came to as he hit the ground. The bully boys were back and they were ready for him. They carried sticks and they wore boots and they used these boots as much as their weapons. They knew what they were doing. They worked him over systematically, using the sticks on his arms and legs and their boots on his stomach and ribs. They largely kept away from his head, wanting him to be conscious and to experience his punishment, but they were working towards it. He vomited green bile. They waited for him to stop and then the blows to his head began. He knew that he did not have much longer to go. In all his pain, the thought came to him that it was a pretty pointless way to die, but he knew that would happen very soon.

It did not. He was suddenly aware that the thugs had gone. His vision was blurred; images enlarged and then diminished with the throb in his head and the agony of his breaths. He saw three people running towards him, two ordinary gendarmes and Georges Cadot.

'Oh, Alec, Alec,' said Cadot. 'Pick him up—gently, mind.' The two gendarmes pulled Ross to his feet and wrapped his arms round their shoulders.

Half walking, half dragged and led by Cadot, Ross was taken home. Cadot banged on the door. Ross tried to say, 'No-one here,' but his words were choked by blood and vomit. Cadot ignored him. The door was opened by Inez. *Still here?* thought Ross, and even in the condition that he was in, he noted that the money he had left was still on the table—or most of it: some must have been used to buy the provisions that stood beside his cooker, and the room was cleaner than it had ever been. He absorbed all this before he blacked out again, and this time not momentarily. The two gendarmes carried him upstairs and laid him on the bed. Cadot spoke briefly to Inez, telling her what had happened, and then all three left.

When Alec came to he had been washed and dressed in one of his shirts. Inez was standing by the bed. She took charge. She told him not to speak. With surprisingly skilled hands, she checked him all over, feeling his ribs with particular attention.

'Nothing broken,' she said, 'but you are very badly bruised. It'll hurt for three days.' She disappeared for half an hour and came back with some bandages and medicines. Again, with surprising dexterity, she made him more comfortable. 'I have only been able to get six aspirins for you. I shall try again tomorrow. But I have a laudanum drink and you will sleep.'

***

He did sleep, but she had been right, it was fully three days before the pain had at least substantially abated. For that time, she did everything for him, dressing his wounds, feeding him, helping him with a bottle when he needed to urinate and supporting him as he struggled to the lavatory.

Initially, they talked very little. Alec, in any event, could scarcely speak. His right jaw had been kicked, and the bruise stopped him from opening his mouth to any degree. The experience of dependency was a very novel one for him. He could not remember ever having been so reliant on another human being, and no woman had known his body in such detail since his babyhood. By the fourth day, he could move around the apartment and his speech was back to normal. He tried to tell Inez how grateful he was to her. She would not accept his gratitude.

'You saved my life,' she said, 'And because of that this happened to you, so now we each look after the other. That is the nature of the world.'

Later that day, Cadot came in with a bottle of *eau de vie*. The three of them sat down at the table and shared it. 'I feared this would happen, Alec,' said the *brigadier*. 'These men are animals. You humiliated them and they were bound to try to punish you. I had Hulot keep an eye on you, and fortunately we weren't far away. We know who the three men were and they've been taken care of.' Alec looked up.

'No, no,' said Cadot, 'they live, but having had their legs broken as they were, they'll limp for the rest of their lives. The message has been given: none of that gang will touch you again, but be careful.' He turned and looked directly and meaningfully at Inez. 'You too.'

Back to Alec: 'This peasant world of ours was never like England. Our civilisation is very thin and very recent, and what has happened since 1940 has destroyed even the poor thing that it was. Our life—it may not look it—but it's a jungle. We look after each other as well as we can but at the end of the account, it's every man for himself. Remember that, *mes chers*, whatever anyone tells you.'

After he'd gone, Inez and Alec talked as they had not done before. Inez's story was simple enough. She had lived as an orphan in Figuères, about twenty miles south of the Spanish border. Alec was not surprised to learn that she'd been a nurse. When the Francoists started shelling the town, she had moved towards the border with the others of the *Retirada*. She'd reached Perpignan the very day that Alec met her. Like many of the Catalans on either side of the border, although she spoke both French and Catalan, she had no Castilian Spanish. On her way towards France, the Francoists had caught up with her and that was where she had been raped and bayoneted. A short story, but a violent one in a brief life: she was just twenty-one.

Alec's story was difficult for her to comprehend. The culture, the conventions, the institutions were entirely foreign to her, but she accepted him as a man who had saved her life and was, therefore, a kind man. She could see, too, that he was a man who needed her. As far as she was concerned, she was quite simply now his woman, and since Alec did not demur, she took his acquiescence for consent.

Till this night, they had slept side by side, chastely, Inez taking care not to hurt the bruised Alec, but tonight, after the long unburdening to each other and stimulated by Cadott's *eau de vie*, they made love. They did so at a leisurely pace. Each enjoyed the other. This was not the quick release which was all Alec had known of sex. For the first time, he realised that making love was, indeed, the best description of what they were doing.

***

So she was his woman as she always put it and he, he supposed, was her man. She joined the little group of the Café Gambetta, a welcome addition to its feminine element. Peter, as always, tended to the strong and silent, but the group was a harmonious one. They were conscious that they were exiles in alien surroundings and that life was precarious. That made them all the more anxious to live life to the full, and they had many congenial, bibulous evenings. Inez, initially nervous of the others and guarded, very soon relaxed and was clearly at ease. She was, as many were, a little over-awed by Peter, but she and Veronica were good friends, and when Alec was away, she often accompanied the gentle, quietly amused John on trips around Perpignan and beyond. She found him a sympathetic confidant.

As a Jewish refugee, she had no prospect of obtaining work in Perpignan, but she volunteered to nurse children at a house that Edith and Hilda had established not far from Perpignan, at La Coume. With food and rest, her appearance changed. Her body became fuller and her hair longer and Alec realised how beautiful she was and how lucky he had been. He was not, however, a particularly observant man. At any rate, if he noticed that after some time Inez was washing some strange bandages every month, he made no mention of the fact.

Chapter 21

The broadcasts at the café covered a wide variety of topics: the availability of foodstuffs, or an announcement about an assembly of the *Légion Française de Combattants*, the group whose members had climbed the Canigou and renamed it Pic Pétain. The *Légion*'s assemblies were little more than an excuse for beating up Jews and doing a little looting.

Indeed some announcements related explicitly to the Jews. They had been facing more and more hostile treatment. At the start, German policy had been to push them out of the Occupied Zone and let Vichy look after them. Of the French and the Germans, it was the French who made life more difficult for Jews in France. Almost from the start, Vichy began to legislate. The propaganda was crude and vicious, portraying the Jews as incapable of national solidarity, hook-nosed and avaricious, to blame for France's defeat. The government passed anti-Semitic laws defining *Jewishness*. Penalties against anti-Semitic defamation were annulled. The *Statute des Juifs* excluded Jews from most professions, and later laws confiscated their property. Within a year, about 40,000 Jews were imprisoned in camps in the south. Hiram Bingham, the splendidly partisan American vice-consul in Marseille, counted twenty-seven internment camps of one sort or another. As the Spanish prisoners were gradually removed from the camps, their places were mostly taken by Jews. In the camp at St Cyprien, just south of Perpignan, it was rumoured that there were no less than 7,500 Jews, although their numbers were being reduced fast by a typhus epidemic.

Alec and the others were not clear how much of all this was known to the ordinary French man and woman, but it seemed to them that ignorance could only be achieved at the cost of a very real effort to keep eyes and ears closed.

When the so-called Grand Rafle took place in Paris and 13,000 Jews were arrested in a single operation and moved to the Vél d'Hiv, the great cycling stadium, a German commission was touring the camps of the south. Veronica and the others who regularly worked in the camps saw the convoys of black German cars arrive. And as it happened, Alec walked past the Mairie in Perpignan just as the Germans arrived that evening. There were at least eight German officials, and one was accorded considerable deference by the others.

Alec watched the choreography of their reception by the French municipal officers. It was a pitiful, fawning affair, the French dwelling on the expressions of their masters like whipped dogs. Passers-by stopped to watch, they too cowed. What by? Alec instinctively saw the German delegation as the embodiment of evil, but when he thought more, he had to acknowledge that this was an intellectual appreciation, based on what he knew, rather than what he saw. What he did see was power, authority. That was what the French hosts and the spectators were acknowledging. The Germans didn't look like animals or sub-humans. On the contrary, they emanated the confidence that flowed from evident intelligence and ability, and that was much more dangerous than unfocused evil.

Within the delegation, there was a hierarchy. It was partially revealed by the uniforms that some wore, but not all were in uniform, and the man who dominated the gathering was one of those in civilian clothes. He was tall, grey-haired and wore a well-cut tweed suit. In his manner and his gestures, he could have passed for an English gentleman. He turned to engage with the Frenchmen around him, smiling out to the onlookers, making jokes that appeared to be genuinely well received. Alec realised that the impression the man conveyed was essentially of decency. And he had the indefinable attributes of leadership. Surely, this was the essence of the problem. The fight was not with amorphous forces of evil, but with power and leadership. Unlike the democratic regimes, could fascism be mortally wounded by killing a leader? Alec had seen enough of the army to be sceptical about the effectiveness of the military machine, but surely assassination of an individual was not beyond the scope of ingenuity? Hitler was obviously the ideal target, but there were other indispensable agents of the Reich, like the man he was looking at. Alec wondered whether he could ever nerve himself to look down the barrel of a revolver at another human being, perhaps one that looked, like this one, thoroughly *nice*, and pull the trigger.

***

Would Alec have been so affected by all he saw in and around Perpignan if he was not living with a Jewess, bound to her indeed by an increasing intimacy that was far from being purely physical? Was it the persecution, the rape, the bayonet thrust that she had suffered purely because she was Jewish that provoked his disgust? Perhaps not entirely. But he *had* changed and was changing. The influence of experience was belatedly coming to bear on a man who had been woefully immature for far too long.

In Damascus, he had seen Jews and Christians and Muslims living together peaceably in the same streets, all combining to promote learning and scholarship that for centuries had been far in advance of anything that existed in the west. He remembered too what Walter Benjamin had told him of the cultural Zionism in which the Jews of the Austria-Hungarian Empire had contributed to the artistic and intellectual achievements of *Mitteleuropa*. But all that was theory, and as Alec made his way on a mission of observation to Rivesaltes, to the north of Perpignan, a sorting centre for the industrialised process of exterminating the Jewish race it is impossible to say that his sense of affront was not stimulated by the thought of the smooth curve of Inez's belly defaced by the cruel stab of the anti-Semite's weapon.

At Rivesaltes, he spent a day on the hills above the little town, ostensibly sketching. He could see pitiful batches of Jews arriving, prodded from railway trucks into the camp, stumbling, barefoot, carrying pathetic bundles of property.

Many of the children were incontinent from the effects of dysentery. At intervals, other groups, already documented and processed, were hustled aboard trains that left from the other side of the camp. Alec could see that the men had been segregated by now from the women and children.

Alec had often heard it said that war brought out the best as well as the worst in human nature. He had often doubted that, though lately in his companions in the café he had found evidence to support the proposition. There was, however, no shortage of evidence to challenge it. The corruption or at least corruptibility of human nature was demonstrated in the way that the war had flushed out, along with the black marketeers and minor gangsters, large numbers of nasty, bully boys who made up semi-official bands of thugs like the *Légion Française des Combattants.* When the Perpignan section of the *Légion* was launched at the Café de la Bourse, it soon had 11,000 members from the Pyrénées-Orientales Department alone. It supplied grim-faced guards of honour for Pétain on his provincial tours and its leader in the department, Colonel Jean-Jacques Rufiendes, joined along with his fellow officers in a Fascist salute for the Marshal.

The collaborationist *Milice*, whose members had put Alec in bed for three days, was technically separate, but both organisations were amorphous and incoherent and their members were less interested in political philosophy than in the opportunities for licensed banditry and for persecuting those they considered undesirable—Jews, homosexuals, gypsies and racial minorities.

The *Milice* evolved into an organisation especially committed to capturing and torturing the Resistance. They increasingly identified more with Germany than with Pétain. The *Milice* were kitted out with black uniforms and black berets. Their first assembly in the department was in the Paris Cinema in Perpignan. Their aims were for solidarity and discipline and 'against the Jewish leper'.

The anti-Semitism of the regime was in the forefront of Alec's mind when he reported on his visit to Rivesaltes at the café that night. Peter was particularly well informed. Jews from the region were joined by others, rounded up elsewhere and brought south by long, slow and circuitous railway journeys, housed in cattle trucks. They were allowed to bring just one piece of luggage and there was no sanitary provision. He told the others that in nine months alone 40,000 Jews had been deported from France to Germany—or further afield—including 6,000 children. A quarter had come from the south, most from Rivesaltes. He was in no doubt that the bulk of the deportees were going to immediate death.

Veronica was able to report that on her visits to the camps for the Spaniards, she'd seen that the Jews had been segregated from the gentiles, ostensibly so that they could celebrate Passover together. The accommodation they were put into was the poorest in the camp, with little protection against the weather and only straw to sleep on in company with vermin.

No mention of deportations or anything of the sort appeared in the *Malicieuse* or the *Intransigéant* or *L'Indépendant*, and although there were some items in BBC broadcasts, they provoked no great reaction.

Peter said the Resistance was aware that Jews were being deported from France to Germany and Poland in numbers. They were taken at rifle point, clubbed round the head if they resisted and frequently beaten to pulp on the street. Children were separated from their parents, wives from their husbands. Over 2,000 had gone from Rivesaltes alone ultimately to a camp known as Auschwitz.

Anti-Semitism had been a powerful influence in France for many years, exemplified in the Dreyfus case little more than a generation earlier, and the Pétainists represented only one of the many anti-Semitic strands in society. But while Alec and the others were not, therefore, greatly struck by the fact that there was no huge interest in France about what was going on, it seemed to them amazing that these morbid statistics, if they were known in England, did not seem to be exciting the wrath of people there. Alec could only assume that England was ignorant. He determined to bring the facts urgently to Cantley's attention.

After all this, the group was in sombre mood as they made their way to the Café Gambetta, where they ate their meal with less than their usual gaiety. Alec saw his friend, the *brigadier,* in a corner table with the Widow, Hulot. Alec and Georges Cadot exchanged a nod and a smile. Alec looked at the genial Cadot, masticating enthusiastically and teasing the serving girls, and wondered, not for the first time, how much he knew of what was going on in his name, of the deportations from the camps, of the beatings up. The policy was dictated at the highest level, from Pétain himself, but its implementation involved police just like Georges. People could choose not to open their ears, but they couldn't entirely close them either. The Archbishop of Toulouse had spoken out against the treatment of families like cattle. The Resistance press, if not the official newspapers, referred to it.

Those who wished to, and who were perhaps far from hostile to the policy, could dismiss all this as anti-Nazi propaganda, but Georges Cadot had to send his men out every day to execute the policy. Alec knew he was no zealot: his philosophy was the antithesis of dogma. Surviving was his only aim. But how could he look so comfortable when he was complicit in all this? It was a question for Alec too, when he came to think of it: was he too complicit in acquiescence?

He turned his attention to Edith and Hilda. Their demeanour was slightly different from usual. They were sitting very close together and talking only to each other. They talked with particular animation, but almost too brightly. Before the rest had finished their meal, the two women got to their feet and prepared to leave. Veronica seemed aware of something special and gave each of them a long, close embrace.

Afterwards, Alec asked her what it had all been about. 'They didn't want anything said—no emotional fuss. They have to go. The International Commission isn't happy that they should be here if the Germans move into the Unoccupied Zone as everybody thinks they will.'

'Why so sad to leave? They'll be together and in safety, won't they?'

'You don't understand. It's not safety they want; it's being able to do something. You must have seen how happy they have been without any safety, just because they were making things a little better for these poor children. Anyway, they're not going to be together. Hilda's being sent to Egypt and Edith will be working in a maternity hospital in India. They couldn't be further apart.'

'Surely, they could stay together? They've both got their own money, haven't they?'

'Of course, they could,' said Veronica with some acerbity, 'but they've surrendered their individual freedoms in order to work where they can best be employed. They've often been apart before. They may be Quakers, but they submit to discipline as willingly as nuns. They met when they were working close to the front with people who had been displaced by the war in 1914, but Hilda's been to Vienna, Switzerland and Greece, and Edith's been all over the place, even to China.'

'But they love each other, don't they?'

'Of course, they do. You know that. But they wouldn't love each other as much if they didn't know that each of them was prepared to sacrifice personal happiness for others.'

Inez said very little in the course of the evening. As they left the restaurant, she admitted to Alec that the scale, the organisation, the formality of the campaign against her race had shaken her. In Spain, in her youth, Jews were accepted and a familiar element in society, and the viciousness of the Francoist thugs an exceptional aberration. She was shaken to find it was part of a larger and terrifying whole. But what Alec sensed had moved her most was the love of Edith and Hilda and what Veronica had said about it. As they made their way back to the Rue des Cordonniers, she clung tightly to Alec, and he was conscious of his responsibility for someone who might be morally stronger than he, but was still infinitely vulnerable.

Chapter 22

Quite soon, after the departure of Edith and Hilda, Alec made a trip to Salses, where there was a seventeenth-century castle built by Louis XIV's Minister, Vauban. It was a powerful example of his military architecture and well-designed to withstand seventeenth-century Spanish canon fire. It was of little value, however, in defending the coast against an allied invasion and Alec's true purpose was not to make sketches of Vauban's work, which he did, but to make notes about the concrete gun emplacements that faced out over the gulf of Lyon.

He then made his way inland to the village of Salses proper, where there was one of these sympathetic little farmhouses that seemed to be able to avoid the consequences of rationing for those who could pay. Here he met one of Garrow's agents, who had a message for transmission to Peter and John. The agent who brought the message was a young officer who had become part of the escape organisation because he had spent school holidays in Switzerland. His French might have been adequate for ordering a meal in a tourist resort, but could not have begun to fool the farmer's wife if she had chosen to listen. The message, as usual, was *en clair*, not in code, but in very legible English. Alec never quite got over his astonishment at how few precautions were taken to escape detection. He knew that parties of *évadés* on the Pat Line continued to be intercepted regularly by the Gestapo before they reached Vichy France, and he was scarcely surprised.

With that part of his business done, Alec decided make a proper inspection of the camp at Rivesaltes of which Veronica had often spoken and which he had observed at a distance from his vantage point in the hills. He wanted to extend his investigation into France's policy towards the Jews so that he could report more fully to Cantley. He could not believe that if Britain were aware of what was going on, she would not declare her abhorrence as she had so far failed to do. What was going on was an outrage to civilisation, and the Allies surely must condemn it and declare its ending to be a principal war aim.

The day was bright. The Tramontane was blowing, not hard, but enough, as the Catalans said, to brush the clouds from the sky. In the strong sun, the air was warm. All the same, Alec chilled as he reached the site of the camp, a vast, flat area of some six hundred hectares, originally designed as barracks but found to be unfit to house horses. Even on a dry day, the beaten earth within the barbed wire held pools of water and muddy potholes. Rectangular concrete blocks had been erected in a hurry. Their roofs had not been maintained and few had windows or doors. At the centre of the compound, there was a cooking area, which consisted of no more than a long metal grill under which miserable fires of scrub and broom smoked. Filthily clothed women swathed in what appeared to be rags and with bits of cloth tied round their feet to serve as shoes shuffled round the fires which were heating tubs containing an approximation to soup.

Here and there were groups of children, sitting empty-eyed, apparently receiving some kind of instruction from men and women struggling to educate them. Some older boys kicked balls around and groups of adults sat round an individual who gestured didactically. Gaggles of women with children in their arms sat together in lack-lustre conversation. There were numerous groups of card players. Alec could see the hut which served as lavatories. Down its centre ran a long pipe with holes in it like a gigantic flute. Men and women perched over these holes side by side.

He could see into dormitory huts. They had no furniture other than a long platform on which lay straw mattresses and ragged blankets. There were no provisions for heating. Near the gate, he saw a Red Cross party, two women and a man, handing over tinned and packeted food. They were surrounded by a shouting crowd of children. A line of men with linked arms kept the children back to allow the delivery to be effected.

Apart from this squealing group of children, the remarkable feature of the camp was its silence. There was a subdued hum of conversation, but nothing more. Alec was quite close to the barbed wire but the people he saw through it passed by apathetically without looking at him. No one spoke to him and he spoke to no one.

***

On his return to Perpignan, it was to learn that the Nazi grip had tightened dramatically. Veronica had mentioned the possibility of the Germans moving in to the Unoccupied Zone when she had told Alec about the departure of Hilda and Edith. As the weeks passed, there had been increasing talk of this. Veronica had been particularly concerned. She regarded it as a seismic move from decency to chaos. The military men, Peter, Garrow and now John, spoke of it as a certainty. Inez feared it as a development that would make her vulnerable position more vulnerable still. Alec feared it for her sake.

The notion that the Unoccupied Zone was in any sense free had long been exposed as a myth. The tentacles of German power spread through the south. Pétain did his masters' bidding; indeed, he usually managed to anticipate it. The organs of the Vichy state were the agencies of Germany. The swastika was often seen in the south as German soldiers and officials came to confer, inspect and direct. Although the Zone was not technically occupied, there was no shortage of Germans.

America's entry into the war had created a new imperative: Peter saw it as inevitable now that Germany would want to control the Mediterranean as well as the Atlantic coast. Vichy France counted out the last days of its theoretical independence. The end was precipitated by two events. The British and Americans were both now in North Africa. Technically, this territory was part of Vichy France, and the distinction between Unoccupied and Occupied Zones was now meaningless. Secondly, the British shelled a French fleet on the Algerian coast at Mers-el-Kébir when it had refused to put itself out of the reach of German control. The action was a horrible necessity for Britain, but the death of 1,200 French sailors did much for collaboration, and Germany formally took control of its whole coast. The pretence that the Unoccupied Zone wasn't part of the Reich was at an end.

So this was what Alec learned when he returned from Rivesaltes to the Place Jean Jaurès in time to hear the broadcast news: German soldiers had crossed the demarcation line. Any notion of independence vanished. The future seemed totally black as Alec and Inez made their way back to the Rue des Cordonniers that night. The camaraderie of the evenings in the café and the excitement of the intrigues and derring-do had infected him with a sense of purpose and fun. But now it seemed that all had been an illusion. They had all been running around like ants, absorbed in their own world. He had come back from Rivesaltes as depressed as ever he had been. Now the consolidation of the evils he had seen in the even greater evil of Nazism left him wholly demoralised. Could they do no more than float rudderless in a sea whose waves he could not control, no more than inanimate flotsam? Was there no compass with which to lay a course?

***

It wasn't long before the Germans arrived. The first soldiers reached Perpignan before noon on the following day, 11 November 1942. Their organisation was impeccable. Within hours, German street signs had been erected, the Todt Organisation, responsible for military engineering, had taken over the Chamber of Commerce, its eagle displayed over the doorway. There were machine gun posts on the bridges over the river and other posts at important junctions within the town. The evidence of detailed preparation was remarkable: this was just one town out of thousands which were occupied in the same way, all in the course of twenty-four hours. Before the day was out the swastika flew over the Castillet and there was even a skeleton garrison on the coast.

When Alec and the others gathered at the Café de la Loge that night, they could hear tanks trundling through the town. Cars and trucks drove through the Place itself, including a large open car containing officers and flanked by motorbikes. An obvious target for assassination, thought Alec. The noise of the vehicles all but drowned out the loudspeaker announcement, which talked of important strategic points on the Mediterranean coast of southern France that were now under the protection of the German and Italian armies.

'The passage through France was effected in an astonishing and rapid way without incident,' said the loudspeakers. Peter arrived back from the frontier post at le Perthus where he had seen German officers shaking hands with the Francoist troops on the other side.

Almost immediately thereafter the better houses in the area were requisitioned. This happened on a big scale in Perpignan. In smaller villages, the impact of the invasion was limited. As Alec moved around the region on the following days, he found that some villages had just one German stationed in them, and the man often seemed to have settled into a friendly relationship with the local people. One man pointed out to him was a little Mongolian, a Russian prisoner of war who took care of the mules for the troops that had settled in Banyuls. The local children seemed to have adopted him as a pet.

Chapter 23

A few days later, Alec made his way as usual to Port Vendres. It was a changed scene. A routine that had not hitherto been disturbed by the war had now been interrupted. Stripped to the waist, soldiers were constructing concrete barricades. All along the coast between here and Perpignan, where Hairy Watson had come and gone with impunity, the beaches were being mined, barbed wire was strung up and barricades linked to pillboxes were built against the risk of allied invasion.

He continued to investigate the impact of the arrival of the Germans on the region and within the week was able to report to London that Perpignan was the base for the troops stationed in the *Département*. There were about 25,000 of them in the town and the surrounding villages. Hotels and houses were requisitioned and the evidence of the occupation was inescapable.

The military police, the *Feldgendarmes,* patrolled in pairs, wearing a strange semi-circular breastplate which hung on chains from their neck. In stations they were at the platform barriers, searching luggage for weapons or food. Requisitioned buildings were guarded by sentries standing outside them on small wooden platforms. The brothels in Perpignan were few and discreet, but they now displayed a sign indicating whether they were for the use of Germans only or *open to civilian gentlemen*. German planning was thorough.

Though some of the non-commissioned officers could be arrogant and offensive, most of the commissioned officers that Alec met seemed to be educated and sensitive, and ordinary soldiers were not oppressive in dealing with the civilian population. If someone declined to reply to an enquiry or a pretty girl turned her back on an advance, the rebuff was usually met with a smile. Discipline had been well instilled, and Alec amused himself, when approached by a plain-clothed agent, by asking to see the man's identity card. He wondered what would have happened if he had made the same request in England.

In the Café Gambetta, off-duty German troops ate and drank every night. The individuals varied a bit, but as in most cafés and restaurants, a pattern seemed to establish itself and some of the groups became more or less fixed and the faces familiar. Because the Café Gambetta was not cheap, even for Germans, there tended not to be many ordinary soldiers, but the same groups of officers and senior non-commissioned officers, *Feldwebelen* and *Unteroffizieren,* were around on most evenings.

At one table, in the opposite corner from that used by the group, there was a sinister figure, a Captain, a *Hauptman*, of a cadaverous expression, usually flanked by distinctly subservient juniors. He tended to stare straight across at them. Alec and Inez wondered what he made of them, who he thought they were.

135

Peter seemed not to care and, unperturbed by the Hauptman's challenging gaze, nodded to him as he sat down and more than once sent an order of beers over which was acknowledged with an unsmiling nod of the head.

The local population was not alienated as Alec had expected. Indeed, he was intrigued that the staff of the restaurant seemed to welcome the invaders without any sense of resentment. He asked Amélie, the large and usually flustered wife of the proprietor, what she thought of them.

'Nice enough men,' she said, 'I can't complain at all. They behave very well. They're quiet and serious. I've had our own soldiers in here many a time who behaved very much worse.'

That seemed perfectly true. As Alec made his way backwards and forwards along the coast, he saw no signs of Hunnish atrocities. He saw soldiers handing sweeties to children, a fat Sergeant sitting with a little Catalan girl on his knee, showing her a photograph of his own children. Off duty, some soldiers gave a hand to the farm workers and Alec even saw one helping to unload a fishing boat at Port Vendres.

Some of the soldiers were from subject races, Poles and Czechs, emaciated and often lacking fingers from frostbite on the eastern front. There were scrawny youths too, whom local matrons sometimes mothered in substitution for their own boys, imprisoned in Germany.

Rather than embitterment, humiliation and subjugation, Alec sensed a feeling of solidarity in which all, the German soldiery as well as the Catalan residents, felt themselves victims of common calamity. Even before the arrival of the Germans, the year had been a bad one. The weather was appalling in its effects on a rural community. There had been a long period of drought which had ruined the harvest. Then the fruit crop had been destroyed by hail. There was little water to drink, let alone to water the fields. Although the black market seemed to supply almost anything that anyone with money could need, for the less fortunate, the majority of the population, even the most basic foodstuffs were in seriously short supply.

To add to all that, in the middle of the summer the government announced what was called the *Relève*. French workers were required in Germany. In theory but not in practice the scheme was voluntary and, again only in theory, for every three volunteers, one French prisoner would be released from Germany. In reality, this was deportation, the use of able-bodied Frenchmen as slave labour to keep the German war economy going. It seemed perverse to Alec that the German troops in Perpignan were seen not as instruments of oppression, but at worst as examples of the injustice of the world.

Alec was left largely to his own initiative on what he reported to London, as indeed he had been in Damascus. There he had enjoyed assessing the opposition to the French occupation, and now, in France, it interested him to investigate and report on the extent of opposition to the German occupation.

There were of course some who resisted, many of them the Communists so hated by the Pétainists, but while the war seemed to be moving in favour of the Germans, resistance was limited and fairly ineffective. Alec had seen a patriotic demonstration of sorts in Perpignan on 14 July, to mark Bastille Day, a celebration which had been officially abolished by Vichy. Hundreds of people filled the Place Arago wearing rosettes of red, white and blue. They sang the Marseillaise and chanted *Bread for the Workers*. He noted that their chants and songs were pretty effectively drowned out by the Collabos' chant of *Death to the Gaullists*, and nothing lasting came of this other than arrests and punishment.

Support for Resistance and recruitment into the *maquis* didn't increase until the introduction of the *Relève*. With effective conscription for forced labour, the numbers of youths volunteering for resistance soared. Alec would have liked to read this as a patriotic reaction, but had no doubt that it had been prompted more by a desire to avoid working in labour camps in Germany.

All the same, it changed things. There had been isolated incidents of sabotage before, but now resistance really began to develop. The telephone lines of the German Headquarters in the Hôtel de France were cut; the iron ore transport cable from the base of the Canigou was sabotaged and supply interrupted. Convoys of guns and tanks were held up by interference with rolling stock on the railway.

In the countryside, some bands of the now enlarged *maquis* and other uncoordinated and unruly groups lived off the land and occasionally carried out minor acts of sabotage. London was anxious to know the strength of this informal Resistance and to see if it could be channelled into an organised military effort under the direction of the SOE. In the course of gathering information, Alec asked many questions. The response he got was consistently critical.

'They're no patriots,' he'd be told. 'They're reds from Spain who steal our chickens and live off our work.' Others resented the repercussions. If the *maquis* did succeed in blowing up a bridge, the German reprisals were disproportionate. But the local reaction was usually that the Germans were quite entitled to react as they did and the *maquis* had no business to be behaving as *they* did.

As well as reprisals on innocent civilians, draconian action was sometimes taken against the *maquis* themselves. One evening, in the café, there was particular talk was about Valmanya, a village on the higher shoulder of the Canigou, which had been the main gathering point for the *maquis* in the area. There was some doubt about what had happened there, but the talk was of particularly harsh punishment.

Alec reported on all of this. He stressed his doubts about the commitment of the population to Resistance, the lack of evidence of moral outrage. This line of enquiry seemed to interest London, and he was frequently asked for more information on how much partisan support a second front would receive. He also supplied as much detail as he could on what could be seen of the treatment of the Jews and on the evidence of elimination of Jewish populations throughout Europe. He received no response. When, in exasperation, he asked whether London knew what was going on and accepted his reports, that enquiry went unanswered.

Chapter 24

Inez enjoyed working at the children's home at La Coume. Her gentle authority was ideal for reassuring children of all ages who had been subjected to unspeakable horrors in their short lives. The home had no extensive amenities, but the volunteers who ran it poured out affection to children who had lost their families in the disruption of the Spanish Civil War. Some were reunited with a parent, but most were not and probably never would be. The Church and other agencies supplied the home with enough food, and plenty of toys and games were gifted, but what was very difficult was what La Coume was really there to do, to supply stability and reassurance for damaged, vulnerable victims of an upheaval of which they could understand nothing.

Some children, on the surface at least, reacted well. Siblings were mutually supportive. Other children sometimes seemed to find it easy to make friends and create their own little communities within the larger La Coume family. Many others were less fortunate, withdrawing into the nightmare of their own worlds, remaining speechless and untouchable. None of the volunteers had any qualification for dealing with these children. A few made the mistake of handling them as if they could briskly be made to pull themselves together, but most of the women (the volunteers were all women) quickly came to realise that they were dealing with injuries, and injuries that would take time to heal. Most of the boys and girls did slowly react to love and respect; some never would.

Inez had a special relationship with one five-year-old boy, whom La Coume had named Valentin and she called Vally. He was one of those who were originally badly affected and almost mute. Thanks to Inez's persistence, he began to talk and smile. Slightly against her better judgement, because she believed that in the long run Vally was best served by integrating with the other children, she sometimes brought him home with her when she had an afternoon off. When this happened, Alec tried to be there too. He enjoyed seeing Inez and Vally together. This was a tender relationship of a sort he'd not seen before. Inez was a natural mother and instinctively understood how to handle the little boy. He followed her round the house like a little puppy, and was now robust enough to be teased and in turn to play tricks on her.

Often, they took Vally out to the country for a picnic, and these almost family occasions were as near as Alec could imagine to bliss. Here he saw in reality the image he had dreamt of when he married Barbara, a vignette of father, mother and gambolling child: an idyll. Like a boy, which he had never really been, he played with Vally. He threw a ball; they chased each other. His relationship with Vally wasn't as close as Inez's. This he attributed to the natural order of things, the difference between the feminine and the masculine personality, but he did regret it a little. Vally tended to look at him in a sideways manner, avoiding direct engagement. Or he would run up to Alec, with a ball perhaps, but at the last minute, as he handed it over, would avert his gaze.

Although Alec never mentioned this to Inez, she knew her man, and that it disappointed him. She watched carefully, and one cold day, when the three of them were in the house, she said, 'You know, Alec, I think your moustache frightens Vally.'

'How could it frighten him? It's not much of a moustache.'

'I don't know. But I think it worries him. He doesn't want to look at it. He wants to see you, but not the moustache.'

'What could he have against moustaches?'

'Something to do with the bad days before he came to La Coume? A soldier with a moustache? It's just an idea. We'll never know, because you'll never get rid of that moustache of yours. I can't imagine you without it.'

'Nonsense,' said Alec, heading out the room. 'Vally is much more important than a few hairs on my upper lip.'

When he got to the bathroom, he looked at his moustache in the mirror. He'd never really thought about it very much. During the earlier war, a moustache was more or less required of officers—indeed at the outset of the war it had been obligatory. Anyway, Alec, like most young officers, thought it made him look older and less like a schoolboy. After the army he'd been used to it, and now in wartime Perpignan more men were moustachioed than clean-shaven. But as he looked at it objectively, it looked a rather odd and superfluous piece of fluff. It succumbed quickly to a preliminary assault with a pair of scissors, followed by a surprisingly painless application of a razor. All that was left was a smooth and disconcertingly white crescent above his mouth.

When he re-joined the others, Inez looked at him amazed. 'Incredible. I never thought you would do that. I thought it was so important to you. I'd have expected you to cut off a limb first.'

Alec was greatly surprised by her reaction. 'I told you it meant nothing.'

All the time they were watching Vally. He was building a little castle out of books with his back to the door when Alec had entered the room, and it was some time before he turned round. When he did, he didn't initially look at Alec. He started towards him with one of the books in his hand, and only when he was quite close to him did he look straight at him. At once, he registered the change. He stopped and laid his book carefully on the floor. Then he straightened up and carefully studied Alec's face for most of a minute. He said nothing. Then he walked slowly up to Alec, looking steadily at his face as he had never done before, and quite slowly and deliberately ran his lips back and forth on the spot where the moustache had been. It was a formal bonding. Alec was too moved to speak, and there were tears in Inez's eyes.

That night, in bed, Inez cuddled close to Alec, and she too nuzzled the newly accessible skin. 'How you have changed, Alec,' she said.

'It was only a moustache.'

'That's not what I meant,' she replied.

***

On the following night, Alec and Inez were in the café with the others as usual. The disappearance of the moustache caused a reaction he had not expected. As soon as he came in and ordered their drinks at the bar, Angélique, the proprietor's wife, took a step back.

'What a change! I like that.' And she put her arms round him, squeezed him to her, gave him a kiss on the lips, which she had never done before, and then another one.

Veronica's reaction was very similar. She noticed the change at once. 'You're a different man,' she said. 'I could kiss you.' And she did. It was a long, moist kiss, and Alec enjoyed it. He looked towards Inez, but she was smiling, amused, unconcerned.

If Peter saw the kiss, he too was unconcerned. But he too was interested in the change in Alec's appearance. It seemed to go beyond the removal of a few hairs. 'You're out of uniform at last.'

'What do you mean? You've never seen me in uniform.'

'On the contrary, I've never seen you in anything else. But you seem to be taking it off.'

Chapter 25

By now, the process of getting across the frontier was very different from the happy hiking of the early days. Alec was fascinated to recall how relaxed and free of danger it had been at the start when Frau Mahler and her musical scores had headed south. Inez, whose passage north had been much less comfortable, had difficulty in accepting that it had been little more than a scramble for those going in the other direction at the same time.

There were safe houses in Perpignan, bars like the Continental Bar on the Place Arago, which afforded shelter. The network of serpentine streets in the medieval heart of the town, and houses with doors on several sides, provided cover that was difficult to police. The object was to get the *evadés* from there to another series of safe houses on the Spanish side of the border, at the end of which British intelligence agents escorted the escapers to Madrid, Gibraltar or Lisbon.

The arrival of the Germans pretty well closed the route in and out by sea, and the only escape was over the mountains. The early, low-level route to Figuères, where sympathetic Spanish rail workers had helped *evadés* get to Barcelona and the British Consulate, had to be abandoned in favour of higher and grimmer regions. Now the route for the Pat Line men involved hard climbing to heights of up to 8,500 feet and over the least travelled parts of the mountains. The reason that these parts were not travelled was precisely because the going was so hard. There could be snow at almost any time of year. Even when there was not, it was bitterly cold in the mountains at night and the men were neither clothed nor shod for expeditions of this sort.

British intelligence kitted the *evadés* out with food, clothes and footwear. Often the footwear was no more than rope-soled espadrilles. Occasionally, the soles were made from old tyre treads. The British also supplied bribes and train tickets and camouflaged leather bottles and flasks of cognac.

The escapers were entrusted to *passeurs* who navigated the remote cols across the frontier, through the Cerdagne or Andorra. Sometimes a Spanish *passeur* took over for the descent on the south of the border ridge. The *passeurs* were usually paid in Spanish money, about 1,500 pesetas for each crossing. That was good money, but a lot more would be paid as a reward for treachery.

Spanish border guards, who were ill-paid and ill-fed, did not go out of their way to police the border very seriously. If they caught an *evadé* crossing the border, they would probably only send them back. The greater risk was from German patrols. As time went on and it became clear that an escaped serviceman contributed importantly to the allied war effort, the patrols were stepped up and often supervised by highly trained SS and Gestapo units. Germany patrolled the hills much more systematically than Vichy had done, and a considerable number of escapes went wrong. There seemed to be patterns, periods when particular routes regularly failed, and Peter and John spent more and more time in the mountains, trying to sniff out betrayals and weak links.

The fate of captured guides was not pleasant, whichever side of the border they were caught on. No question of imprisonment as prisoners of war by Vichy and the Germans on the French side, or by Francoist soldiers on the Spanish side, where they were republican rebels. Some guides acted out of political principle, as well as for reward, others purely for money. The latter were particularly unreliable, as ready to give their charges up for cash as they were to save them.

Even when the *evadés* reached Spain, their danger was far from over. The Guardia Civil was a much more professional outfit than the border guards. If they caught escapers, they were perfectly capable of handing them over to the Germans. If that wasn't what happened, then the *evadés* were sent to one of a number of small concentration camps. The conditions there were grim, grossly inferior to those in a POW camp in Germany. It could be many months before diplomatic representations secured the release of prisoners. So it was as important to avoid the Guardia Civil on the Spanish side as the German patrols on the French side.

Chapter 26

The visit to Georges Cadot's family farm, the *mas*, for the *cargolade* had been considerably postponed as a result of Alec's ambush in the Place de la Loge. Alec wondered if the fact that he and Inez were openly together caused the policeman a problem. The occasion had been proposed as a family reunion and as Alec and Inez were invariably together when Cadot was in the café it would be impossible to exclude her. But her Jewishness had been acknowledged by Cadot when he first met her just minutes after Alec had saved her.

Alec's ponderings were probably ill-founded, because after a few weeks, when Cadot renewed the invitation, he made it very clear that Inez was to be included. Indeed, he always made his appreciation of Inez's attractions jovially evident. Alec thought this no more than jocular badinage, but Inez reacted differently and found Cadot gross and predatory.

So Alec put the hood of his car down and with Inez at his side, drove up the valley of the Têt towards Prades, where Pablo Casals had found refuge from Franco, and where he was to remain for seventeen years. Inez sat beside him in the early summer sunshine, her hair moving gently in the wind. Alec looked at her, her profile seen against the freshness of a landscape not yet parched by the summer's sun. She was very beautiful. Alec, seeing her in a moment of clarity, realised that she was indeed more than beautiful. She shone with strength of character, an unmistakeable integrity. He was filled by appreciation of her importance to him.

Alec was aware that when he was away and Inez was not at la Coume, she and John Miller often explored the country surrounding Perpignan. There was an easy complicity between them in shared jokes and experiences. They were a good-looking couple. John's skin had bronzed in the Mediterranean sun. His fair hair was not far from the tone of Inez's darker blonde. Inez was much closer to John's age than Alec's.

Alec had frequently felt the stirrings of a new possessiveness. Nothing more than that: Inez's commitment to him had always seemed total and reassuring. Now for the first time, with this novel perception of what she was and meant to him, he realised he had perhaps been too simple.

'You spend a lot of time with John—I hope he never misbehaves himself?' he said in what was meant to be a neutral tone.

Inez turned to look him full in the face and laughed openly and unaffectedly, 'Of course not. I wouldn't let him anyway. You know I am your woman and no one else's, Alec. He's simply very nice.'

'I'm *sure* he's very nice. You are a very beautiful woman.'

She coloured slightly. Compliments from Alec were rare. 'Thank you, Alec,' she said slowly and deliberately. 'But I know what to allow and what not to allow. Anyway, he wouldn't. He has a woman in London he will marry when this war is ended and he needs no more. He is a complete man.'

'What do you mean *complete*?'

'I mean he is entire in himself. He's enough. He needs no more. Peter is the same. But there's something fierce in *him*. I like John but I'm a little afraid of Peter. He burns with his purpose. John doesn't burn. He is quiet, sure of himself, but he is complete. He needs no-one but the girl he will marry.'

'And what about me?' said Alec, 'Am I complete?'

'No, dear Alec, you are not complete. I saw that on the day you saved me and took me to your empty little house. It was a shell and you were like a shell too and I knew that I could make you complete. With me, you are complete and that is why I will be with you. Now you are not a husk. Your blood flows and your heart beats.'

'And what about you, are you complete?'

'Certainly completer than you,' she said, smiling at him. 'But only really complete when I am completing you.'

***

The Cadot family *mas*, like the other small farms of the region, was a solid square building of rough stone to which organic accretions had over the years attached themselves, barns, stores, buildings to house animals, a dormitory-like building for seasonal workers who, in the days of peace, had come to pick the fruit. It had been a mixed enterprise, some cows, some parcels of vines, but above all acres of fruit trees: cherries, apricots and peaches. When Alec had first come to French Catalonia, the fertile valleys of the Tech and the Têt and the Agly in spring were unbelievably beautiful, with the flowers of these trees, as in a Japanese print, dominating the landscape. Behind them, Himalaya-like, rose the Canigou, carrying snow on its upper levels past midsummer and then disappearing completely behind a heat haze until the autumn, except when the Tramontane blew, always, reputedly, for multiples of three days, but no-one counted in case the myth were false. Now the labour-intensive cultivation of the fruit was impractical, the itinerant workers had been called to fight or to serve the war industries, the fruit trees were largely neglected, and untended fields reverted to scrub. This was true of Georges's *mas* as much as anywhere else. The heterogeneous group of buildings, roughly forming a hollow square, and with a pleasing jumble of height and rooflines, still made an attractive composition, but there was an air of abandonment, and the surrounding fields looked unworked.

Georges Cadot greeted Alec and Inez warmly. As usual, his embrace of Inez verged on the lubricious. He introduced them both to his sister and her four children, all under the age of eight, two boys and two girls. Alec still found it strange to kiss children, but was reminded to do so by Inez's example, as the children lined up, their faces upturned for a *bise*. They were, all four, remarkably clean and neat and behaved with gravely correct manners as no English children of their age would have done.

This was the first time that Alec had seen Georges in civilian clothes. In his blue, slightly shiny striped suit which passed for the uniform of his elevated office, he was bulky, but out of it, he was frankly fat and he looked shorter. He was very much the Catalan countryman in moleskin trousers, calf length leather boots and a white collarless smock. A red sash round his waist completed his outfit. He had not troubled to shave, and the explicitly rustic garb effectively disguised what Alec knew to be a shrewd intelligence. His sister, Dominique, a little younger, was also built on stout lines. Her dress was an adaptation of his, a voluminous black bell-shaped skirt, white blouse and a red scarf over her shoulders.

Dominique withdrew to prepare food and while she did so Georges proudly showed Alec and Inez over the little *mas*. It had been built by his ancestors early in the nineteenth century. He pointed out a large room on the ground floor which was now the family's living room. This, as recently as his parents' time, had housed the goats in the winter months and, throughout all the year, a large pig.

'The smell upstairs in the bedrooms was appalling,' he said, 'but they kept the place warm.' In what Alec had assumed to be another living room, an antique tractor was parked. There was still no running water. In the void of the hollow square, there was a round well with a rope and pulley. At the far corner, there was an ancient privy.

Georges pointed out where the pig had been taken each autumn to be slaughtered, describing with relish how the blood had been collected from its severed jugular vein to be turned into *boudins noirs* as the year came to an end and food was in short supply. There was a feast on the fresh pig meat that lasted for several days after the slaughter, and then the remains were smoked and used to eke out the rice and flavour the soups which were all the family would eat until the following spring. He explained all this without any sense of self-pity or privation; indeed, it was clear that he looked back to this as a much more natural and healthy life than the one that his countrymen now lived. Papa Pétain had many such admirers.

His sister and the children emerged with trays which carried jugs of rosé wine for the adults and water for the children, together with a huge mound of snails.

'This,' said Cadot, indicating the slimy molluscs with the pride of a *maître d'hôtel* lifting a silver dome to reveal an exquisite culinary confection, 'is the *cargolade.*' He explained the ritual, which had to be followed in every detail. The two older children and the adults were all involved in a production line. The snails were picked up one by one. Salt was then scattered on the unfortunate gastropod. The snail clearly didn't like the salt and started to come out of its shell. At that point, the next in the line smothered it in *aïoli*. Successors in the line then installed the snails on a wire contraption of spiral shape. A wood fire, lit well in advance in a corner of the square, had reduced itself to smoking embers. The cylindrical devices were placed over the embers and the contents cooked alive. When they were ready, the pyramids were brought back from the fire and placed on the middle of a plain, scrubbed deal table that had seen service for very many years. To remove the snails from their shells, it was apparently essential that builders' nails, and nothing fancier than that, should be used, and the snails and their salt and their *aïoli* and their strong garlic flavour tasted very good.

The wine, covered in wet cloths, had been chilled by the process of evaporation, the nearest thing to refrigeration in the homes of the Pyrénées-Orientales. The sight of the condensation beaded on the outside of the jugs, in the middle of a very hot day, was as welcome as the contents.

This meal, or something like it, had been produced in Languedoc-Roussillon for hundreds of years, and its simplicity and the fact that it had cost nothing to produce except the time of the children who had gathered the snails that morning was part of its charm.

The snails were followed by Catalan sausage and some lamb chops grilled over the embers. The Catalan sausage should consist of pork, gristle and spices. Dominique was ashamed of the compromises in its composition dictated by the exigencies of war, but in this mellow situation and flavoured by the smoke of the fire, it tasted very good. After that a salad. Nothing but lettuce leaves, olive oil and a very few tomatoes, but Alec wondered how the people of the Mediterranean managed to make these ingredients taste so much better than the rabbit food of England. Dominique was again embarrassed, this time because she could offer them no pudding, but Alec and Inez were replete and happy and the coffee that ended the meal tasted more like the real thing than the acorn brew that they had become used to.

The grave little children were dismissed to play, and Inez and Dominique went indoors to wash dishes. Georges fetched a bottle. He moved his seat closer to Alec's and poured them both glasses of an innominate homemade *eau de vie*. It was now late afternoon. The wind that had been blowing in the morning had disappeared and there was a sleepy warmth in the sheltered courtyard in which the woody smoke still hung in the air. Neither man spoke very much. His heart warmed by the geniality of the occasion, Alec thought what a decent fellow Cadot was, perhaps his only real male friend in Perpignan. Indeed, how many male friends did he have anywhere?

Then, exorcising this maudlin line of thought, he wondered again. How much did he really know this inscrutable Catalan, whose immobile, side-of-beef face served as a mask to conceal his true feelings? He had unquestionably saved Alec's life when he had been attacked beside the Castillet. Why had he done that? It seemed to Alec that for Cadot, life was a series of transactions rather than relationships.

Alec had noticed him looking at Inez in the course of the meal, not lasciviously, as wouldn't have been unreasonable, but coldly and appraisingly, as if inspecting a piece of stock which one day he might or might not buy. While Georges had always been perfectly kind to Inez, Alec knew that he was frankly anti-Semitic. Alec was ashamed to recall that, like many of his class, he too had in the past spoken disparagingly of Jews, seeing the very word as a derogatory term. His time in Syria, when he looked at the Jews beginning to dominate the British mandate of Palestine, had reinforced his prejudice. Now, he saw things differently.

As Inez and Cadot had indicated on the evening he had rescued her, everyone except Alec himself seemed to know instinctively that Inez was Jewish. Alec could still not understand why. She was far fairer than most Spaniards and he liked to tell her that Hitler would have thought her so Aryan that he would have had her for his wife. All the same, he could see this was not the reaction of others. He and Peter knew from information that was not available to the readers of *L'Intransigéant* something of the fate of those who were deported to Auschwitz and the other camps in the east. He was repelled by the deliberation, the *system*, which lay behind this, the same perversion of human nature as he had seen inspiring the frontier guards at le Perthus.

Reason had always been his lode star and the yardstick by which he regulated his life. To begin with, it was the replacement of reason by Fascist prejudice that offended him, but seeing this unthinking hatred directed at Inez in the eyes of those who looked at her with contempt brought a personal element into his reaction which surprised him and indeed worried him.

After a period of what is often described as companionable silence, but in truth had been filled by quite intensive reflections on Alec's part, Cadot jerked himself fully awake.

'Alec,' he said, 'it has been good to have you here today. You have long seen the policeman, but now you see the man, you and your lady.' Was there a sneer? Alec thought probably not. 'You've seen me,' Cadot continued, 'as I am, a very ordinary man, a country man, a family man. I am sorry I have no wife. But here I am, on the *mas* that my family has worked for almost a hundred and fifty years. Most of us here are like me. Even in the town, our true links are with the soil. Everyone here either works on the land or is within a generation of working on the land. That means that we are really quite simple. We grow things, we eat them, we sell them, we're family people, we trust our families. We don't trust others very much. We have to get the better of them in our bargains at the market otherwise they will eat and we will not.'

He was looking far beyond Alec, his eyes ranging over the hills. He sounded sleepy and relaxed. 'So I am a *brigadier* of police. People think I have done well and so I have, but not because I am a clever man or a very good policeman. What I do is that I understand people. I know what they want and I know what I must do to make them happy. I learned very little at the school and left it at the age of twelve. I don't know that I've learnt a lot since I left school but I have learned one thing, and that is that you need to provide people with what they want. I don't greatly care about the Germans or Vichy or any other government. At the end of the day it's getting food from the land, making money from others and having enough to eat. We're just insects, fleas that live off bigger fleas. My aim is to look after my own. I would rather help another Catalan than a German, but that's only sentiment and if I have to survive then it's the Germans I must serve for the moment and they're the people I sell my peaches to. They have come and they will go. They were here in 1870 but they went away. They were here in 1914 but they went away. They came here in 1940 but they will go away. What we have to do, dear Alec, you and I, is to make sure that we are still here when they do go.'

There was a long pause. Alec had some difficulty in filling it. At length: 'But Georges, this is all cynical stuff; what are you trying to say to me?'

The policeman gave a long, slightly despairing sigh and shook his head a little as he replied, 'Alec, what you must do is to shake yourself out of what you learned at your school in England. Life is simpler than you think it is and not so nice either. I have protected you. I even saved your life. And I did it partly, and I admit this although it's no part of my creed, because I liked you, and I'll go on trying to help you as long as I can. But don't relax. When you came here, you were a prickly cactus. I used to talk about the umbrella you had swallowed. Now it seems to me, because I am not quite as stupid as I sometimes claim to be, that you're in dangerous waters. When you were an awkward young man, you were safe enough. What I am saying is this: don't become a man of principle. I think that's the danger for you. I know how fond you are of your young lady and I don't blame you. She's very pretty, but she's even more vulnerable than you are because of what she is.'

There was another long pause, during which neither man spoke. Then Cadot continued, 'You'll have noticed that there are no big trees here. Do you know why?'

'No,' replied Alec, 'I hadn't really thought about it.'

'It's because of this Tramontane that blows so hard. We have none of the great trees that decorate your parkland in England. What we have in abundance are cork oaks. Do you know why?' Alec did not know why.

'Because, my dear Alec, they bend with the wind. And they make themselves useful—their bark is used to bottle our wines. If you want to survive, Alec, you must be prepared to bend with the wind too and to make yourself useful.'

***

Alec had found the first part of the day absurdly pleasant. Being with his beautiful Inez, being admitted to a special family occasion—these were rare experiences for him and he had felt himself physically relaxing as he would have done in the warmth of the sun or the heat of a bath, but the conversation with Georges had dispelled that sense of relaxation as surely as the blast of the Tramontane blows away the clouds. He was much less happy on the way back to Perpignan than he had been when he had driven out in the morning.

Inez too seemed disturbed. She wanted to talk about the women in Alec's life. This was a topic which concerned her, concerned rather than obsessed her, but one to which she returned from time to time. For obvious reasons, she felt something in common with Salema, a woman picked up on a foreign shore and ultimately abandoned.

'I never understand, Alec,' she said, 'how you could leave her like that. Did you give her no hint, no warning?'

'No,' said Alec, too tired to have to go over a narrative that had been explored many times, 'no, that was the whole point. She was wanting to change things and I had to go while I could.'

'But don't you see that was cruel?'

'I don't know that it was cruel. I had never said that I would stay and I left her better provided for than she would have been if she'd never met me.'

'But you let her think that you would be together always. You misled her. You hurt her. The money is nothing. She was your woman.'

'I never asked her to be my woman. I never told her I was her man.'

'But Alec, don't you see, how can I know that you won't do exactly the same to me? How am I any different from Barbara or Salema?'

'Because you *are* different from them. I didn't love them. They just happened to be there. I never knew Barbara. I admired her, because she was remote and desirable, and I suppose beautiful.' Inez did not look pleased by the admission. 'But because I never knew who she was I never thought of how I related to her, of how we differed, or how we were the same. We never came together. There was much less to know about Salema. With her, it was just convenience and proximity. Convenience for her as much as me. I suppose I never felt her my equal, which was bad, but she probably looked down on me too, my softness, my lack of fight. With you it's quite different. We *know* each other. We fit together. You're certainly a better person than me, kinder and nobler, but I don't look up to you any more than I look down on you. I just see you as part of me and me as part of you. We make up one—as you say, you make me complete.'

There were tears in Inez's eyes after this speech, the longest declaration Alec had made to her. All the same, she was not satisfied. 'But still, how do I know that you won't abandon me like you did them? You left Barbara behind just as much as Salema. You have deliberately left her memory far behind you.'

'Oh, come on, Inez. She *died*.'

'Yes, and then you forgot her. And Salema? You told her you would marry her. And all the time you had planned to leave her. You lied to her.'

Alec didn't feel it would help to say that he had had no choice if he were to get away from Salema. Instead: 'You must know that I wouldn't do that to you; this is quite different. Salema never said that she was my woman and if she had, I would have told her she was nothing of the sort. You told me that you were my woman and that pleases me and I tell you now that I am your man.' Inez looked relieved. This was the closest to a commitment that she'd ever heard from Alec or—she guessed—would probably hear again. But the effect of what he had said was spoiled, rather than enhanced, when he added, 'You must believe me, it is the truth.' Inez, as a Catalan, knew that the truth was as real as a handful of wine.

Chapter 27

In the days following the cargolade, Alec found himself thinking increasingly about what Inez had said about Barbara and Salema. He had never worried about hurting them because it hadn't occurred to him that he might have done so. He could see that his approach to life had been self-centred. To begin with that could be blamed on his upbringing, even if later his solipsism was the self-imposed consequence of the experience of vulnerability. Now he began to feel guilt and confusion. He was happy with Inez—and Vally. He luxuriated in this new contentment. But nothing seemed as simple as it once had done. Helping one person meant hurting another. Now he wanted both to help and not to hurt, and it was not clear to him how to go about either.

He and Inez went for a picnic with Vally, along with Veronica and Peter. It was warm and happy and domestic. Alec saw again the realised dream of a family group; of a kind of happiness he had never known. He was determined to translate this snatched war-time happiness into the days of peace. Veronica seemed to have guessed at his thoughts.

'I can picture the three of you after this war, Inez. Do you think Alec would make a good father?'

'Oh yes,' said Inez with confidence.

'And you'd make a very, very good mother,' said Veronica.

There was perhaps more being said between the women than Alec could understand. 'I want Vally to have a better life,' he said.

'Yes, fate started him off with a pretty poor hand,' Veronica said.

Alec just stopped himself from correcting her. He had meant a better life than *he* had had. Crass to point that out.

Reflectively, not critically, Peter: 'But are we all simply to wait for this cosy domesticity to arrive? Isn't it our responsibility to work for it, to make it happen? We can be quite comfortable if we want to close our minds to what's happening all round us.'

Veronica was too thoughtful to say anything to spoil the idyll, but Alec was discomfited by seeing her nod in assent—discomfited not least because she and Peter were enunciating the dilemma that increasingly gripped him. In his frustration, he said what he felt: 'I know what you mean. But I have no idea what to do. I feel increasingly indecisive.'

'You're right, Alec,' said Veronica. 'You've changed a lot since I first met you. I don't mean for the bad. Quite the reverse. You're more sensitive and thoughtful. You used to think you knew exactly what to do, but now you see the complications.'

Inez wanted to support her man. 'I like you the way you are, Alec. Franco's bastards and the Germans have no doubts, and look at them.'

Even Peter was reassuring. 'Come on, Alec, less of this Hamlet introspection. I shouldn't have started philosophising. You're taking risks every day. You're working for the right cause. You're not a soldier. You're not bound to take an active role, and it's to your credit that you do voluntarily what I do as part of my job. You're entitled to domestic felicity too.'

Alec appreciated this from a man who didn't throw compliments around. But it didn't satisfy him. He *was* doing something, as Peter had said, but he didn't believe it was enough. Going on with the routine was one thing. He was hungry for a bolder step, something that would give him entitlement to the happiness he had stumbled into.

Chapter 28

The next day was Easter Friday. Inez had the day off from work at the children's home and she and Alec awarded themselves a day's holiday together, a quiet manifestation of their emerging domesticity. Even if Alec didn't articulate the thought consciously, it was a fact that each of them wanted the other and that together they had no requirement of the ebullience of the group as a whole. It was Inez who was the organiser of the day. She had hinted at surprises. Alec was the passive participant, but very content in a relationship of a sort that he had never before experienced.

Although by now he considered himself an old Perpignan hand, his experience of the town was limited to the accessible parts, the Place Rigaud, the area around Le Castillet, the Place de la Loge and the broad streets of the New Town running to the shady Boulevard of Les Platanes. He had not carried out the more intimate explorations of the ancient town that Inez had, sometimes with Veronica, often with John, but most of all on her own. She was vitally curious and, extroverted, talked to anyone she met, plying them with questions.

She led Alec first through the Quartier St Jacques, densely populated, run-down but lively, south of the cathedral on the slope of Lepers' Hill, Puig des Lépreux. This, she told him, was once the *aljama*, the Jewish Quarter.

'There were a lot of us, you know,' she said, 'here, and in Gerona and in Barcelona.' She talked about its vibrant days in the thirteenth century and of the literature and art of the time. After the exile of the Jews, this working-class quarter had been taken over by Gypsies and North Africans. The cooking smells and the skin colour of the people who bustled through the narrow streets reminded Alec of Damascus. When he said so, Inez became silent and Alec was aware for some moments that his capacity for leaving his women behind was being remembered.

As always, her quietness did not persist. Soon she was tugging his hand and dragging him up the hill to a huge, castle-like structure that dominated the highest point of the town. Alec had often seen its concentric star-shaped walls from the lower town but had not been curious enough to know more. This was the Palace of the Kings of Majorca, originally built by Jaime le Conquérant.

The route to the Palace took them past the medieval Arsenal and the headquarters in the town of the Foreign Legion. Alec felt that he could be in French Colonial Africa. The houses in this area had a distinctly colonial appearance, flat-roofed, square, painted in pastel colours. In this part of the town, as elsewhere, there were many palm trees and columnar cypresses that created an oriental feel.

They entered the palace by a high arched passage. The air was cool compared with the heat outside. The walls of the palace on the outside were defensive, high, tapering away from the road, built of narrow red bricks and perforated by almost no windows. Inside, there was much more decoration: pink marble and elegant columns, wells sheltered by elaborate canopies.

The presence room in which James II had held court was vast. A modern drawing on the wall illustrated the way it would have looked in the thirteenth century: the king at the head of the high table flanked by his lords, the other tables occupied by knights and their ladies, troubadours, entertainers. There they would have eaten dishes delicately seasoned with the spices of the east, followed by sweetmeats, nougats and sorbets made possible by the ice-houses Alec had seen in the hills. It all evoked the courtly life and the romance of chivalry, Peter's special subject.

The architecture, the detailed, exquisite carving of the capitals, the sheer size and confidence of the place all spoke of a sophisticated and evolved society. Alec wondered how it compared with England at the same time. Thirteenth-century London he imagined to have been much more parochial than this cosmopolitan meeting place of cultures. The Silk Road that brought the riches of the east and all its spices came to these Mediterranean shores at the same time as the Moors, coming round the south and through Spain, carried their learning, the fruits of the ancient world that had been lost to the west.

***

Alec and Inez wandered around the palace, little of it restored but most of it surviving reasonably well in a benevolent climate. As he looked at the colours of the masonry, light blocks alternating with black ones, and at the way in which the whole building was grouped in a series of courtyards, he was reminded again of his time in Damascus. This time, he didn't mention that. The recollection was even more marked when they approached the Chapel Royal and he looked at its door decorated by abstract designs and arabesques, just as the great houses of Syria had been.

In the lower chapel, the range of different coloured marbles, some rose, some pink, many in the subtlest of pastel colours, created a wonderful effect. A frieze composed of Arab designs ran round the room and Alec could see, repeated, the letters that made up the Muslim word for God. He thought of those days when Christians and Jews and Muslims could live and work together in amity. When he thought of what Christians were doing to Jews in the present time, he could not but feel despair.

Here was the oldest Royal Palace in France, surrounded by the huge walls that Vauban had added in the seventeenth century. As Inez led him round the imposing throne room and then to the double-decker chapels of the Donjon, Alec had a sense of the magnificence that had existed briefly in the thirteenth century and of the flamboyance of the culture that had preceded the Aragon Conquest.

Finally, Inez took him to the very top of the palace. This was the highest point in the whole of Perpignan. As they looked down from its topmost tower, the Tour de Homage, they could see some traces of the Moorish gardens. Looking further away, across the city, over the plain and towards the sea, Alec saw a landscape that was rich, fertile and peaceful. It was too remote for him to see evidence of the decay and abandonment engendered by war. It was possible, even for an unimaginative man, to picture what he saw as a medieval tapestry, full of peasants making hay and nobles sporting with hawks and dogs and hunting boar.

The view through 360 degrees was exceptional. The sea ran the full length of the eastern perspective. Looking round clockwise from the edge of the sea he could see the Albères running up into the *massif* of the Canigou which in turn merged with the Corbières hills as his eyes came back again to the sea. In the foreground lay Perpignan, still in appearance a medieval city, a city of the south, of the sun, an exotic gathering of peoples.

On this clear, sunny day, there was scarcely a cloud in the sky, but as on other occasions, the Tramontane wind brought airs down the Rhône valley that were forced up over the summit of the Canigou where they formed distinctive jets and clouds high above the peak. In Alec's mind there were complicated thoughts as there had not been when he walked into Perpignan to his meeting with Inez.

As he turned to descend the tower, out of the corner of his eye he saw in the courtyard below him a group of young Catalans, male and female in a circle, their hands joined and lifted above their shoulders.

'What's going on here?' he said to Inez. Immediately they saw him, they dropped their hands and disappeared. Inez looked amused.

'Never mind. I'll tell you about that later. Remind me by saying "Sardane".' Alec let her enjoy her mystery.

By the time they had reached the courtyard, it was deserted. They sat in a corner, in the shade, and ate a picnic lunch. In the course of her wanderings in the town, Inez had got to know people who always seemed to have something interesting to exchange for a few centimes. Today was fairly typical. Fish was not rationed and the little fish that they used for frying and making soup cost very little. Inez had found them each a little seafood pie called *tielle Sètoise*. They ate these with fiery pieces of toast, rubbed with raw garlic and dampened with tomato pulp. They drank, sharing a bottle they had brought with them. It was red wine, *arosé*, diluted with water. It was relaxing and they sat close together afterwards, looking out over the Mediterranean, Inez's head on Alec's shoulder, his arm round her. They talked little.

Alec reflected how much her touch and closeness mattered to him. This was a novelty for him, something he had never been aware of in the days of his more functional, transactional relationships with Barbara and Salema. He was aware of that, and glad of it, and recognising that, he hugged Inez all the closer.

His eye fell on two lizards, mating in the shade at the foot of the ancient castle wall. Motioning towards them he said, 'You know I always find something exciting about that, something exotic. It reminds me that I am right at the heart of the Mediterranean world, with all its dust and spices and smells.'

Inez threw her head back and laughed up into the sun, her face and hair more golden than ever. 'Alec, you are wonderful. Only an Englishman could be excited by watching copulating lizards!'

Alec laughed. He realised how Cadot would have responded to his admission with some comment about Englishmen needing to watch lizards fucking in order to stimulate their own libido. He looked at Inez, her face still tilted upwards, full and relaxed as it had not been on that first day in front of the Castillet, her hair longer and sun-gilded, and he knew that he would neither have been able to laugh at himself in this way or to confess the romance he found in the meridional existence before he met her. An Alec Ross savouring the poetry of life was not one which his parents would have recognised. Remembering what Cadot had said on the day of that meeting, it seemed to him that if he had indeed been born with a figurative umbrella within, to stiffen him inside and to protect him from the outside world, Inez had removed it totally painlessly. He squeezed her hand.

She responded with a reciprocal squeeze, and said, 'Dear Alec, I may be only half your age, but you are only half as grown up. I have understood you like a little boy right from that first day I came home with you. It's taken you longer, but I think you are getting to know me and that's what I want to do today. I want to tell you a little about my world, this Mediterranean world, half Jewish, half Catalan. It's time for the next stage.'

***

Alec had been aware of some hesitant, intermittent, booming noises. As they came down back through the Jewish quarter, passing the Couvent des Minimes, a Franciscan sixteenth-century foundation, the noise became louder, and when they reached, just a little further on, the church of St Jacques, its source was revealed. He was amazed by the sight of scores of figures clothed in black robes that reached the ground, wearing tall hoods like elongated witches' hats which covered their faces entirely but for two grim eyeholes.

The men—and there may have been women there too—were forming up into a procession in silence. The road was crowded with spectators, but they said not a word. Inez spoke to Alec in a whisper. In the distant past the Brotherhood of La Sanch had been founded in this church, in gratitude for a miraculous cure. The Brotherhood originally had the function of protecting condemned criminals on their way to execution, to spare them the ordeal of walking through hostile crowds who frequently tore them to pieces or lynched them before they reached the executioner and before they could make their confession. The Order protected them by the hooded robes. The condemned man, Members of the Order and the executioner himself were identically dressed to avoid identifying who was the condemned man and who were the brothers who were there to support him and afford him an opportunity for expiation.

Over the centuries, the procession had moved from its original purpose to commemorate the Passion and death of Christ. The church regarded the whole thing with suspicion. From time to time it had been proscribed, but its tradition was dear to the people of the region. Inez told Alec that similar processions took place in other places, like Salamanca, but the tradition was strongest in Perpignan and here it was still important for the people, whose view of Christianity had for so long emphasised concentration on suffering.

They reached the church in time to see the procession move off. All was disciplined. At the head of the parade, a figure in red robes intermittently rang an iron bell. Behind him, the penitents marched to the beat of muffled, black-veiled drums. The whole effect was impressive and frightening. For the Protestant Alec, images of the Inquisition were impossible to eliminate. The procession moved very slowly. This was inevitable as some of the penitents carried hurdles supporting *misteris,* representations of the different scenes of the Passion. The weight of these tableaux was enormous. Inez told Alec that each of the men carrying the heavier ones was bearing a weight of up to 50 kilograms. He could well believe that. The enormous *misteris* swayed and rocked, like ships on a wave, on the shoulders of the half dozen or so men who supported it.

The whole effect was powerful. This was no holiday jamboree: the slow beat of the drums and the occasional tolling of the bell had a hypnotic effect. The only other sound that broke the silence was the rhythmic noise of the penitents' shuffling feet. Not all wore shoes. Some were barefoot. Some even moved on their knees.

The crowd moved with the procession, following in its trail, preceded by the *misteris* and crosses. From time to time, there was a tap on the cobbles from a staff to allow a change of load-bearers. During this pause, the crowd and some of the penitents quietly sang traditional Easter hymns and Catalan *goigs*. A double tap of the staff signalled resumption of the march.

Thus the procession slowly moved to the town's cathedral of St Jean. In the square in front of the cathedral, the procession made its final stop. The *misteris* were carefully lowered and carried through the great double doors of the cathedral and the crowd slowly dispersed. The emotional effect was inescapable. No one spoke.

***

Inez had taken Alec's hand in hers, and she led him away from the cathedral through the Place Gambetta and the Place de la Loge in front of the medieval merchants' house, the Loge de Mer, still decorated by a weathercock in form of a ship, despite the fact that the sea which had lapped the edge of the town when the Loge was built was now many kilometres to the east.

On their way, they walked through the maze of narrow streets that surrounded the Place de la République. In the Rue de la Poissonière were the stalls where spices were sold. There were the elaborate piles and pyramids Alec had seen without great interest in the Grand Bazaar in Damascus, and the same smells of herbs and spice and lavender and Aleppo soap that here he found intoxicating. The scale was smaller, but they spoke of the same world, the same indivisible culture of the Mediterranean and the Levant.

They made their way to the edge of the old town and the Castillet, the gate tower at the foot of which Alec and Inez had met for the first time in memorable circumstances. Alec and Inez certainly remembered the occasion and often referred to it as they walked past the Castillet. Even today, they exchanged an acknowledgement as they approached the building.

Inez took Alec inside. They climbed the stairs to the top floor. There, Alec knew, was a room which had been discovered not long before, when masons broke through a sealed wall. They found the body of a child, which on contact with the air had dissolved into dust. The clothing belonged to the late eighteenth century. Had this been Marie-Antoinette's son, the Dauphin, who had been used by the revolutionaries for bargaining with the Bourbon family in Spain? They passed the door to this chamber and Inez opened an adjoining door, which led to a very small room, little more than a cupboard. All it contained was a table and on that table a paraffin lamp burned.

'Now we go,' said Inez, 'and I'll explain.'

***

They sat at a table in the little Café du Castillet, which looked across the Place at the building from which they had just emerged, and ordered acorn-juice coffees. Inez smiled, conveying a sense of satisfaction.

'Well, Alec, I hope you know a little more about me than you did on the day when you saved me here.' Alec made to interrupt, but Inez raised her hand and said, 'I know you do in many ways. But today I've tried to explain a little more about what matters to me. You've seen the Jewish quarter. There, when Western Europe—and your England—were still barbarous places, my ancestors were producing philosophical treatises that are now preserved in Paris. From the Palace of the Kings, Jaime Le Conquérant and his son presided over their empire. They absorbed all the civilisation of the Moors—their cooking, their art, the learning of the ancient world that had been lost to Europe in the Dark Ages.

'You have seen the strength of the Catholic faith and its mysticism,' she continued. 'It's not part of my Jewish heritage, but I'm a Catalan and it's part of the Catalan tradition. The point is that all this has built up over a thousand years—it's what civilisation consists of. That's why we have to fight against the Germans. We mustn't have another Dark Age.'

Alec couldn't deny that. He did not know how to reply. He tried to buy time. 'And what was the paraffin lamp all about?'

'That's part of me again. You know that le Canigou is special for us Catalans?'

'Yes,' said Alec. No one could live in Perpignan for a week without being aware of that.

'What you won't know, because it doesn't happen during this war, is that in June every year, on the Fête of St Jean, near the summer solstice, the Catalans light a great bonfire on the summit. We go up from both sides, perhaps even more from our side in Spain, to les Cortalets. You can reach that by track and from there it's a climb of about three hours to the top. At les Cortalets we have a huge party. It's to celebrate our bonds, the fraternity that links us on both sides of the frontier. I remember going there as a little girl with my parents. People sleep in tents or under a blanket. You take your food and you cook it on great bonfires and it's very simple and very special. The paraffin lamp you saw is carried to the top of le Canigou to light a great bonfire on the summit. As soon as it's burning, young men run down with flaming torches to all the villages in the Albères on both sides of the border, and from the flames they carry they light bonfires in all the villages. The whole mountainside burns with the flame of the Canigou. And one very special burning brand is carried all the way into Perpignan and it re-lights the lamp there which is kept alight all year. From that lamp is carried the flame that lights the next year's bonfire, so the flame of the Canigou is eternal.'

'And that was the point of the lamp we saw tonight?' asked Alec.

'Yes, but that flame we saw tonight is even more special, because the Germans and the little puppet Franco forbid the fire on the mountain. That flame in le Castillet is all we have. We must guard it till this evil war has ended. It is the flame of Catalan liberty. It must not be put out. It will burn again.'

'But why is the fire forbidden? What's wrong with it?'

'Because this isn't some harmless tradition. It threatens Vichy France. It threatens the German Reich. It's about individuality and independence. And Franco fears it most of all. It threatens the new order he has created in Spain. I told you to ask me about la Sardane. I knew you would forget,' she said laughing. 'You saw these people starting to dance. They were going to dance la Sardane. It's a very ancient folk dance of these parts, very sad and slow and haunting. Until Franco, people danced it outside after church every Sunday. But it's a symbol of Catalan independence. Now if they dance it their legs are broken.'

'Oh come on,' Alec interrupted. 'Surely not. This is the sort of atrocity story that comes out in every war. It's a myth.'

'It's not,' she said, irritated. 'I have seen the Falangistes do it. They swing their rifle butts and I've seen them breaking the legs of women and men, and even children. Do you know that you go to prison for speaking Catalan—or for that matter Basque at the other end of the Pyrenees?'

'No.'

'Well, if you're *lucky*, you go to prison—but for dancing the Sardane or speaking Catalan or flying a Catalan flag or criticising Franco, El Caudillo, you're just as likely to get a bullet in your head—or a bayonet in your womb,' she added.

After a moment or two: 'So now you know a little more about me. You know why I came to Perpignan. But I didn't come just to escape. Just like the flame that burns over there in the Castillet to return one day to the mountainside, so all we treasure must be preserved.' She looked very tired. She stretched. 'Now, Alec, let's go home.'

***

When they made love that night, they did so particularly tenderly. They had long been coming together in a very different way from that first coupling on the night of the meeting outside the Castillet. Even then there had been a reciprocity that had been a revelation to Alec, quite unlike the brief release that Barbara and Salema had offered. Inez was not simply a receptacle for ejaculation. Indeed, the orgasm, though ultimately so urgent, was in a sense the least of the experience, which was much more to do with closeness and intimacy and reciprocal giving.

The abandonment of self began, as these things do, with a kiss, which was melting rather than aggressive. That set the tone for all that followed. Inez was no passive participant. The pleasure was hers as much as Alec's, and that in itself set the experience apart from what he'd known before. She moved with him and against him. She responded and initiated, and what they achieved, they achieved mutually. Each time they made love, they bound themselves more closely together. Long before they reached their climaxes, they were lost in each other, they felt themselves one body, spiritually as much as physically.

Attaining this stage in their relationship had not initially been easy for Alec. For this taut, private man, perhaps constrained by character, but certainly confined by his early circumstances and institutional upbringing, sex had been a need, but a need of which he could not be proud, an admission of lack of control. It was to the credit of Inez that he had moved so quickly to maturity. Though far less experienced than he—her rape at the hands of the drunken Nationalist soldier had been almost her first sexual encounter—she was in sex, as in so many matters, more mature than Alec. The centrality of sexual pleasure to love, the acceptance of sexual desire as normal and natural may have been no part of the Anglo-Saxon mould which formed Alec, but was taken for granted in the Mediterranean world which was her cradle.

Briefly, Alec had, indeed, been almost shocked by what were wanton ways by the standard of provincial England, but he remembered Georgie's whisper about his 'ways'. In a sense that whispered admission licensed for Alec what Inez enjoyed. He liked to think that Georgie had been in some way telling him in advance that Inez was good for him. But more importantly, and less occultly, he could not fail to see for himself that Inez *was* good: good for him and good in herself.

She gave herself. She gave herself whole-heartedly to the children's home. She gave her support and sympathy to Veronica whenever she was troubled. Peter rarely looked in need of support, but after some of his more difficult expeditions he was desperately tired. Inez sensed this at once and often contrived to ensure that he and Veronica were left quietly by themselves.

So, did Alec realise that she loved him? He did. Did he realise that he loved her? He did. He even told her. The first time he did so, he had said the words

159

pretty well spontaneously, in the midst of passion. His immediate reaction was of surprise at what he had uttered, but that was followed by the no less surprising realisation that he had truly meant what he'd said.

Now, by different routes, these two days—the visit to Cadot's *mas*, and now exploring her world—had brought Alec closer to Inez than he could have thought possible. He knew her, he felt, in her entirety, and there was no reserve on either part. Maybe, in truth, he could never know her in her entirety, but he was right to think there was no reserve on either part.

And did Inez believe that he loved her? Yes, she did. She understood him very well. She knew he loved her. What she did not know was what his love would ultimately mean. She understood well that Alec had never committed himself in any real sense to Barbara. She knew that he had fled from commitment to Salema in Damascus. She believed that their relationship was different. She wanted to believe that. But she never freed herself from the pain of the dagger of doubt. She, unlike Alec, did not know whether she knew her partner in his entirety.

Chapter 29

Alec would never know whether he truly had seen Cantley go into the Commissariat de Gendarmerie, but not long after the day at Cadot's *mas* he did hear from him, even if only vicariously. He went as usual to Port Vendres and collected his message from his friend the purser. Then he had gone to la Frégate and opened the envelope. It was an instruction to meet Hairy Watson at the usual place on the cliffs above Paulilles a week later.

Alec made his way there with a great deal of difficulty. The German patrols and lookout posts rendered this sort of exercise very much harder than it had been, and his cover as an artist wouldn't carry much weight if he were caught in the middle of a dark night, whether or not he had his painting materials with him. It rather pleased him, however, to feel that he was running real physical risks like the others and being a real spy rather than a subsidised informant.

He had some concerns for Hairy's safety. The creek at Paulilles was too narrow to be guarded in the same way as the potential invasion sites, but approaching the shore in any kind of boat was full of risk. Alec, like all the others, was fond of Hairy. His bellows in the Café Gambetta as he met new escaping Britons, had become a byword: 'I'm Hairy, what about you?'

Alec had realised, long ago, that the English chose to hide any hint of intelligence either behind pomposity or facetiousness, and some of the most extraordinary buffoons he had met turned out to be very astute indeed. He thought that Hairy was probably highly intelligent.

He certainly was a buffoon. He was also decidedly overweight. Alec could hear him grunting and panting noisily and without a care for who might be waiting for him, long before he reached the top of the cliff.

'Ahoy, ahoy,' he bellowed, though he must have been well aware of the German patrols. 'Heave to!' he shouted when he saw Alec, 'and assume a stooping position. The Royal Navy's here.'

He was a remarkable figure. His bushy beard was more extravagant than ever and he looked very much like the bearded man in the Popeye cartoons, Popeye's rival for the hand of Olive Oyl.

He was wearing a dark blue sweater on which were woven the words, 'HMS Skylark. Trips round the bay our speciality!' He pointed at his sweater and asked Alec, 'Don't you like it? I had them made specially. Don't wear them a lot in Portsmouth or at the Admiralty, but they help morale aboard the Good Ship Hairy enormously and I like to think that if we ever get caught by the Germans, they'll give the Boches an idea of what the Royal Navy's made of.'

They sat on a rock which served as their desk when they did business at Paulilles. 'You may not have noticed,' said Hairy, 'not being a military man, but this place is absolutely swarming with horrible Huns. If they're not going to be friendly to me, then Hairy's going to keep out of this neck of the woods.' He took a cigarette out, offering one to Alec. Alec declined it and said that lighting matches wasn't an awfully good idea.

'Quite, quite,' said Hairy, lighting a cigarette all the same. 'I come today as an emissary from on high, to be precise from a little fellow in Whitehall who declined to give me his name, rank and number but told me that if he said that he was from a tight little island, you would know who he was. That mean anything to you?' Alec said that it did.

'Well, I come not so much as Hairy of the RN but as Hairy of the FO, a beplumed and helmeted imperial messenger. I come with a message far too precious to be committed to paper. I was made to memorise it and was then tested. I passed with full marks, better than I ever did when I had to learn the principal parts of Latin verbs, which have stood me in very good stead in my naval career. I am now to impart the contents of that message to you. When I am satisfied that you have absorbed it, I shall set fire to you and swallow the ashes.'

He then imparted his message, the essence of which was that the war would go on for some time and there would be a lot of nasty fighting, but that with the Americans in, as well as the Russians, final victory against Germany was a certainty. Alec was to understand that Cantley was, as at the end of the First World War, now looking beyond the end of the present conflict. The Nazis would be defeated, but they would be defeated largely by Russians, with the aid of Communists in the occupied countries. What was important was to ensure that when peace came, the apparatus of resistance to a Russian enemy was not destroyed. The Germans, the Vichy French and the Spanish Francoists might not be to our liking, but they would be our essential allies in the war against Soviet Communism which was going to be the defining struggle of the century. Accordingly, while continuing to do his bit in the role in which he was presently placed, Alec was not to be too zealous.

A bit less criticism of anti-Semitism, too. It would annoy Spain. Keep going through the motions of waging war on Fascism, but not too officiously: that was the nub of the message which he was asked to put into practice and to communicate to Peter and Garrow. They were to look *beyond the horizon* and assemble a network of reliable men who they could work with in the fight against the communists. Above all, they were to be cautious of the Resistance, which was infiltrated by committed Marxists.

Hairy left a bottle of whisky with Alec as he always did on these occasions and then climbed laboriously down to the beach to be rowed back to his ship. Alec could clear him quite clearly singing sea shanties as he went.

Left alone, Alec felt very solitary. Ever since he came to France, he had been coming closer to a philosophy that had been quite absent before. He could see good and evil and the necessity for fighting for the former and against the latter. What Georges had said to him at the *mas* had undermined that philosophy a little, but Georges was a simple peasant. What he had just been told, in the unmistakable cadences of Cantley, was the elaboration of policy by civilised men in positions of power in democratic institutions, but in essence the message was the same as Cadot's—forget about ideals: self-preservation is what counts. Cantley had been pretty chilling in his arguments about *realpolitik* a decade earlier in Damascus but then Alec had been politically agnostic. His slow conversion during the Perpignan years had been filling him with the beginnings of the convert's zeal. Now he had either to lose his newfound faith or to fuel its flames so that it could destroy Cantley and all his works.

Chapter 30

Exactly one week later, Alec set off on another expedition, this time to the north, to Marseille again. It was a mark of his enhanced position in the Perpignan cadre of Pat Line that he now carried out his mission alone.

His mission concerned the continuing case of Harold Cole. Clearly a traitor in the eyes of everyone who had studied his case, Cole still contrived to avoid the consequences of his treachery. Alec and Peter and Garrow and O'Leary were convinced of his guilt, and innumerable men and women were being summarily despatched daily on the basis of far less evidence than had built up against Cole. Yet for some reason this man always seemed to be given the benefit of non-existent doubts. The fact that his evil aura caused Caskie's sensitive antennae to twitch was arguably insubstantial reason for executing him, but there was much more solid evidence against him and it was on the basis of that evidence that it had been decided that Cole should be executed on sight when O'Leary had his meeting in Gibraltar.

But Cole had not fallen into the hands of the British, who would have shot him summarily. He and his wife had instead fallen into the hands of the French, the Direction de Surveillance du Territoire for Lyon. Although this was a Vichy organisation, its head, Louis Triffe, was a brave man who was committed to the allies and the proposition that resistance organisations should be protected. Bizarrely, he, a Vichy official, was now conducting a court martial on behalf of Vichy's enemies. Yet again Alec wondered who was fighting whom.

Triffe knew what O'Leary and the others had decided in Gibraltar. Added to that, in the course of the investigation Cole had confessed to his treachery to Triffe. But Triffe was insistent on seeing justice done openly, and he wanted hard evidence. Although his sense of allegiance was commendably flexible, his insistence on correct procedure was not.

O'Leary and Peter asked London for a definitive ruling. They were told to await a response which would be broadcast as a personal message by the BBC. These messages were a regular feature in an addendum to the BBC French News. The news was broadcast each night at a quarter past nine and it was followed by a series of these bizarre special messages, meaningless to most of those who listened, but of vital importance to the few who were engaged in the clandestine war.

They began with the words, 'And now here are a few personal messages.' The personal messages were opaque: *The blind fiddler plays, but no-one hears.* Or *The moon is shining on the still water.*

So, on the evening after his disquieting meeting with Hairy, Peter and Alec left the others in the café early and headed for a safe house near the Continental Bar. In this case, the coded phrase that would confirm that Cole was a plant would be *the brown cows fill the field.* If he were innocent, *the rabbits skip in the sun.* They sat beside the little receiver in a little room no bigger than a cupboard in the middle of the house, and listened to interminable incomprehensible and improbable messages. Their surreal quality had a cumulative effect that was irresistibly bizarre and Alec found it difficult not to laugh. Eventually, however, reality broke in: the cows were in the field. It was to carry this authoritative ruling on Cole to Caskie, for onward transmission to Triffe that Alec left for Marseille.

***

He contrived to arrive at the Rue Forbin in the early evening. Caskie opened the door. 'It's good to see you again, Sandy.'

'They usually call me Alec.'

'Aye, well, if you've no objection, I'll be calling you Sandy. Sandy Ross has a good Scots feel to it. And I knew a Sandy Ross in Islay.' (He pronounced it as 'Eye-lah'.) 'Aye, well, Sandy Ross, how is the search going?'

'Well, I'm not actually searching. I've come with news.'

'Just so, just so,' said Caskie in a tone that did not imply agreement. 'Come in, anyway. We are just about to eat and you'll have to keep your strength up. A man can't search properly with an empty belly.'

He ushered Alec into the communal eating room. He pronounced a blessing and they sat down to a copious, if simple, meal with plenty of good rough red wine. There were fewer occupants in the room than the last time, but as before, Alec and Caskie sat at a table by themselves and took care not to overhear the discussions that were going on around them. Equally, they confined their own conversation to the everyday and commonplace.

After the meal, which was quickly despatched, Caskie took Alec upstairs to his monastic little study. Caskie sat at his desk, Alec in a threadbare armchair. He reported on the judgement of London. Caskie listened gravely. When Alec had finished, he sat in silence for a moment.

'I knew it, of course, but unfortunately, the second sight is not evidence in a court of law. Very well, I'll pass the news on to our friend Triffe. It's sad, but Cole will have to go. We cannot allow one bad man to put at risk the lives of so many good people.' After a moment's reflection, he added, with emphasis, 'There are a *lot* of good people.'

'Unfortunately, there seem to be even more bad ones,' said Alec.

'No, no, Sandy, lad. There are a *lot* of good people and just a very few really bad ones. Most people are in the middle, capable of being one or the other. It's my job to work for them.'

After another moment or two of reflection, Caskie got up briskly and produced a bottle of what turned out to be an excellent malt whisky. He poured a generous tot for each of them, adding to his own glass an equal measure of water. He motioned his glass towards Alec, who reciprocated. They sipped their drinks.

'I remember young Sandy Ross well,' said Caskie, his eyes remote as he dwelt in his memory. 'He was a fine big fellow, like his father, William. They were crofters. We crofters, Sandy's parents and mine, all of us worked together. Big William had a horse and it did the ploughing for us all.' (He pronounced the word as 'plooch-ing'). 'Sandy was turning into a fine horseman, what you would call a ploughman.' (The pronunciation was something like 'ploochman'.) 'Then the Kaiser's War came along. Like many Islaymen young Sandy joined the Merchant Navy.' Again, Caskie dwelt in his memory for some minutes. They drank in silence.

'Then Sandy's boat was sunk by a U-Boat. Not one man was saved. It was no surprise to Sandy's mother. She had the second sight. On the night when Sandy's ship went down, she heard a tapping at her casement. She got up and there was nobody there. The next morning, she told the minister what had happened, three days before the telegram arrived.'

Caskie poured out two more measures of whisky. This time, Alec followed his host's example and added water, finding that it liberated subtleties of taste which his first glass had never revealed. Caskie noticed his reaction and nodded.

'Aye, Sandy it's better that way. We'll make a Scotsman of you yet.' After a moment, his tone changed to the slow cadence he had adopted while talking about the Kaiser's War.

'Aye, it must be twenty years since I saw her, but I remember Sandy's mother as if it were yesterday. She was a fine good-looking woman, as tiny as Sandy and William were big, a little deer calf beside two great staggies. She had beautiful black hair, but it went quite white overnight, on the night when she heard the tapping at her casement.'

Another pause and change of gear from the past to the present. 'Well, Sandy lad, and how was your journey, how is your quest?'

'I don't know that I'm on a quest,' said Alec.

'Oh come, laddie, we're all searching for something, but you are more than most. I could tell that when you were here last with Peter Graham and Pat O'Leary. They know where they are going, but you don't. You are a good man, but there is something you need.'

Alec shook his head, smiling, and held his hands up in surrender.

'Well,' said Caskie, 'I'll give you one piece of advice. There's one thing you must know if you hope to find what you're looking for.'

'Where it is?' suggested Alec.

'No, no, no. *Where* doesn't matter in the least. What you must know is *what* you're looking for. If you know that you'll find it as surely as the sun comes out of the sea in the morning and returns to it in the evening.'

This time, Alec was to sleep in a room of his own and not in the communal dormitory. Caskie showed him to the door of the room and then stood for a moment looking deep into Alec's eyes.

He shook him by the hand in a formal way and said, 'Have an egg with your breakfast tomorrow. You need to keep your strength up for your search. I'll be up and away long before you get up in the morning so I'll say good bye to you now.'

Caskie was right. He had gone before Alec got up in the morning. There was, indeed, an egg for him at breakfast. He ate it and some bread and drank some good coffee. As he opened the door of Number 46 Rue Forbin, he emerged from the twilight calm of the house, whose shutters were never fully opened, into the vibrancy of the Vieux Port, with all its noise, sharp smells and colour. Alec sensed, simultaneously, relief at returning to a world which he understood and some slight sense of guilt that he was more at home in these meretricious surroundings than in the calmer, spiritual world of Donald Caskie.

Chapter 31

The pace of events was quickening. The relaxed, amateurish tempo of the early days had gone. No more sightseeing trips with Veronica. No more vague wanderings with sketchpad in his satchel. The mood was much tenser, activities focussed. All were aware of danger. That's not to say that the mood was grey or less fun; paradoxically the tension gave a febrile edge to existence. Life could not be lived so intensely forever, but for the moment the intensity, the flow of adrenaline, was intoxicating. All of the conspirators felt the closer for it, and for Alec and Inez—perhaps also for Peter and Veronica—it gave a special sharpness to their relationship that might never have developed in normal circumstances.

Alec and Peter required to make an expedition into the hills. They needed to know exactly what had happened at Valmanya. There was still much talk about an engagement at the Resistance base on the high Canigou, some sort of retaliation by the Germans for *maquis* activities, but no clear news had emerged. Customarily, the Germans were careful to publicise the extent of their vengeance—its whole purpose was to deter—but this time almost nothing had been said. There were hints that there had been some over-enthusiastic involvement by the *milice*.

Their journey took them to a desolate scene. Where the village had been, not a building remained, only dismantled habitations and blackened ruins. There were a few, very few people around. Alec and Peter came across one man leading a donkey, with a crude coffin slung askew across its back. He told them what had happened.

The Germans had been embarrassed by the way in which Valmanya, because of its remote position well up on the *massif,* had operated openly as a *maquis* base and in particular as a key point in an escape line known as the Henri Barbusse line that operated from Belgium, through France to Spain. The problem was that whenever it was approached, the *maquisards* just vanished onto the summits.

The Germans decided that something had to be done, so they approached in strength, expecting to find a deserted village which they would destroy. Almost all the inhabitants had indeed made themselves scare, but four very old people had refused to leave, thinking they were too old to be harmed. They deluded themselves. The Germans had been quite merciless, delighted to be able to be making an example of them, rather than simply burning some empty buildings.

The four were beaten and tortured before being executed and the Germans ordered that their corpses were to be left where they lay. There they lay for eight days. A younger woman of thirty-one also remained. She had thought that the

168

fact that she was four months pregnant would save her, but she too over-rated the Nazi sense of decency. She was raped by fourteen soldiers in front of her two children. Then she and her children were shot.

After the Germans and *milice* had stolen everything they could and killed the domestic animals, they had set fire to the whole village. They sat around watching the flames and drinking the contents of the cellars and at dawn set out with their vehicles and machine guns to flush out the *maquis*, who were still on guard on the ridge above. It was a short, one-sided battle. Those who could escape took refuge in the upper heights of the Canigou, but about eighty *Résistants* had been wounded and thirty dead were left behind.

Looking at the coffin, at recently dug graves, at perhaps fifty burned-out houses, Alec felt sick. But when he tried to commiserate with the mule-driver, he realised that their views did not coincide. The man, one of the dark, solid men of the mountains, did not quite approve of what the Germans had done, and did squarely condemn the *milice* for their cruelty to their own countrymen, but there was a distinct element of sympathy for the German reaction in the face of intolerable provocation. There was a case, it seemed, for saying that the Germans had their job to do, and that the uncommitted countrymen, of whom the muleteer was one, also had *their* job to do, and that the *maquisards*, largely Spanish communists, lived off the crops and stock of honest men, and made life difficult for both the Vichy French and their German allies.

As they headed back down the hill to the valley of the Têt and the road to Perpignan, Alec found himself infuriated by what he regarded as a perverse view of a very straight-forward conflict between good and evil—indeed monstrous evil. He said so to Peter several times in several ways, and was goaded by his lack of response.

'This kind of thing is happening all the time now, and I don't begin to understand it. If Germany and fascism and so on is so very bad—and surely, we all agree it is—why do we keep trying to find excuses for the bastards? Look at that fellow—old people tortured and killed, a pregnant woman raped. Scores of his fellow-countrymen—his own people—killed or wounded. And he tries to find excuses for these Nazi swine.'

Peter grunted, but didn't reply. Alec was normally respectful of Peter, perhaps excessively so. He liked and admired him, but his quiet authority, his apparent possession of a private hinterland, had always engendered caution. Now, however, he was irritated.

'Even you, Peter—you fought in the other war. You've been injured. You know what all this is about. But you buy drinks for that Junker, Mueller, in the café. He's practically your chum. But he's not your chum—he's your enemy. Are we fighting the Germans or playing a game with them? *Donald Duck* forsooth! Is this a war to the death to defend civilised values, or just a bally game?'

Peter had his pipe in his mouth. Now he took it out to reply. His expression was considered and firm, but he wasn't in the least angry, as Alec was. He spoke as if explaining to a dull pupil.

'Alec, my dear old friend, you've changed a lot since I first knew you. I'll be frank—to begin with, I thought you were a cold fish. In fact, you rather annoyed me by your lack of commitment, by standing aside and failing to engage.' Alec tried to interrupt, but Peter waved him aside. 'No. Let me finish. I'm not a great talker, but I was a lecturer and now I'm going to lecture. I admit I got you wrong. Veronica—who is very fond of you, you know—has told me a bit about what you've done and so on. Plus, I've got to know you properly. Plus—and I do believe this—you've changed a lot over this last year or so.'

Alec sat back and waited for more. This dissection of his character incommoded him, but it was clearly being done in a kindly way and for what Peter thought good reasons.

'The thing is that, like many converts, you may be moving too far in a new direction. Be careful about that. Games have rules. When the rules go, that's when you have to start worrying. Be careful you don't go too far away from the game. You may meet more than you want to. There have always been wars. There always will be. All right, in this war I think we're on the side of right—although there will be lots of Germans who would disagree. But mostly wars are fought because one country wants another's money or territory or for prestige or to divert its citizens from their grievances. We don't get the chance to decide whether we think the reasons are good ones. We have to fight anyway, and all we can do is to be true to our own values even if our country isn't doing so. So we stick to the rules. There's a certain beauty in doing that, thinking of courtesy and chivalry and so on. Take that away, and we're no better than insects or animals.'

Alec could hear Veronica in these words. Peter continued, winding up his lecture. 'Life goes on, war or no war. Look at your pal, Cadot. He always seems to me to be the ultimate survivor. He reminds me of that story about King William. A boatman took him across some river when he was on the way to fight a battle. Maybe it was the river Boyne and the Battle of the Boyne. I don't remember. Anyway, at the end of the day, the same boatman took him back across the river. He asked the king, "Tell me, who won the battle?" The king didn't give him an answer. He just said, "Why, what does it matter to you? You were a boatman this morning, and a boatman you'll remain whoever won the battle." Cadot reminds me of the boatman. War matters, but it doesn't matter all that much.'

For the rest of the way back to Perpignan, Alec and Peter travelled in unembarrassed silence, as was often the case when they were together. Alec believed that Peter did, indeed, like him, and he was pleased by that. He had not always been sure. He also felt he knew Peter much more intimately than he had. He was far from sure, however, whether the philosophy that had just been expounded to him was inspirational or utterly cynical. Whichever it was, Peter's position was not his. He ached at the evil that was being done to Inez's race and to defenceless infants like Vally and to all those whose lives and chances of happiness were condemned by the ambitions of evil men. He had no wish to fight the ranks of their followers: they were as innocent as the followers of good men.

But he burned to be able to make a sacrifice for good, and his inability to do so gnawed at his newfound and undeserved happiness.

Chapter 32

The following day was a Wednesday, the day for Alec's weekly game of draughts with Cadot in the Café Gambetta. Before it, as usual, they ate together. Their conversation during the meal was desultory as was often the case. Georges tended to withdraw into reflection and Alec was never an energetic conversationalist. Inez was still at la Coume with her children. Veronica, Peter and John were at another table. Directly across from Alec and Cadot sat the cadaverous Hauptman Mueller. As usual he was flanked by junior officers. Mueller, as always, seemed to have his eyes fixed on Alec and the others.

When they had finished, the table was cleared. The squares of a draughts board were inlaid in the table. Alec set out the draughtsmen and they played. Alec won much more often than he lost against Georges, and tonight victory came even more easily than usual. However, instead of setting out the pieces to seek his revenge, Georges swept them into a leather drawstring bag which was their home. He was preoccupied and not happy.

Alec waited for him to speak. After a moment, the large gendarme leant forward, his face very close to Alec's, and spoke quickly and quietly, anxious to convey a painful message.

'My dear Alec, when you amiably came to my sister's *mas,* I spoke to you very openly. I delivered the contents of my heart. I told you that I am only here because I am useful. Life is difficult these days. Those whom I must serve are unhappy. They see you here doing what they know not. There are others.' He waved in the direction of Peter's table. 'My masters are no more interested in the war than I am but they have to live with *them.*' He jerked his head at Mueller's table. 'People ask me, "What does this man Ross do? Does he spy? Does he help our enemies escape?"' Alec tried to interrupt but Cadot waved him back with irritation that was not counterfeit. 'No, no, Alec, do not insult me. I may not be a man of intellect but I am not a fool, I do not ask. I do not need to. They say to me, "he sits there with a Jewess in sight of you and the Boches. How can you allow this?"'

The reference to Inez stung Alec. He said, 'But you are our friend.'

'Yes, I am your friend. I have saved your life, and I have for the beautiful Inez impeccable regard, but I am at my limits—even beyond them.'

He could see that bringing Inez into it had made Alec angry. He tried to mollify him, 'I don't pretend, Alec, that I like the Jews. I don't. They are alien, they are not part of my country and they feed on us. But that doesn't mean I like what the Germans do or what our government does to please the Germans. These raids, these *rafles*, go too far. Thirteen thousand Jews arrested at the Vel' d'Hiver, that's too much. And since the Boches entered into our Zone, it's even worse. You know that next week this man Barbie comes from Lyon to tell us what to do. You know of him?'

Alec did, indeed, know of Barbie, already known as the Butcher of Lyon, the man who had arrested Jean Moulin, the most distinguished of the *Résistants*. The stories of Barbie's torturing, his use of dogs to abuse women prisoners were well known. Quite recently, Peter had told Alec how Barbie had treated a Resistance leader, beating him, skinning him alive and then plunging his head into a bucket of ammonia.

'I do not like all this,' continued Cadot, 'but we are supposed to be *collabos* and the Maire asks me how I can collaborate when I allow a Spanish Jewess to sit in the full view of our conquerors night by night. I say because she is the mistress' (Alec glared and Cadot quickly changed the word to *femme*, which could mean wife as well as woman), 'the wife of my friend. They say France has no friends, only interests. I say, but my friend gives me information. They say, what information? And I have no reply.' They sat in silence for a moment. Alec's face was burning and he felt as if he was the focus of attention in the room. Veronica and the others carried on their conversation however, oblivious of the tension between him and Cadot.

Across the room, Mueller drank on. Cadot continued, 'I told you at the *mas*, Alec, you must bend with the wind, you must give me something. Just give me *something*, some useless *évadé*, some hapless soldier who will make no difference to your war. Just tell me when and where. They will spend the rest of the war in a comfortable prison camp. You will have lost nothing. The outcome of the war will be unaffected, but I will be able to say, look what this man does for me, touch his woman and we lose him. All will be well.'

Alec struggled to keep his voice down, 'You ask me to betray my country, my countrymen. You know I can't do that.'

'Why not? I do that every day of the week. I don't imagine I know what is best for my country—I just do what I have to do and that is what you must do, Alec.' He repeated himself: 'You must,' he paused, '*must* do this for the sake of your woman. Politics, the war, they are too big for us to understand, but you love your woman, do you not? *Politics*,' he expostulated. 'The dogs bark, the caravan passes.'

When this choice was put to him, Alec knew, more strongly than ever, that he did, indeed, love Inez. 'Are you telling me, Georges, that if I don't betray my comrades, you will sacrifice Inez? Is that the threat you are making?'

Cadot shook his huge, impassive face slowly, 'I am not threatening you and it pains me to say what I do. What I say is that my protection of Inez will be valueless if I have given nothing to my masters. To say this is not to threaten, Alec; it is the truth. Barbie arrives in a week and one week after that, we have a conference. If I have no names from you, I can do little more.' He got to his feet, and stumped out of the room, bowing formally at the Hauptman as he left. Alec's eyes pricked with impotent anger. Veronica, seeing he was now alone, smiled across at him, but Alec was in no mood for conversation. He got up and walked out into the night.

Barbie was as clear an example of the organisers of evil as he could imagine, and now, this man's timetable was to determine Inez's fate. The conjunction grabbed at his intestines. He felt sick and light-headed and stumbled as he walked along the Rue des Cordonniers.

Chapter 33

He slept not at all that night. The direct threat to Inez made him aware of his need for her as never before. Even more than that, he felt indignantly defensive of her. If it came to a choice between saving her and betraying British servicemen, he had no doubt what the choice had to be.

But the implications, the execution of that election, were another matter. Every instinct that had been implanted in him by his background and upbringing, his school, his time in the army, all now reinforced by the camaraderie of the group and the sense of a common mission, all this made it impossible for him to imagine doing what he must surely have to do. Through the long night, Inez lay asleep beside him. He could feel her breath on his face and one of her arms lay over his chest. She felt small, soft, innocent and vulnerable, childlike. And yet, every time he thought of going in cold blood to Georges Cadot and telling him where the Gestapo could find their victims, he recoiled. It was as if he knew that he had to put his hand in a fire but could not find the resolution to do it.

Often, after sleepless hours, the worried man will finally nod off as the dawn approaches, but Alec was far too disturbed for that. From time to time, he looked at his watch on the table beside his bed and saw the hour for rising approach, reducing, minute by minute, the time left before he was required to act.

***

But not long before he would have risen to face the day, there was an insistent banging on the street door below. He went down to find Peter looking sombre and concerned. He wasted no time.

'For a long time, we've been worried about betrayals.' Alec felt a grab in his stomach. Had Cadot spoken to Peter?

But that wasn't what it was about. Peter reminded Alec of their meeting in Marseille, with Garrow, when they heard that Cole had fled. That had been the day when John had come back to Perpignan with them. It appeared that the interception of prisoners on the way to Marseille had stopped with the disappearance of Cole.

'Good, then they got the right man,' said Alec.

'I'm afraid that's not necessarily so,' replied Peter. 'Almost immediately after the betrayals on that route stopped, they began on the route south from here. I'm very clear that all we did was to move the traitor from one place to another. Cole certainly was as guilty as hell, but he wasn't the only traitor and the other one's here now.'

'Oh come on. Who do you suspect in our circuit?'

'That's pretty obvious, isn't it? Who comes away from Marseille, ending the problems there and moves south just as they begin here?'

'It couldn't be John, if that's what you mean. He's far too gentle and decent a chap.'

'I'm afraid that's exactly who I am accusing. I've not rushed to judgement. I've analysed the pattern. The change in events after he moved here could have been coincidental, but I've been watching the situation for a time. There are no interceptions of shuttles he doesn't know about. There are no incidents when he goes out with the *passeurs*, but on two out of three other passages, the Germans are there. To add to that, the *passeurs* themselves escape. They're not trying to close the line down, just to grab our men.' Alec found this all hard to believe and said so. Peter would not be shaken. 'I want to go on a little expedition into the hills with John and see what he has to say, but if the worst proves to be the worst, I need a witness that justice is being done, and as you've been involved with him from the start and are well disposed to him, I need you.'

Alec and Peter headed off in Alec's car. John had been told that Peter wanted to reconnoitre a potential route. They picked him up and drove south till they reached the range of the Albères. There they headed up to an elevated *balcon*, a few hundred feet up, overlooking the plain of Roussillon, but with the bulk of the Albères rising sheer to its south. On the ridge below the summit, there was a chain of peasant villages. They headed for one of those, Laroque-des-Albères. Laroque was elevated, built like most of the villages in concentric circles round a medieval castle. It was perched high on the ridge and had an unbroken outlook in all directions, particularly to the north where Perpignan and the bulk of the German troops were to be found. Because of its remote position, and the opportunity for observation it offered, it was the hideout for a concentration of rascals, *quasi*-outlaws who roamed the Albères on both sides, rustling a little stock, carrying contraband and participating in the struggle against the Germans and Vichy. A little cabin just beyond the village was actually called the *casot des trabucaires*, the bandits' hut. The *passeurs* who were based in the village were, unusually, regarded as a hundred per cent reliable.

***

The three men left the car near the old château and the Catalan church, a solid building that like most in the region looked designed as much for defence as anything else and had in its time indeed served as an armoury.

They walked up a little lane behind the village, passing the ruins of an ancient chapel. The lane reduced to a narrow track. Its base was stones placed there by the men who had used the track for a thousand years. After climbing up it for perhaps forty minutes, Peter indicated a junction, an imperceptible gap in the thick brush which no stranger would have noticed. They turned aside here and onto an even narrower path.

Till now, Peter had been stopping frequently and checking in all directions for signs of patrols. Now that was no longer necessary. The deep brush formed a canopy over their heads. They continued to move in silence, however, and if anyone broke a stick or disturbed the vegetation, they received a reproving scowl. Even now, hidden from sight, Peter slowed the little column down and frequently stopped for a moment, listening for suspicious sounds. The narrow path was crossed repeatedly by tracks made by wild boar. They neither heard nor saw any adult boar, although four little piglets ran in front of them, and then panicked off up the hill, squeaking. Peter made them sit still a full ten minutes after that. By now, the sun was well up. The shade protected them but it was warm and airless. The climb was very steep and they were breathless and sweaty.

Alec marvelled, as always, at the complex, intricate pattern of the clandestine maze of interlacing routes that covered the countryside. Some of the tracks were quite substantial and would have allowed a two-wheeled wagon to be dragged up by a mule. These routes had been created to allow access to soldiers and supplies for the chain of military forts that ran along the highest peaks, built to allow the French to maintain the security of their border against the Spanish. Some of the forts had been built by the ubiquitous Vauban in Louis XIV's time, but some were a lot older. There was always a direct line of sight from one to at least two others, so that signals could quickly be passed to Perpignan in the event of an attack. They ran down the coast and also up the valley of the Tech. So the chain continued all along the line of the Pyrenees, the Tour de Madeloc, the Batterie de Taillefer, the Batterie de Santa Engracia.

The tracks that led to these forts had to negotiate steep inclines that involved dramatic zigzags and adapted themselves to the torturous situations of the hillside. They were impressive examples of seventeenth-century engineering. The lower side of the track was built up with substantial pieces of masonry, sometimes to a height of six feet or more. The higher side of the track was often cut into solid rock. The surface was composed of large blocks of stone, flat enough for a wagon's wheels to cope with some difficulty, but sufficiently irregular for the poor mules to keep their footing.

In the early days, before the Germans were present in numbers and these ancient forts reoccupied, Alec had often gone up these military tracks in the course of exploring and recording the coastal defences. The forts were very substantial buildings, consisting of solid dressed stone tapering up from the mountain summits, pyramid-like, the huge blocks cut to fit each other unsecured by mortar. They were massive structures, built to withstand cannon fire, although Alec found it difficult to imagine how they could ever have been approached close enough to have been invested.

The sense of history was profound. Alec had been particularly impressed by Bellegarde, an important defensive position, not on an isolated peak but commanding the obvious crossing point on the Albères at Le Perthus, that gap in the hills that Hannibal and those elephants had used, later the point at which the Via Domitia, the main route still into and out of Spain, found its way to Italy. In its arid surroundings, it made Alec think of a colonial post in North Africa rather than metropolitan France, its sense of isolation compounded by the melancholy graveyard in which lay the bodies of soldiers who had died here, veterans, some of them, of the Napoleonic campaigns.

The military routes into the hills were largely avoided by the escapers. Forts that had been occupied by the French a century before Napoleon were now occupied by the Germans. They looked out from the forts not so much to Spain as to the Mediterranean coast, but their troops made their way up and down the same routes on which ancient cannons and cannonballs had once been hauled.

The routes which the *evadés* used made up a confusing, vestigial tracery that spoke of the life of the hills. Some of them had been illicit routes that smugglers and those escaping authority had used for hundreds of years; others led to the chapels dedicated to martyred saints, to villages that could only be approached on foot or by mule, to upland pastures to which animals moved in the system of transhumance, to graze in the summer months.

Until the nineteenth century, the plain of Roussillon, low-lying and undrained, had not been suitable for agriculture. In any event, its foetid marshes were the breeding ground for disease-carrying mosquitoes. It was only with the drainage schemes that accompanied the extension of the railways that agriculture moved down to the plain. Until then it had been on the hills that vines, olives, even cereals grew, and on the hills too that pasturage was to be found. The little hamlets that still existed on the hills, some now severely depopulated, others abandoned, had been where the life of Catalan Roussillon took place and the tracks that joined them were the circulatory system through which its life-blood flowed. By these tracks, people moved to exchange their goods, to find their mates, to alleviate what was otherwise a lonely existence. So the tracks that they had used were well formed and had been carefully maintained. They spoke to Alec of the cheapness of labour in past times and of a slow and unchanging way of life.

These tracks were much narrower than the military ones. They could cope at best with the width of a mule bearing wooden framed panniers on its sides. They had been constructed without the gunpowder available to the soldiers. There was no cutting into the rock. Their progress was circuitous and serpentine.

It had taken Alec a very long time to learn to navigate his way over the hills, and even now he had to stick with only the parts that he knew. Peter, in the nature of his work, had a better grasp, but even he was only an amateur. The real men of the hills like the shepherds, many of them now *passeurs,* were in a different class.

As soon as agriculture started to move down from the hills onto the plain, neglect set in. The Catalans had a saying that a cow made the best fireman. They meant that grazing kept the hills in good order. Once grazing—and cultivation—stopped, it wasn't long before scrub started to grow, and it grew fast in these warm climes. The process had accelerated with the outbreak of war. There were now few sheep or cows on the hills. The grazing that was done now was chiefly carried out by wild boars, chamois and ibex, both goat-like animals with horns, the ibex with a particularly distinguished ornamental pair, and marmots, dumpy beaver-like animals that lived in burrows. The bears of the upper Pyrenees were rarely in evidence.

The result of this decay and abandonment was that the hills through which Alec, Peter and John climbed were densely clad in forest—cork oak, beech, pines—and in scrubby brush, all of which concealed the paths on which they moved. The paths were obscure. An occasional cairn marked an intersection but meant little to an outsider. Some of the best paths turned out to be those created by the wild boar, and in his first few months Alec followed many such paths with great confidence only to discover that they stopped abruptly and led him nowhere.

***

Their climb took them at times along the retaining walls of the terraces. On top of the smooth stones of the wall, flints and iron-stone moved under their feet. This produced a bell-like tinkle, which was echoed by the slightly deeper tinkle of the bells of the few cows which still grazed in the meadows.

For the first three or four hours, they moved up a succession of ridges as their path took them over a series of summits. Alec savoured the poetry of their names: the Coll de la Dona Morta, the Coll de la Placa d'Armes, le Pic des Medès, the Coll de Cerbère. The sense of being part of an ongoing and ancient civilisation thrilled him, linking him, as he thought, to the times of the Phoenicians coming to Port-Vendres before the Romans named it the Port of Venus. The ancient names of the mountains were those they had had for centuries and were not dreamt up by eighteenth-century classical enthusiasts. The continuity of the Mediterranean civilisation clashed with the squalid reality of taking a man up on the hills to assess his treachery and very possibly to execute him summarily.

They necessarily moved in single file, John in front, Peter next, a revolver in his pocket as Alec knew, Alec himself last. Peter and John talked in low voices, although from time to time Peter requested silence. Alec didn't join in, but he could hear most of what the others were saying. He was impressed. Although the conversation was mainly on trivial matters, Peter brought it back, just now and again, to operational matters. Alec could tell that he was assessing John's credibility. He wondered if John had any inkling of this. If he had, he didn't reveal it.

For Alec, as he reflected, and against all his instincts, the circumstantial facts presented an inescapable conclusion. As Peter had said, there had been almost no setbacks until John arrived. After that, there were regular interferences with the crossings, but never again as Peter had said, when John was one of the party, and his *passeurs* seemed to have a remarkable and happy capacity for escaping arrest. That conclusion clashed with Alec's every wish. He truly liked John, who was open and vulnerable, without the crust with which Peter and the others defended themselves. His brief concerns about the relationship between John and Inez had gone and he recognised it as an expression of John's embracing kindness, nothing more.

But as they walked, Peter bit by bit threw out the pieces of evidence. He didn't do so bluntly. There was no question of an accusation, more an incremental reflective discourse, and John responded in a similarly dispassionate tone, not seeming to perceive that a case on which he required to defend himself was emerging. Alec didn't know what conclusion Peter was reaching but, for himself, he could despairingly see little hope that John could dislodge the inevitable conclusion. What could this civilised and balanced man, less driven, more human than the others, say in the face of the accumulating evidence? He had no wish to be called upon to cast a vote in Peter's little *ad hoc* court martial. In any case, what would they do if they both decided Peter were guilty? The evidence could be no more than circumstantial and suggestive. And Harold Cole, against whom the evidence was infinitely more damning, seemed repeatedly to avoid its repercussions. But there was that revolver in Peter's pocket.

They reached a substantial beech wood. Beneath its dense canopy, there was a thick drift of the last season's fallen leaves. They were dry and made a crisp, almost ringing sound as the men moved through them. Peter frowned disapprovingly, and they moved more slowly and gently till they emerged from the wood and made their way out of the shade and on to a steep sheet of limestone scree, a mix of large boulders and loose shale. They clambered across and up the sheet. Crossing the boulders was easy, but on the loose scree they risked disturbing a stone that would clatter noisily down the slope. They negotiated this part with circumspection. Alec was aware that if they attracted attention, they would be horribly visible in the bright sunshine against the background of the reflecting limestone.

Having gained a long, level ridge after le Puig del Tourn, they made their way along the edge of one of the upland meadows, towards a *cabane* where the shepherds would have slept while their flocks were up for summer grazing. Peter stopped them in the shelter of a pine grove some distance from the pastureland and the *cabane*.

They watched the building for some time to be sure that it was unoccupied and then advanced along the edge of the clearing. At this point, they could see two of the ancient forts. There would be a German patrol based in each of them and Peter made the trio move very slowly, keeping low and always with tree cover between them and the forts. When they reached the far side of the meadow, they again had the benefit of dense cover. As they straightened up to move into the protection of the gully, they heard two shots.

They instantly dropped to the ground and lay there without moving, their faces deep in the grass. After perhaps five or ten minutes there was another shot, this time followed by the barking of dogs.

'Bugger,' said Peter. 'Dogs are the very last thing we want.' He jumped to his feet and motioned the others to follow him. He ran down to the bottom of the gully. There was a river flowing in the depths of the gulley, and he plunged in, followed by the other two. It was knee-deep and not wide—not more than five yards across. It was, however, fast flowing, fed by the melting snows on the Pyrenean summits, and its bottom was very uneven, with very deep holes between the boulders. It was composed of pools and then fairly fast glides. The bottom was muddy and slippery and once all three of them had had an awkward fall which threatened to sweep them down-stream.

Peter grunted, 'Won't do.' He took his trousers off and motioned to the others to do the same. They copied him in tying the legs of their trousers together to use them as ropes so that the three men were linked together. Alec, at the end of the chain, realised belatedly that his untrousering had been redundant, but was too embarrassed to dress again. Instead he hung his trousers round his neck. He ruefully smiled at the others. He received a grin in return from John but no response from Peter.

They waded forward up the gully. Intermittently, they heard the odd gunshot, but, more worryingly, the barking seemed to get closer. Peter seemed clear that the dangers of being seen or heard were less significant than the dangers of leaving a scent for the dogs. They splashed forward quite noisily towards the head of the valley, into which the stream descended by a series of cascades. Between the men and the head of the valley there were a series of rock pools. They followed Peter into first one and then another. Eventually, they were in a deep pool where the water reached their waists. It was surrounded by boulders and in front of it was a waterfall and the almost precipitous head of the valley. Here they enjoyed almost total cover. Alec silenced them and they remained stock still, hoping that they had covered enough ground in the river to ensure that they had left no scent. They could still hear some barking although it no longer seemed to be getting any closer.

At length, they could hear no more barking. By this stage, they hadn't heard a shot for some time. They waited in total silence for forty-five minutes by Peter's watch. It was unbelievably cold in the water. To begin with, the coldness had been a welcome after the heat of the climb, but the snow-melt wasn't warmed in the shadowy valley, and in no time, Alec had lost any feeling in his feet. Once he had got used to that he could tolerate it. No feeling meant no feeling.

In his thighs and groin the pain of the cold—and it was real pain—was however a different matter, quite intolerable. The discomfort was intense, perversely more like burning than anything else. His testicles ached as if they were held in a vice. He half wished that the lack of feeling was not confined to his feet, but he suspected that if it spread further his circulation would close down completely. As it was, he shuddered with the cold. He noticed that his teeth didn't chatter as they were supposed to do, but that his whole head was shaking. He looked at the others. John exchanged an expressive acknowledgement of what he was going through, but Peter didn't communicate his feelings. Alec tried on several occasions to nerve himself to ask Peter if he could get onto dry land but was too much in awe of him to do so.

At last, to his relief, Peter nodded to them to follow him to the riverbank. The three moved with enormous difficulty. The trouser rope came into its own. Stumbling and shivering they reached the shore and threw themselves onto the grass in a patch of sunlight.

There was immediately a sharp whistle from a point not far away, just where the rising riverbank formed a horizon. Instantly, Alec and Peter turned their gaze on John. John reddened but said nothing.

'Just what was that,' said Peter, addressing the question, it seemed, exclusively to John.

'It sounded awfully like a whistle didn't it, Peter?' said John.

'And why would anyone be whistling at us on a bare mountainside where our nearest neighbours are two units of Germans?' asked Peter narrowly.

'I have not the slightest idea, Peter. I have no more understanding of the situation than you.'

Alec was inclined to believe him. John spoke like a man completely baffled but adamantly making it clear that he was telling the truth. Peter let matters go at that, but it seemed to Alec that the inquisitorial nature of the expedition had moved into a new phase. He was now certain that John knew he was under suspicion. Alec found himself admiring John's philosophical recognition of that fact.

The three men wormed their way to the edge of the clearing. They could neither see the lips of ground immediately above them or be seen from them. They kept absolutely still and listened intently for the sound of anyone approaching. When, after a tense ten minutes, there had been no sound or any repetition of the whistle, they relaxed to the extent of noticing the effect of the sun on their wet and frozen bodies. Quite soon, Alec felt his crotch and thighs return to normal and his violent shuddering stopped. What was exquisitely painful, however, was the pain in his legs and particularly his feet as the feeling returned there in a series of sharp, knifelike stabs. No one spoke, but he imagined that the other two were experiencing similar phenomena.

After what Alec guessed might have been half an hour, Peter motioned to the others to bring their heads to his. He whispered that he was going to climb up to the top of the bank. If anything happened, they should drop back to the river and get downstream as quickly as possible.

All three squirmed to the edge of the tree cover. Alec and John remained there while Peter ran across the clearing in a monkey run and then hauled himself onto the steep bank, keeping his belly on the ground. He moved as the experienced and trained soldier that he was, keeping his head down and turning his hips to push himself up first by one leg and then by the other. He moved noiselessly, at the cost of progress that was painfully slow.

Alec watched John. He seemed to be wholly absorbed in what Peter was doing. Alec found that he was holding his own breath as Peter's head approached the crest. There he waited for a moment, like a stalker about to sight his stag. But as his head broke the skyline there was another loud, sustained whistle.

About to turn tail, Alec was transfixed when he realised that Peter, in the face of this challenge, had not dropped back. Instead, he continued to rise above the skyline. His shoulders started to shake. The effect was surreal and mesmerising. It was only after a moment or two, when Peter turned towards the others that they saw that he was in fact convulsed by silent laughter. He waved to them to join him and disappeared over the lip.

When the other two reached him, Peter was still shaking with laughter. 'We've been freezing our balls off for the sake of a bloody marmot,' he said

'A what?' said Alec and John simultaneously.

'A fucking marmot, a cuddly little thing like a giant guinea pig. There are lots of them up here. They don't do anybody any harm. They're companionable little buggers, and all they do is whistle. They whistle to each other to communicate and they whistle very loudly indeed when they get a fright, and that's what this little fellow was doing.'

The nervous release made the whole incident feel a good deal funnier than it was, and it was several minutes before they pulled themselves together. Peter was the first to do so. For a few minutes, his habitual self-control had wavered. Uncontrollable laughter was not part of his usual demeanour, and Alec had never heard him swear before. He looked a little shame-faced.

Chapter 34

It was now late in the afternoon. Peter said that there wouldn't be time before night fell to reach the observation point from which they were to work out routes and meeting points, the ostensible reason for the expedition, indeed the only reason for it as far as John Miller was aware. He led them with infinite care back to the *cabane* that they had examined earlier in the day. The light of the setting sun would be directly in the eyes of any guards in the German forts, but all the same he made them move very slowly, insisting as usual on pauses every ten minutes or so. As before, they observed the *cabane* for some time and listened for the sound of any occupants before approaching it.

When they entered it, they found it clean and dry. There was a doorway on the side further from the Germans. There was a bench along one wall, a broken table, an empty fireplace and a few candle ends. There were some twigs and firewood. The hut was clean and it smelled only but strongly of wood smoke.

The men hadn't planned to be away overnight. They had no food. Peter and John carried water bottles. Having filled them up from the river they had plenty of water but they were too cold to be thirsty. The cold was indeed going to be a problem. The sun had never warmed up the massive walls of the *cabane* and its floor of beaten earth kept it as cool as a wine cellar.

'How about a fire?' asked Alec.

Peter shook his head. 'Sorry, the Germans would see the smoke. Once it's completely dark we can think about it, but only if there's cloud-cover. Wood smoke's very visible against a clear sky.'

He was looking slightly embarrassed. 'I'm sorry. I did that rather badly today. I should have thought of the marmots long before I saw the little chappie.'

'But what about the shots?' said Alec. He couldn't see that Peter had been in any way remiss.

'Oh, I wasn't hugely bothered about the shots. They were from shotguns, not rifles. Quite a few people have hidden away a hunting gun and a few cartridges and try to shoot a boar when the Germans aren't around. What threw me wasn't the shots, but the dogs. Looking back, they were probably involved in the shoot too, because they didn't seem to be looking for us, but the Gestapo do use dogs in the hills. They're very effective, and that was what set me off on the wrong direction.' He relaxed a little. 'I managed to get through the last war without developing trench foot, but as a result of that marmot I may well end up catching trench testicle in this one.'

***

184

Alas, the sky remained clear. This not only ruled out the fire but meant that the mountain air became very cold indeed, once the sun had gone down. There wasn't much talk. They were all tired and talking in whispers. In any event, in Alec's opinion the suspicion that had crystallised around John had created a barrier to any genuine conversation. As soon as darkness fell, they lay down hoping to sleep. Their clothes didn't provide much warmth or even insulation from the cold floor, but it was only after a time that the cold overcame their inhibitions to the extent that they allowed their bodies to touch in the hope that they would be warmer that way.

Alec knew it would be by design rather than by chance that John was sleeping furthest from the door. Alec was in the middle and Peter was in the coldest position, right in front of the empty doorway. Alec didn't sleep much, and he doubted if the others did either. At one stage, he must have dozed off, however, because he was awakened by John climbing out, presumably to go for a pee. He noticed that all the time he was out of the hut, Peter remained seated at the door watching where he had gone.

Next morning, they continued upwards. After about an hour and a half, they emerged onto a little plateau of meadow immediately behind a high rock, the Roc Grévol. Peter motioned them down. He swarmed forward to the rock and from there spied out the land below them. He came back satisfied and they sat on the grass in a circle, facing inwards. Peter drank from his water bottle. So did John, but not until he had offered his to Alec, who accepted with gratitude and guilt.

When they had recovered their breath, Peter said, 'I'm afraid I haven't been entirely frank with you, John. This little expedition isn't entirely about spying out routes. I suppose it *is* a little to do with spying in another sense.' He stopped. He was clearly not finding the interview easy.

John had scarcely spoken all morning. He held Peter's eye and said, 'Oh, so what does that mean?'

'I have, I'm afraid, come to the conclusion that you are not entirely what we thought you were. I wanted you to have the opportunity of putting your case forward. Let me tell you my worries.'

Peter started to repeat what he had told Alec on the previous day, but before he'd got very far, John motioned him to stop. He still looked entirely calm and unsurprised. 'I shan't embarrass you by making you continue,' he said. 'I could, of course, deny everything and you haven't got the kind of evidence that would convict me in a court. I was studying law when the war broke out, did you know? But you have quite enough evidence to justify killing me. You are a professional, and so am I. I'm doing what you would have done if our situations had been reversed and now, you're going to do what I would have done if that had been the case.'

His surrender was so complete and so charming that Alec found himself saying, 'I'm really sorry about this, John.' John turned to him and laughed. 'Exquisitely English,' he said.

He turned back to talk to them both. 'The funny thing is that I feel exquisitely English myself. My surname is the same as the Hauptman in the café. I am Johan Mueller, not John Miller, but very much the same thing.'

'Yes,' said Peter, looking more moved than Alec had seen him, 'very much the same thing.'

'The happiest years of my life were in England. I was a student at Cambridge reading law when the war broke out. May I have a cigarette?' Without waiting, he took out a silver cigarette case and offered it round. No one but he smoked. He lit his cigarette and continued, 'Yes, I met a girl from Girton when I was there and we were going to get married when the war ended. She gave me this cigarette case in fact. Her name and address are inside. I wonder if you would see that she gets it—if anything should happen to me?'

'Of course,' said Peter.

'I'd rather you didn't tell her how it all ended though.'

'I won't, but if it's any consolation to you I don't think you've anything to be ashamed of. As you've said, if the war had come to England, I'd be doing exactly what you're doing,' said Peter. John smoked on for a moment or two.

'In one of the college chapels in Cambridge, not mine, there's a memorial to the men who died in the First World War. On it, amongst all the English names, is the name of a German who had died fighting against your country. I thought that was awfully nice, awfully English. It wouldn't have happened in Germany. I wonder if they'll put my name on the memorial at Selwyn College.'

'If I survive the war, I'll do my best to make sure they do,' said Peter.

When he finished his cigarette, John took another from the case. 'I think I'll go for a smoke in the woods over there. Would you mind giving me your revolver in case I need to defend myself against a wild boar?' Peter handed him his revolver. In exchange, John handed over his cigarette case, 'Please do look after this.'

'Of course I will,' said Peter, who was controlling his emotions with difficulty. He pushed his hand forward and shook John's. 'You're a brave man and a good man. We understand each other.'

John said, 'You're both of these things too. I like you both very much.' He walked over to Alec and shook his hand too, still smiling. Having lit his second cigarette, he slowly walked away. As he entered the woods, he turned slowly and bowed to Peter and Alec. They stood in silence, looking at the ground. After a few minutes, there was a crack of a shot.

Until then the air had been full of the sound of the cicadas. With the shot came utter silence. After perhaps a minute and a half, the noise of the cicadas resumed. Alec had learned that the cicadas produced their remarkable racket by rubbing their rear legs together. Was that all a human life amounted to, ninety seconds of silence when a cicada stopped rubbing its legs together?

After a minute or two more, Alec went off in the direction John had taken and came back a few moments later, carrying his revolver.

***

Peter and Alec descended in silence to the car. As they walked, Alec's thoughts were of the suddenness of John Miller's death, his reduction from a fine—yes, a fine—and brave man to an inert corpse all in the time it took a bullet propelled from a .38 revolver to penetrate his brain. Could this man who had so recently shared his water flask with him, this John, this kind, thoughtful, sensitive man whose last thoughts had been to spare Peter the embarrassment of stating the case against him, be no more than the physical evidence that now lay on the forest floor? Surely, all that was so individual and authentic could not just be eliminated forever by nine and a half grams of lead? He couldn't believe that the grand concepts of Walter Benjamin, Peter Graham's noble ideals or, above all, everything that was so peculiar to Inez—her candour, her devotion, her sheer goodness—were not more than that. If it were otherwise then truly he was forced back on Veronica's rejected vision of men and women as mere insects, cicadas indeed.

Happily the more he thought, the more he felt reassured. The very evil in the world that had come to preoccupy so much of his thoughts made him conscious of another force, maybe not equal and opposing, but surely inextinguishable, which expressed itself in a spirit of revulsion against these horrors and in a determination to replace them with something that was recognisably good. That spirit, that recognition and the souls that it inspired could never be stifled by something as commonplace as death. The souls and not the cicadas must prevail.

***

They drove back for most of the way still in silence. Alec's heart was very full and he suspected that Peter's was at least equally full. He had to work to suppress his tears for the loss of a gentle friend who had been almost a family member for him and Inez. At length, he felt it was time to talk.

'Weren't you worried about handing him your revolver?' he asked.

'No,' said Peter, 'not in the least. I knew who I was dealing with. The English are not the only people who have a code of honour you know.'

He said no more for some moments and then broke out, 'I hate this war! It's the squalor, the personal betrayals that I hate. Last time around you fired your rifle at people you couldn't see and they fired theirs at you. You weren't involved. I could cope with going out on a night patrol in no man's land. But having to do what we just did with a thoroughly decent man, whom I liked very much, is different. It was the same for him. Fighting his war involved deceiving people that he liked. Then you add to that the bestiality of the camps and so on and the anti-Semitism. People like the French, the countrymen of Racine and Molière, and the Germans, heirs to Schiller and Beethoven, are treating the Jews or the Gypsies as if they were sub-human—torturing them, killing them like rats. It wasn't always like this. I know there's been anti-Semitism for centuries. In the fourteenth century the leaders in Perpignan wrote to the king of Aragon saying that everything would be tickety-boo if all the Jews became Christians. But it wasn't so clinical, so degraded as it is today. You know that swine Barbie's coming here next week?' Alec nodded: he knew only too well. 'He's going to teach them new tricks, even nastier ways of killing Jews in the most degrading ways that can be thought of. It's not exactly the Europe of Roland and chivalry, is it?'

***

It was quite late when they got back to Perpignan, and they made their way straight to the Café Gambetta. Alec felt he had to shelter Inez from what had happened. When she asked where John was, he simply said that he had left.

'Left? Just went away without telling anyone?' she asked. Alec could see where this might lead, but knowing how fond she'd been of John, he thought on balance that he should protect her from the truth.

'Yes, he had to move on,' he replied lamely.

'Ah, I see,' she said. 'Just like you in Damascus.' With an effort, he said no more. His silence was unfair to John, but an explanation that would have done himself justice would have given Inez unspeakable grief.

Alec saw Peter talking gravely to Veronica. He suspected she must have known the purpose of the day's expedition. She seemed to understand what had happened with very little explanation.

Alec had little appetite that evening, but he did need more wine than usual to dull the pain. Further along the table, he could see Peter drinking even harder, with the determination of a man who means to get drunk. While he was watching, he saw Veronica move very close to Peter. She already had one arm round his waist and was holding his hand. She kissed him long on the lips. As she withdrew, she saw Alec looking at her. This was the first time he had seen such a public display of affection. She winked conspiratorially at Alec.

'This is no dilettante,' she seemed to be saying.

The skull-like Mueller sat opposite, surrounded as usual by his little court. His gaze looked more hostile than ever, and not without reason. Peter's table was drawing attention to itself. The general noise in the café was not enough to drown out the occasional word of English, and Peter, by now thoroughly drunk, was reciting the filthier verses of *Eskimo Nell*, ones reputedly written by Noel Coward, banging his glass on the table in time with the rhythm of the poem.

Finally, Mueller's self-restraint broke. He snapped to his feet, his chair grating on the stone floor. He was staring straight at Peter. Everyone fell silent, Peter's voice trailing off in mid-verse. After standing motionless for a moment, Mueller marched across the café, bearing down on Peter. Three or four junior officers and under-officers followed him, some with their hands on their holsters. Peter stood up unsteadily facing the Hauptman. Veronica stood up too, close beside Peter. Alec moved closer to Inez, shielding her body with his.

It wasn't clear whether the Hauptman was going to assault Peter or arrest him. He was no more than a yard from him. A muscle worked on his jaw. He himself appeared uncertain of what he would do.

Finally, in a quiet voice that crackled with anger, he spat out at Peter in clear, but heavily accented English: 'If you must speak in your own language, have the goodness to do so quietly. Otherwise you insult my intelligence, and honour requires that I react accordingly.'

There was a moment's stand-off, then Peter replied, in a controlled voice, 'You are quite right. It was very bad manners. I apologise.' The Hauptman and his supporters returned to their seats. Peter and Veronica got up after a moment or two and moved to the door. When he reached it, Peter turned and bowed formally to the Hauptman, who nodded curtly in response.

Chapter 35

By the following morning, Alec's plan was pretty well fully made. John's execution had brought home to him the personal nature of betrayal. Like Peter, although not quite as magnanimously, he could see that John was not a betrayer. He was a German fighting the British. But it had been bad enough to see him die in cold blood. Even more awful for Alec to betray his own countrymen whose deaths might well be a great deal more unpleasant than John's.

On the other hand, something had to be done. It had to be done if Inez was not to die, and the manner of her death and what might happen before it was unthinkable. On a wider level, too, something had to be done. He could no longer observe, uninvolved, a world in which unspeakable evil was being done while others sacrificed themselves—Edith and Hilda to the dangers of the life they had chosen and then the pain of separation, Veronica to the proposition that men were more than beasts. Garrow and Caskie and Peter—and John—accepted the prospect of death and torture on a daily basis. So did Hairy Watson, disguising his courage behind his tomfoolery. It was true that Alec himself had come to be taking quite substantial risks. From simply gathering intelligence, he had moved on to being part of the escape line but a fairly detached part of it. It was a role for which he no longer had any real stomach. Cantley's instructions had revolted him. To pretend to fight Nazism while secretly wishing it well was far worse than any sort of treachery that John had been involved in. It was treachery without idealism.

So what could he do without losing Inez and without betraying his fellow countrymen? He could, as before, run away. Not, of course, this time leaving a woman behind. Although Inez still doubted him, he would never abandon her as he had abandoned Salema. It had taken many years and Inez's reaction to make him feel guilty about Salema, but now he did. He even felt, rather less reasonably, guilty about Barbara. He hadn't run away from her, but he'd never truly committed himself to her. He had not left her: it was she who chose to escape from life, but he had never tended her memory or much thought about her after he had seen her buried at Menton.

The nature of war as he now saw it was far too complicated. Cantley's cynical geo-political notions were too vague and fluid. Alec needed enemies who could be identified, but who were they? The Muellers, Johan and the Hauptman—were they enemies? They seemed to him to be decent men whose lives were governed by civilised codes of which he could only approve. He could take no pleasure in killing men who were no worse than he was, simply born in a different country.

The evil that he could see was organised, systematised evil, the kind of evil that Stalin, currently Cantley's friend and soon to be his enemy, was wreaking in the Soviet Republic, the kind of evil of the industrialised killing of the Jews with gas chambers and extermination camps that Peter had been talking about.

His decision was to attack this last revolting misapplication of human ingenuity. He would go from Perpignan, with Inez. He could easily go to Paris and lose himself there—perhaps even move on back to Britain. But as he went, he would knock out one of the Princes of Darkness. No prince within Alec's reach was darker than Klaus Barbie. He knew that Barbie would arrive in Perpignan in two days' time. After his conference with the German command in Perpignan and their collaborationist friends in the Mairie, he would drive down the Avenue de Grande Bretagne, the road that runs from the station to the Castillet, to the Préfecture. This he knew from Cadot. Barbie had just been awarded the Knight's Cross of the Iron Cross with Swords by Hitler for capturing Moulin and for all he had done for the Reich. At the Préfecture, the Maréchal's representative was to promote him to the highest level of the Légion d'Honneur to add to the Führer's decorations. Surely, it would not be too difficult to make sure that he never reached the Préfecture?

***

And yet even now Alec shrank back from the implications of the conclusion he had approached. In his mind, there remained an icicle of self-doubt. He had never killed a man. Indeed, in spite of his years in the army, he had never seen a man killed. There were few people in the world that he could imagine deserved to be killed more than Klaus Barbie, but would he be able to nerve himself to melt that icicle, to put his hand into the fire?

When the choice had seemed to him to be between betraying one of his countrymen and seeing Inez sent to the camps, he had always known that if he could not bring himself to betray, he could avoid his dilemma by fleeing to Paris with her. That option still remained. Fleeing responsibility was what he had done before. Doing something decisive to alter the change of events for the better was a novelty, and an element that could be added on or left aside. The Ross of Damascus would not have intervened. Indeed, the idea of intervening would never have occurred to him. But perhaps the Alec Ross of Perpignan was a different man. The strutting *Jeune Milice*, their beatings and killings, their slogans about Jews, the reduction of other human beings to something lower than the level of animals, the way he had seen perfectly ordinary people twisted and perverted: all of these things he knew to be wrong and he was aware that there could be a duty which the younger Alec would never have conceived of to try to do what he could to restore the world to reason and normality. His concern was not the rightness of what he planned to do: rather his own moral strength. Could he, looking into Barbie's eyes, pull the trigger to kill a man he did not know?

A way of testing his resolve was available. Barbie was engaged in a tour of the southern cities of which the last stop would be his visit to Perpignan. Before that visit he would be in Marseille. Someone had to brief Caskie and Garrow about the double role of 'John Miller' so that its implications could be addressed. Alec volunteered to go. He hoped to see enough evil in Barbie's eyes in Marseille to nerve himself to kill him in Perpignan.

***

He took a train that left very early and arrived at the British Seamen's Mission at 46 Rue de Forbin at seven in the morning. Donald Caskie, wearing a light cream suit and soft hat and carrying a walking stick was approaching the door as Alec prepared to knock.

'Sandy Ross, I thought I might see you again soon,' he said, and asked Alec to hold the large sack of food which he'd been collecting for the last hour and a half while he opened the door.

Inside there were two airmen and four soldiers from the Fifty-First Highland Division. Caskie addressed the latter in Gaelic. The food was piled on a table and two French boys started making sandwiches and tea. In another room, on the ground floor, were six legitimate inmates, shipwrecked sailors who could not be interned under international law.

Donald Caskie took Alec upstairs where he found Ian Garrow and Pat O'Leary. The information about Miller was accepted pretty calmly and Garrow, O'Leary and Caskie clearly thought that Peter had handled the matter well. There was no suggestion that Miller's activities had compromised the line generally and there was a sense that Peter could sort out any problems from the Perpignan end.

The three men in Marseille had their own problems. In recent weeks large numbers of men sent to Toulouse to cross the Pyrenees well to the north-west of Perpignan were being apprehended. These were soldiers who were expected to be able to find their way over the higher but more open mountains without guides, so the problem didn't lie with the *passeurs*. When they were caught, the men were returned to Marseille to be interned in the Fort St Jean. Donald Caskie had been interviewing them there and was convinced that there was a treacherous member of the French Resistance passing information to the Gestapo.

There were some differences between the three about the best way of dealing with the matter, and this, rather than Alec's news, was their main preoccupation. Before an agreement could be reached, the meeting broke up. Garrow had to leave.

As Caskie showed them out, he addressed Alec: 'I sense that I won't see you again in this world, young Sandy, so I wish you well. May the wind always be at your back.'

***

The team from the Rue Forbin was keeping an eye on activity at the docks, where it was suspected that an important troop movement was taking place. A watch was kept in relays, and Garrow was due to take over at eleven that morning. Alec and he walked to the dock gates on the Quai des Belges. On the corners of the two roads that joined on the Quai there was a number of small cafés, nameless, very simple with benches and stools outside for the benefit of thirsty dock workers at the end of their shift. Alec and Garrow, who was carrying a copy of *Paris Soir*, sat down and ordered *demis de pression*. Not long afterwards someone who looked like a sailor who had been sitting in a café across the road reading *Midi Libre* folded up his newspaper and slowly walked away. There was no eye contact between him and Alec and Garrow.

The police were conspicuously present in connection with Barbie's visit. He was expected at the Préfecture on the Boulevard Garibaldi, just two blocks away, at one o'clock. It was natural enough in the circumstances for Alec to raise the subject of the visit. Garrow needed no prompting. He told Alec the story he'd already heard from Peter about the Resistance leader who had been beaten, skinned alive and then had his head immersed in a bucket of ammonia. He was able to supply more chilling information. Recently, Barbie had arranged for forty-four Jewish children to be taken from an orphanage and sent to Auschwitz. Alec now had known many professional soldiers and he was used to seeing them coping with terrible events by maintaining an impassive front. Garrow was usually such a man, but on this occasion, he controlled himself with difficulty. What nauseated both men was not just the torture and interrogation. No doubt most armies resorted at times to pretty dubious techniques. What was particular about Barbie was that the forms of torture he used appeared designed for the torturer's amusement rather than simply extracting necessary information. And Barbie did not simply preside over his organisation: he delighted in personally participating. One little girl of thirteen who was suspected of being Jewish was presented to Barbie. He stroked a cat as he told her what a pretty girl she was. For the following week, the cat stroker pulled her out of her cell every day and attacked her open wounds to obtain information. Another woman had been hanged from handcuffs with spikes inside them. Barbie himself struck her on the back with a spiked ball attached to a chain.

So it went on. The story that was best known was how Barbie had tortured Jean Moulin, the charismatic Resistance leader. Red-hot needles were pushed under his fingernails. Screw-levered handcuffs were tightened on his wrists until they broke the bones. He was whipped and beaten and when he was reduced to a coma Barbie had him put on display.

Alec left Garrow and walked the two blocks to the Préfecture. He arrived about ten minutes before Barbie was due to reach the building after a very short drive from the railway station. There were perhaps two hundred civilians waiting to see the Gestapo chief. Alec could see gendarmes at various points on the route, not stationary or posted at fixed intervals but in evidence all the same. In front of the Préfecture was a Gestapo honour guard and on the steps of the building, waiting to be presented to Barbie a group of German officers and Vichy officials. Alec was able to position himself at the front of the crowd, directly opposite the Préfecture.

There was a scattering of onlookers all along the route from the station and Alec heard some cheering, fairly muted, which alerted him to the arrival of the official car. The hood was down and the car drove slowly so that the spectators had an opportunity to see the Butcher of Lyon resplendent in his medals, including the one Hitler had so recently awarded him specifically for his role in the Moulin affair. The reconnaissance told Alec that killing Barbie in a motorcade was technically not difficult.

The car stopped at the Préfecture gates and Barbie and his ADC descended. Barbie was of slightly more than middle height, quite handsome. His left shoulder was higher than the right and his gait a little awkward as a result of an injury in the First World War. His stiff collar and his epaulettes carried much gold braid, as did his high, peaked cap. His appearance was assured and confident. If Alec had only seen Barbie's face in repose, he might have had difficulty in identifying him as the source of so much evil, but his face did not remain in repose. As he moved from person to person, he revealed an almost electrical sense of energy. It was as if contact with others switched on a powerful dynamo.

His eyes were the most significant part of his appearance. Once engaged in conversation, or making the short speech which he gave from the top of the steps, they flashed and darted. But his face and his hands were not much less expressive. There was a hyperactivity about the man which had a galvanic effect on those to whom he spoke. His eagerness to communicate was reflected in their desire to respond. Even allowing for the sycophancy of a picked audience, Alec was disturbed to see how willing they were to respond as Barbie wished them to. They wanted to please. Alec couldn't hear Barbie's words but he could observe his energy and its hypnotic effect on those around him.

Having seen this phenomenon, and knowing the ends to which it was being directed, Alec left Marseille intellectually confused. On the one hand, he was satisfied that he might have seen a terrifying force for the dissemination of evil. On the other, he couldn't say that he had seen evil itself. He had wanted to see Barbie not as a fellow-man, but as the distillation of evil. From what he *knew,* Barbie may well have been—no, certainly was—just that. But that wasn't remotely what he'd *seen.* Barbie had been no brutish oaf. On the contrary, he was obviously intelligent, charming, responsive and sensitive to his interlocutors. Alec had seen pictures of Hitler in repose when had looked banal and insignificant. His fear had been that Barbie would look like that—unworthy of martyrdom. But what he'd seen in Barbie was something more difficult still— a man not below the level of his fellows, but in some ways above it.

In the course of a long, slow and sad train journey back to Perpignan, Alec felt himself empty and depressed. He had hoped to gaze into Barbie's eyes and recognise the evidence of evil so profound that he would return charged with a transforming energy that would sweep away all his scruples. He had failed utterly to capture that vision, and try as he would over the long journey, he failed to displace what he had seen with what he knew. Barbie persisted as a man, not a devil.

It was only as the train approached Rivesaltes that his outlook changed and he suddenly found himself thinking of concepts rather than individuals. It was his sense of smell, and not his intellect, that was to alter the course of his history—and not only his. From his window, his eyes fell on the camps which he'd visited just weeks earlier. The railway line ran past the sidings where he'd seen the Jews and other undesirables arriving for sorting and then departing for further processing. He could see gaggles of disheartened inmates shuffling around the parade ground. He remembered the starved, dehumanised husks, the children with their swollen bellies and dead eyes, the silence, the pools of ordure and urine. Indeed, as the train moved slowly past the huge camp in the heat of the day, he could smell that shit and piss. And that stench reminded him of the dripping cattle trucks he'd seen at Platform One at the Centre of the Universe, when a kindly nun, faced with a labour of Hercules, had at least tried to give a little water to those who were dying for lack of it.

This industrialised slaughter, this grim desecration of humanity contrasted itself with a more recent image, the slickness of the shiny convoy he'd seen in Marseille outside the Préfecture: a well-oiled machine run by a man of perceptible ability. What he thought of that man, however charming he might be, was entirely irrelevant. It was the machine that must be stopped, and that could best be done by striking at the man who ran it. With that revelation, everything seemed childishly clear and all his earlier qualms seemed bizarre and self-indulgent.

Chapter 36

Inspired by this insight, Alec's agonising ended. He felt as if he had been released from blinkers. He was energised and ready to act rather than think. Over the next day, he completed his planning. He reconnoitred the route from Perpignan *mairie* and worked out the best point of interception. It would be at the far end of the Avenue de Grande Bretagne, the end closer to the station. Killing Barbie, provided he again used an open car, would not be too difficult if he could get a decent angle of fire. What was more critical was extracting himself from the scene before he was seized. But from the spot he had chosen, in the dense crowds that Barbie would attract, he reckoned he had a good chance of slipping into the station and away to Paris.

He completed his arrangements in the awareness that he was alive as he'd never felt before, elated, light-headed, untroubled by doubts. He assembled as much cash as he could and stowed it together with only his most essential belongings into his artist's satchel. In that too he placed the service revolver that he had never surrendered after he left the army. He checked that the chamber was fully loaded. He even went out into the country in his car and fired two rounds at targets just to make sure that he and his weapon were in good shape. He returned it to the satchel. There were four rounds left.

He said nothing of his plans to anyone except Inez. Even she could not know everything. He could not tell her about his plan to assassinate Barbie. If anything went wrong, it was essential for her good that she knew nothing. He told her simply that Cadot had warned him that her life was in danger and that the pair of them were going north to Paris and to lose themselves there. He had a task to perform first, he said, but he would join her on the train. She was to take, like him, only essentials. He would arrive at the station at the last moment and she was not to wait for him. She was to be on board and in her seat in plenty of time and he would find her there.

Remembering Damascus, she was full of suspicion. There Alec had jumped on a train leaving Salema behind. 'This time you are putting me on the train and you are remaining.' For hours, the argument went round. She had long since come to trust Alec in a general way, and she wanted to believe him. He told her again and again that whatever happened in the past, he would not separate from her.

'Nothing but death would keep me from you,' he said. In his elation, he felt divorced from the debate, above it and not fully engaged. His evident sincerity reassured her—but only to an extent, and it was after many reiterations of her concern and his assurances that they went to bed and to try to sleep.

196

Having slept little for many nights, Alec now slept soundly. Inez slept little. With no one else to turn to, she looked to the tribunal of her own judgement. The jurisprudence that was practised there was informed by the values of a simple, rural community to which she added her own experience of persecution, flight and rape. The jury inevitably failed to reach a verdict. She couldn't condemn Alec: she believed in his love for her, though it was different from her love for him. She knew he wouldn't betray her or leave her to her fate in Perpignan. But would he go with her?

***

On the following morning, despite her sleeplessness, Inez was more settled, less emotional. While she still had concerns about what Alec might have in mind, she tried to put them aside. He had made it clear that he had something difficult and possibly dangerous to do during the day, without saying what it was. They agreed that it would be best for her to be occupied and to avoid suspicion by going to la Coume as usual. From there, she would make her way back to Perpignan in the evening. The Paris train left at eight thirty and she would board it at eight o'clock.

Alec had nothing much to do till about the same time. Barbie's conference was to be followed by a meal at the *mairie* and he was to be at the Préfecture to receive his decoration at eight thirty, after which he would be driven back to Lyon. He should, therefore, pass along the Avenue de Grande Bretagne at around eight fifteen. Alec would just have time to slip aboard the train after he had made use of his revolver.

He didn't want to meet anyone or get involved in any awkward conversations in the course of the day, so he stayed in the apartment in the Rue des Cordonniers, reading and dozing, the time passing slowly until he thought of drawing. He started on a detailed sketch of a head of euphorbia which Inez had left in a jug of water. The intricate representation of the tiny blooms, caught in botanical detail, was wholly absorbing. Concentration on the precision of his sketch pushed all other thoughts from his mind and when he next looked at his watch, he realised that he need wait little longer.

He left the apartment, locking the door for the last time, remembering as he did so ushering in Inez when he had first met her and remembering too being dragged there by Cadot's gendarmes after the beating at the Castillet. He headed towards that building and as he came into the open square, he looked across the plain to where the mighty mountain of le Canigou seemed to float. A little late snow on the summit was pink in the setting sun. He had come to love this mountain and he realised that he was unlikely to see it again until the world was at peace. He was convinced, all the same, that he would return. He had a clear picture in his mind of being in a little country property, perhaps rather like Georges Cadot's, with Inez and Vally beside him. He was in a calm mood as he continued on to the Avenue de Grande Bretagne.

As he had expected, a large crowd had gathered to look at the Butcher of Lyon. He wondered if they were revolted by him or there to applaud him—or was it just something to do when entertainment was scarce?

The electric tramway was no longer electric. As the utilities, one after another, surrendered to the needs of the German war machine, electricity, like gas, was a luxury that was increasingly rare. The tram still made its way up and down to the station, but was now pulled by two heavy draft horses. In a way, they took the town back to an earlier age and added to the charm of the scene. They also left their droppings on the road. There was a strong smell of the horse manure that lay between the rails, and swarms of bluebottles enjoyed it until peasants scooped it up to use on their gardens.

Alec thought of Inez, who would have made her way along this same street, either on foot or on one of the trams, shortly before him. He felt invigorated, purposeful, steady. If he had thought about it, he would have said he was happier than he ever had been. He was dictating history, not being manipulated by it, certainly not just playing games. No Donald Ducks. No Peter and his chivalry. No Miller or Mueller and their amorphous concepts of honour. No HMS *Skylarks*. None of Cantley's temporising. What he was doing was not ambivalent. It was clean and simple and fine and he felt good in doing it.

***

Inez was in a very different position. She was physically ill. Nausea was not the problem. She was used to that. It was fear she was suffering from, not fear of the unknown, but fear of something she understood well, the foreboding of an inevitable ending. Her guts churned in her anguish. Leaving Vally had been impossibly difficult, unable to explain, knowing that he would be hurt, perhaps irretrievably, by her disappearance from his life, a second betrayal that would be bound to the first.

It was now very close to eight o'clock. Inez had taken the tram. She was pale and tired and the walk was more than she could face. If Alec, who had never noticed the strips of rag that she used to wash every month, had been more observant he would have noticed that she no longer did so.

When she reached the station, she did not follow Alec's instructions. She did not board the train. She stood instead at the end of the platform, waiting for him. She knew he was not on the train, because she had arrived before it had pulled in. The air in the station, whose roof was covered by smoky glass, was hot and lacked oxygen. The light was poor, and the station was lit, like the street outside, by paraffin flares. They added to the heat, and their oily, black smoke filled the depleted atmosphere with its pungent aroma.

***

Back on the Avenue, Alec took up the position he had chosen on the previous day. The crowd was at its densest where he was. The road curved round the station before heading straight for the Castillet, and this corner meant that the spectators would have a good view of Barbie. Alec had moved his revolver from his satchel to his jacket pocket. The safety catch was off and his hand was round the weapon, a finger resting on the trigger guard. His main concern had been that Barbie would arrive early or late, but with the punctiliousness which endeared him to his masters he was likely to be exactly on time. It was now eighteen minutes past eight. Alec would have time to pull the trigger and be at the station just before the train left.

***

There was a murmur of excitement from round the corner. The car, still out of sight, was approaching and the crowd stirred. All eyes were on the direction from which the car would come. No one had eyes for Alec—except for one man. Directly opposite Alec but unnoticed by him stood Hulot, the Widow, who had shadowed Alec from his earliest days in Perpignan.

Alec stood at the back of the pavement, with a clear line of fire between him and the approaching car. All he had to do was to pull the trigger. The range was no more that fifteen yards. Then he would drop back into a little alley which ran at right angles to the Avenue. A quick run from here to the station would take no more than three minutes.

***

In the hot, airless atmosphere of the station, Inez felt faint and sick. It was darker now and the effect of the swirling paraffin lights was to throw grotesque shadows over the station walls. The loathsome bluebottles which had fed on the horse manure were attracted by the flames and every so often flew into them, fizzed and were burnt to nothing.

***

The car was, indeed, again an open one. It approached slowly. Barbie was waving to the crowds, who seemed pleased to see him. Alec withdrew the revolver from his pocket and started to raise it.

At that moment, before he felt the knife at his back, from behind a hand crushed his throat, and his body was withdrawn into the little lane through which he had planned to escape. No one had noticed anything, except Hulot, who waited for just a moment longer before walking rapidly off towards the Castillet.

***

199

Inside the station, the minutes passed and Inez stood there with her miserable bag of belongings. Alec had not appeared. It had happened again. The train gave a long preparatory whistle. Inez made no move to join it. The train drew out of the station. In despair and misery, Inez slowly walked back to the apartment she'd left that morning, a mortally wounded animal returning to its lair.

***

In the Café Gambetta, the Hauptman sat, emaciated and skull-like. At their usual table were Peter and Veronica. At *his* usual table sat Georges Cadot. It was a Wednesday evening, when Alec habitually joined him for their game of draughts. Tonight, Alec did not join him. Instead, Hulot came in. He looked round carefully and then walked over to the *brigadier*. He bent obsequiously to him and murmured in his ear. Cadot, continuing to chew, nodded. Hulot withdrew. Cadot finished his meal. The leather drawstring bag of draughtsmen had not been opened. There would be other games. He moved ponderously to the door of the café. It was a Wednesday, his evening for the widow Lagrande. Her apartment lay to the right, beyond the Castillet. The Rue des Cordonniers was in the other direction. Cadot remained on the doorstep of the café for a full minute.

Part Five:
Epilogue

Afterwards

While history has not recorded what happened to Inez, Peter and Veronica after the close of this narrative, the record of history is partial, in both senses of the word, and something is known of the fate of some of the personae *of this drama.*

The life of Nikolaus 'Klaus' **Barbie** *has been widely researched. Most of the attention has been concentrated on his vicious regime as Head of the Lyon Gestapo. He had been wounded in the First World War at the Battle of Verdun and was held prisoner by the French. Some have thought that these experiences engendered a hatred of the French that had some bearing on his conduct in Lyon, but his sadism, his personal involvement in torture and the sheer scale of his evil—he is thought to have been personally responsible for the deaths of 14,000 people—surely indicate culpability of a sort that can never be rationally explained.*

The end of the war didn't see an end to Barbie's career—simply a change of employers. The US Army Counter-Intelligence Corps (CIC) recruited him in 1947 to work against communism in Europe. At one stage, he reported to CIC on French intelligence activities in the French Zone of Germany: America was concerned about the extent to which their French ally was riddled by communism. When the French discovered that Barbie, who had been sentenced to death in absentia, was employed by the United States, they asked for him to be handed over. Instead the CIC extracted him from Europe to Bolivia, using 'rat lines' not unlike those which Barbie had tried to close down in occupied France during the war. In Bolivia, he changed his name and as Klaus Altmann was a lieutenant colonel in the Bolivian Armed Forces. In 1983, he was returned to France and was tried on 41 charges of crimes against humanity. He told the court that he had 'nothing to say'. He was sentenced to life imprisonment and died in prison in 1991 at the age of seventy-seven.

Cantley's *life has never been investigated to the same degree and what we know about him is largely based on entries in 'Who's Who' and civil service records. Sir George Marshall Cantley, as he was to become, was born in 1892. He studied law at Newcastle University and in 1914 was commissioned into the Durham Light Infantry. As a result of his forensic skills, he moved immediately into Intelligence and in 1915 was seconded to the War Office. In 1918, he was awarded an OBE (Military) and, although still in the army, was moved to the Colonial Office. In 1920, on leaving the army with the rank of brigadier, he was permanently transferred to the Foreign Office establishment, where he worked for the rest of his life. The nature of his responsibilities is not clear. He was promoted CBE in 1931 and in 1955 he was—unusually—one of two Directors*

General (Political). He was appointed KCMG in the same year. In 1957, he retired from the service. The reason for his retiral, a year or two earlier than would have been expected, is not known, but it is thought that Macmillan's government was concerned about some aspects of Foreign Office policy in connection with the Suez Crisis in the previous year.

He was a member of Whites and the Beefsteak. He had an apartment in Albany and a cottage in Hampshire, where he indulged his only hobby, dry fly fishing for trout on the River Test. He never married. He was found dead in his Hampshire home in 1958. He had been in good health and the cause of his death was never established. Because of his close friendship with Sir Anthony Blunt and Kim Philby, and the unexplained nature of his death, there was some speculation that he had been involved, in some way, in the Cambridge spy ring, but no evidence to support the suggestion was ever put forward.

Major General Comte Albert-Marie Edmond **Guérisse** GC, KBE, DSO ('Pat O'Leary') is widely referred to by those who knew him as the bravest man they had ever known. He ended the war in Dachau concentration camp where he was tortured and sentenced to death. He was saved by the end of the war, when the guards surrendered. He took command of the camp and typically refused to leave until the Allies agreed to take care of the prisoners. After the war, he re-joined the Belgian Army. While serving with Belgian forces in Korea, he was wounded trying to rescue a wounded soldier. He became the head of the medical service of the Belgian army. He died in 1989.

Lieutenant Colonel Ian **Garrow**, DSO, did not return to France after he had been withdrawn through the Pat Line. He served in the Territorial Army after the war and died in 1976. He spoke French with a noticeable Scottish accent.

Brigadier de Gendarmerie Georges **Cadot** retired from the Gendarmerie Nationale in 1946. He had amassed sufficient funds to extend the family mas outside Perpignan. There, he bred pigs and made his own charcuterie. He was a shrewd businessman and a popular figure at the Saturday morning market in Céret. His claim to have been active in the Resistance was accepted, and he was appointed Chevalier de la Légion d'Honneur shortly before his death in 1972.

Edith **Pye** and Hilda **Clark** were reunited. Hilda ended the war in England. She died in 1955. Edith worked latterly in Greece. She died in 1965. Till the end, she remained committed to ending war and alleviating its effects. Edith and Hilda are buried under the same headstone in the Quaker meeting-house burial ground in Street, Somerset.

The circumstances of 'Captain' Harold **Cole's** life remain clouded in doubt. Airey Neave, who escaped from Colditz Castle, the first officer to do so, and reached Britain via the Comète Line, came to the conclusion that Cole (also known as Paul) had been arrested by the Abwehr in Lille, had been threatened with execution, had a 'yellow streak' and was turned. His devotion to the German cause seems however more committed than that narrative suggests. Cole married an attractive young Frenchwoman whom Pat O'Leary had sent out to help him. Unlike him, she was passionately committed to the Allied cause. When they were both tried by unofficial court martial in Lyon she was acquitted *and he was condemned to death. She was caught by the Germans and then escaped.*

As always, Cole seemed to enjoy undeserved luck: he was released to search for his wife, but went instead to work for the SS. He then started to work for the Americans and proceeded to betray his Gestapo and SS contacts. Entirely by luck, he was discovered by the British and identified by Donald Caskie. Even now, he escaped justice. He stole an American sergeant's jacket and obtained sanctuary in Billy's Bar in the Rue de Grenelle in Paris. He was found by chance by two gendarmes on a routine search for deserters. He drew a pistol and was shot dead. His body was identified by Pat O'Leary, just released from Dachau. Cole/Paul betrayed perhaps 150 people, of whom a third died. Greed and self-preservation were his only instincts. He even denounced his wife's elderly aunts, who had sheltered airmen, in order to steal their jewellery.

*The Reverend Dr Donald **Caskie,** DD, OBE, came under increasing suspicion in Marseille and was finally put on trial. Amazingly, he was acquitted for lack of evidence, but obliged to leave the city. He moved to Grenoble and for a time worked there for the university and as chaplain to interned servicemen. When Germany finally ordered the imprisonment of all British-born civilians he was held first in San Remo. When the noose tightened, he was moved to the notorious Fresnes prison, outside Paris, put on trial and sentenced to death by firing squad.*

A German chaplain successfully petitioned for his pardon, and he saw out the rest of the war as a prisoner of war. After the war he returned to the Scots Kirk in Paris, and thereafter was minister in a number of Scottish parishes. He died in 1983 and is buried in Bowmore, on his native Islay, where his father had been a crofter. There are various estimates of the number of British servicemen he helped return to Britain (and in most cases continue the fight against Fascism). The total will never be known, but it is considerable.

***Ross's** friends in Perpignan—effectively the only friends he'd ever had—never knew what happened to him on that night when Klaus Barbie visited the town. They wondered, of course, but not for long. This was, remember, wartime, when strange things happened. About a year later, in London, Georgina Everley, now Mrs Randolph Brand, had a strange experience. She was walking down Whitehall when she saw approaching her what she was sure was Alec Ross. She was so certain that she stopped and addressed him by name, but the man walked past without checking his step. He walked with a cane and his gait was uneven, as Ross's had not been. All the same, she was almost certain it was Ross she had seen, and she found herself quite shaken by the experience. But her husband had been killed in the Western Desert just a month earlier, and she was upset and London was full of ghosts.*

Afterword

Many of my French friends have, consciously or otherwise, helped in the evolution of this book. I particularly want to thank Christine Marcé for her encouraging interest in the project. I apologise to her and to other readers with a close knowledge of the wonderful part of France in which much of the book is set for taking some minor geographical liberties for artistic reasons.

Similarly, although the historical background to the story is essentially true, for structural reasons I have occasionally but only slightly altered the timeline. One or two real characters mingle with the fictional personnel. Where I have attributed words or actions to them which were not their own, I have tried to be true to what we know of them.

I encourage anyone who is interested in the twentieth-century history of the Pyréneés-Orientales (or Occitanie, as the authorities wish to call this region of France) to read two fascinating books by Rosemary Bailey on which I have drawn: *Love and War in the Pyrenees* and *Life in a Postcard*. For further regional background, I have looked at, amongst other things, *Cook's Tourists' Handbook for Palestine and Syria* (1876), *Baedeker's Southern France* (1891), *Cook's Traveller's Handbook to the Riviera and Pyrenees* (1912), *Muirhead's Southern France* (1926) and Basil Collier's *Catalan France* (1939).

There is no shortage of books, some more reliable than others, and some more readable, about France and the Resistance. I mention just one or two of the more accessible ones: Donald Caskie: *The Tartan Pimpernel*, Benjamin Cowburn: *No Cloak, No Dagger*, Peter Eisner: *The Freedom Line* and Airey Neave: *They Have Their Exits*.

Walter Reid
Laroque-des-Albères